The Cord of Scarlet

Marilyn K. Stout

Marilyn Kay Stout

Gal. 2:20

JENNKAY

Decatur, Michigan

For information write:

JENNKAY Publishers
19995 Marcellus Hwy.
Decatur, Michigan 49045

JENNKAY

Library of Congress Catalog Card Number:97-73561

ISBN: 1-891049-00-3

Printed in the United States of America

Books available from JENNKAY Publishers:

Asenath, Daughter of Egypt is the story of the daughter of Egypt's high priest of the sun god Ra. Asenath is wed to Joseph, one of Jacob's twelve sons, a believer in Jehovah, the true and living God. It portrays her struggle between her idolatry and her husband's faith in Jehovah God. $8.95

Michal, Princess is the story of the younger daughter of Saul, Israel's first king, and first wife of David, Israel's best known king. It tells the tale of the tragedies and triumphs of her life as she grows in faith in God. $8.95

The Cord of Scarlet is the story of Rahab's faith from the fall of Jericho until her death. It presents the conflict between her past life as a pagan harlot of the Canaanites and her new life of faith in the God of the Hebrews. $8.95

Coming in 1998:

Dear Jennifer is the true story of Jennifer Kay Stout's life, compiled mostly from her own journals and diaries. It is an excellent book for parents and young people alike illustrating the questions and battles of a young girl's life and the answers she finds in Jesus Christ and God's Word. This book fulfills Jennifer's prayer as expressed in her Bible study journal the day before the Lord took her to heaven in a tragic automobile accident: **"God, will you allow me to have a part in giving the gospel to those who have never heard?"**

To order send check or money order to:

JENNKAY Publishers
19995 Marcellus Hwy.
Decatur, Michigan 49045

Please enclose $3.00 shipping for orders up to three books.

Dedicated
to my husband, Tom, and my children:
Jennifer, Thaddeus, Joshua, Jared,
Christina, Thomas, and Caleb.

Chapter 1

Terror

The air hung hot and heavy as Rahab hurried along the narrow Jericho street, still she shivered and pulled her limp veil over her arms. She stopped before a stone wall rising up several stories from the street and knocked on a small wooden door. Rahab drew in quick gulps of the stifling air and this time pounded on the door.

A draft of cooler air emerged as the door opened and Rahab stepped quickly inside, pulling the door closed behind her. The brighter light of the courtyard in which she stood revealed an elderly man with white hair streaming in unruly wisps over hunched shoulders. Rahab ran to him, seized his shoulders with trembling hands, and said in agitation, "They are here, Zaphnath, they are here! Just across the river!"

The old man folded his arms around her and patted her back with an arthritic claw. She clung to him until her trembling eased and Zaphnath lowered her gently to a rough wooden bench by the wall. He sat beside her with his arm around her shoulders as if to protect her from her fears.

"Yes, child, yes, yes," he cooed as to a troubled infant. "Yes, they are here." He paused and sighed deeply. "And no one can stand before their God."

Rahab straightened her back and pulled away gently. "Perhaps they will pass by without harm." Her voice held a hope her heart did not share.

"Perhaps." Zaphnath closed his eyes and began to hum the gentle lullaby of his habit. Rahab knew that the old man's heart was far away in his native Egypt when he hummed his song. He thought of his beloved wife Asta and his only son, Nuth. He remembered the fearsome time, forty years before, when Asta had been struck in the head with a hailstone as large as a melon and had never again opened her eyes.[1] He remembered the midnight hour when Egypt had cried in anguish and his own heart had died as he held in his arms the dear, lifeless form that had been his son.[2]

The sudden stillness meant that Zaphnath was back with her, there, in his silent courtyard. He opened his eyes and looked quietly into Rahab's wild and wet ones. "Perhaps," he repeated softly, as if there had been no pause for memories. "But they did not pass by Sihon, king of the Amorites or Og, king of Bashan without harm."[3]

"But Jericho's walls are tall and wide." Rahab knew the helplessness of her argument even as she spoke.

"No wall is too high or too strong for their God," Zaphnath answered. Then he repeated, strength in his aged voice, "No wall is too high or too strong for their God."

Rahab leaned close to Zaphnath to look into his eyes. "What can we do?"

Zaphnath answered slowly, "We can do...nothing! When the God of the Hebrews moves there is nothing one can do."

"But Zaphnath, we will die!" cried Rahab, beginning to tremble again.

"Yes, child, we will die. No one can stand before their God."

As Rahab picked her way through the narrow streets of Jericho back to her house in the wall, she felt that she must be caught in some fearsome dream. This could not be. Surely the hand of the Hebrews and their God could not crush her city, her family. Or could they?

---

[1]Genesis 9:23-25

[2]Exodus 12:29,30

[3]Numbers 21:33-35

Rahab glanced around her. The tall, wide walls of Jericho rose to touch the sky as always. The gates remained impregnable. Yet her heart and mind trembled in fear. She reached her door on the inside of that tall, wide wall and was swept inside by the urgency of her fear. Closing the door and latching it in one practiced motion, she leaned her back against it. She would die. And what then? Was death the end of all or only the beginning of some terror she did not know? Surely she, a temple harlot of the great gods should know if there were more, if one's soul lived after death. But she did not know. She had lived her life to please her gods alone and appease their wrath to ease the pain and loneliness in her life. She had given all. But now, facing certain death, she had no peace, no hope; only hopeless dread and ceaseless fear.

With the gentle rap against the door a surge of terror pulsed through her. "It cannot be the Hebrews, yet, here to end my life," she told herself. "They are yet across the Jordan River. But why would someone come to me now when all hearts melt with fear?"

Rahab leaned against the smooth wood and spoke into the door, "What do you want?"

A man's voice replied in the musical Egyptian tones used by Zaphnath, "Open to us. We come in peace."

The voice was unfamiliar to Rahab, and she knew no one but Zaphnath who spoke the Egyptian tongue. Yet she felt compelled to release the latch and open the door.

Before her stood two men. They were strangers to her, indeed. Their clothes and sandals were not of Jericho. They pushed past her into the room and shut the door, latching it again.

For a moment they all three stood silently, and then Rahab knew. They were strangers. They spoke the language of Egypt. But she felt her fears drain away as she looked into their eyes.

"You are Hebrews." she simply stated.

"Yes. We mean you no harm," the tall one answered. "Our great leader, Joshua, has sent us into your city to spy secretly."

"And you will take the city." It was not a question, but a statement. Why did Rahab feel no fear before the men who would slay her?

"Our God will give us the city."

"Your God is mighty and dreadful." Rahab looked steadily into the tall man's eyes. They were not dreadful. He looked like a man of courage and compassion. And still she felt no fear.

"The Lord is strong in love and mercy, also." His voice carried the words from his heart.

"Where is His mercy to victims of your swords?" Rahab wondered at her careless words. Would she anger this soldier of Israel?

"The Lord shows mercy to all those whose faith is in Him."[4]

Another knock sounded at the door, urgent, insistent.

"Hide us," whispered the tall spy.

Without pausing to consider why, Rahab turned and ascended the stairs to her roof, whispering hoarsely, "Follow me." A large pile of stalks of flax lay in order on the roof. Rahab lifted several stalks and said, "Get under these." She rearranged the stalks to cover the men and swiftly descended the stairs to her door.

"What do you want?"

"Open in the name of the king!" came the shouted reply.

Rahab slowly unlatched the door and it was suddenly flung open, pushing her back violently. Soldiers of Jericho streamed in and began to search each corner. The captain approached Rahab and said, "By order of our majesty the King

---

[4]Exodus 20:6

of Jericho bring out the men that came to you and entered your house. We know that they are spies and have come to search out all the country."

From the corner of her eye Rahab watched a soldier ascend her stairs. She quickly said, "Men came to me, but I didn't know where they were from. But about the time of the shutting of the gate, when it was dark, they went out. I don't know where they went. But if you pursue them quickly you'll overtake them. They couldn't have gotten far."

The captain seemed pleased with her words. He shouted a quick order and the soldiers filed out the door behind him. Rahab watched as the soldier descended the stairs and fell into file. She breathed a sigh of relief and ran to the door to refasten it.

Rahab listened at her door. When she heard the march of footsteps pass away from her street, she ran back up the stairs and hurried to uncover the Hebrew spies.

Before either man had time to speak, Rahab said, "I know that the Lord has given you the land. The people of this city are all terrified of you, as are all the inhabitants of the land. We've heard how the Lord dried up the waters of the Red Sea for you when you came out of Egypt, and we've heard what you did to the two kings of the Amorites, Sihon and Og, that were on the other side of the Jordan, whom you utterly destroyed. And as soon as we heard these things, our hearts melted, and there was no more courage in any man because of you. The Lord your God, He is God in heaven above, and in earth beneath. Now, please, I beg of you, swear to me by the Lord, since I have showed you kindness, that you will also show kindness to my family. Promise me that you will save alive my father and my mother and my brothers and sisters and all their families, and deliver our lives from death." Rahab paused from her speech and looked intently into the tall soldier's eyes.

"We, Salmon and Enan, pledge our lives for yours if you promise not to utter our business to anyone," he answered her quietly. "And when the Lord has given us the land, we will deal kindly with you."

"His name is Salmon," she thought to herself. Aloud she said, "I promise I will not utter a word of this."

Enan grasped Salmon's arm and said, "We must leave quickly."

"Is there a way out that doesn't lead into the street?" Salmon asked Rahab.

"Yes," she answered. She quickly led the men down one story to a room with a window which looked out through the wall.

Rahab opened a chest and after rummaging about produced a long scarlet cord. She fastened it securely inside the window opening and asked, "Will this do?"

Salmon looked out the window to the ground below, assessing the height. "Yes, I believe it will work." Then he turned again to Rahab, looking intently into her eyes. "Thank you," he said simply.

Rahab glanced out the window to the Jordan River far beyond and the Hebrew camp, which meant safety for Salmon and Enan.

"The soldiers have gone to seek you toward the Jordan to the fords. Go to the mountain so they will not meet you. Hide yourselves there three days until your pursuers have returned to the city, and then return to your camp," Rahab warned.

Enan grasped the cord and began to lower himself slowly toward the ground far below, but Salmon turned again to Rahab and said, "We will be blameless of your oath which you have made us swear. When we come into the land, tie this line of scarlet cord in the window which you let us down by, and bring your father and mother and brothers and sisters and all your father's family home with you. But whoever goes out of the doors of your house into the street, his blood shall be upon his head. Whoever is with you in the house, his blood will be on our head if anyone harms him. But, if you utter our business to anyone, then we will be free from your oath which you made us swear."[5]

"I have promised," answered Rahab as Salmon stepped out the window and lowered himself into the darkness.

Rahab sat by the window looking out into the night. Campfires flickered like a thousand stars on the far bank of the river. In the midst of the Hebrew camp a pillar of fire reached up into the heavens, illuminating the camp with an eerie light and casting shadows to the very edge of the tents. She wondered at the cause of such a fire. Then she mounted the steps to her rooftop and looked over the top of the city, past the far wall and to the mountains rising in the distance, where Salmon and Enan would seek sanctuary. Leaning her elbows on the battlement of her rooftop, Rahab relived the events of this evening in her mind. Only an hour ago she was a frightened, hopeless woman, facing certain death. Now, the grace of God had been shown to her. Salmon had said that the Lord shows mercy to all those whose faith is in Him. Rahab knew now that she did believe in the God of the Hebrews, the Lord Whom Salmon knew. Her faith was in Him. And He was surely showing her His mercy. The future remained a fearful mystery, but Rahab rested in the awareness that her future was in the Lord, God in heaven above and in earth below.

Three days had passed, and as the city around her droned in misery and fear for the Hebrew camp across the river, Rahab's heart was with two Hebrew spies, hiding in the mountain, fleeing from the soldiers. She stood on her rooftop and watched the colorful tents of animal skins across the river. There, in the midst of the camp, where the pillar of fire had burned in the night, rose a pillar of cloud, stationary, yet constantly billowing toward the

---

[5]Joshua 2:1-20

heavens.[6] Rahab wondered if the spies had returned in safety to report to their leader. Yet, she knew that they must be safe, for they trusted in the Lord of heaven and earth in Whom Rahab had come to trust.

Rahab descended the stairs and, wrapping her veil around her, entered the narrow street. Most that she passed walked quickly, head down. Some watched over the shoulder as if pursued. She walked directly to her father's home and knocked loudly on the door. A servant opened the door and ushered her through a lavish courtyard to a cool shaded pavement where Rahab's parents rested. Rahab bowed low before her parents and then curled on a soft cushion at her father's feet.

"Father, it has been revealed to me that the Hebrews will soon come to take the city. But Father, Mother," she turned, imploring, to look into her mother's eyes, "if you will come to my house when the attack comes, you will be safe."

"Faith, Daughter, it is not as serious as that," chided her father's deep, resonant voice. "Jericho has withstood greater armies than those few slaves from Egypt. We may soon suffer want for lack of commerce with those outside the walls, for I have heard that the king is in great dread of those Hebrews and plans to seal up the city. No matter, we have lived deprived of pleasures before. But we need not fear for safety, daughter."

"Father, the God of the Hebrews is great and powerful. Don't you remember that He destroyed the kings of the Amorites?" asked Rahab. She suddenly realized that her parents did not at all recognize the severity of the situation.

"The God of the Hebrews!" Rahab's father laughed loudly. "Dear daughter, I would rather say that the Hebrews themselves were able to defeat the fools of the Amorites. Their God had little to do with it, except that they trust that He has done it. That is all. We here in Jericho have been sheltered for

---

[6]Exodus 40:38

centuries by our own gods, Baal and Ashteroth. I think it better, don't you, dear daughter, to trust in gods whom we can see with our eyes than a God who has never been seen, even by His own faithful? Rahab, we have nothing to fear from this God. Surely you, a faithful of our own temple, and devoted to the worship of our gods, understand this."

"What did you say, dear?" her mother interrupted gently, "It has been revealed to you? In what way, Rahab?"

"I have vowed not to tell how it was revealed to me. But it is true. You must believe me. You must come to my house for your safety." Rahab's voice rose in volume and emotion as she spoke. But it was clear that her parents were untouched.

Her mother spoke again, with tenderness, "If you are afraid, dear, as we know many are, you may come and stay here, if you wish, until the danger you fear has passed.

"Oh, Mother," Rahab reached out and took her mother's hands in her own. "You are kind. But the danger is not to me. It is to you. You must come to my house to be in safety."

"Well, Daughter," boomed her father, "If we begin to fear, as you do, then perhaps we will come to your house."

Rahab rose to her feet and put her arms around her father's thick neck. "Promise me that you will, Father."

"Oh, I do promise. If we begin to fear that is," her father answered her reassuringly.

Rahab kissed her parents and took her leave. She wound through the streets, past the vendors hawking wares and foods and soon came to the home of her brother.

"My dear sister!" cried her brother when he saw her approach.

Rahab ran to hug him and then, without releasing him from her grasp she said, "Damion, please hear me. This is very urgent."

Damion looked at her with concern and led her to a stone bench, where they sat together.

"Damion, my dear brother, the Hebrews will come and

take the city. When they do, you must come to my house, for you will be safe there. You and your family. Please promise me that you will come."

Damion did not laugh as her father had. He only looked at her through eyes clouded with uncertainty. He frowned as he looked toward the sound of laughter where his children played beyond the garden wall.

"I do fear that you may be right, Rahab. I do fear for my wife and children. I have heard that the Hebrews leave none alive." Damion arose and walked across the stones. He stopped and turned, a puzzle in his eyes.

"But why, dear sister, should there be safety at your house? You live on the wall, which may be penetrated first. Why?"

Rahab rose also and went to Damion's side. She took his hand and said, "Damion, I have come to trust in the great God of the Hebrews. He will keep me safe, and all who will be with me in my house, when the Hebrews take the city."

"How have you come to trust the Hebrew God?" cried Damion. "And how do you know that you will be safe? I don't understand."

"I have taken a vow not to reveal any of these your questions. But, please my dear Damion, believe me. It is true. When they come to take the city you must be with me in my house." Rahab paused to consider her next words carefully. "The Lord, the God of the Hebrews, has shown Himself to me in His great mercy. I believe that He alone is the God in heaven above and on earth below. I believe with all my heart what I have told you. You must believe me, Damion, you must. It will be the only hope for you and yours."

"But you are attached to the temple of our gods. Why do you not trust them to give you safety from the Hebrews rather than the very God who will destroy us?" Damion asked, without mock in his voice.

"Baal and Ashteroth I can see, but I do not know. I have

not seen the Hebrew God, yet, Damion, I feel in my heart that I know Him. He is real. He will save me from Jericho's destruction." Rahab had now avowed what she had not been able to put into words before, but what she knew was in her heart. She quickly added, "And He will save you, also, if you will come to my house."

Rahab left Damion's house with his parting words a hopeful comfort to her heart, "If the enemy comes, I will remember what you have told me."

Rahab's sister, married to a counsellor of the king of Jericho, held her younger sister in disdain. Rahab had rarely seen her since her marriage, several years previously. Rahab dreaded to see her, yet she was a sister, and the only hope for her life and her family was for Rahab to speak to her.

The sun was declining toward the western wall of Jericho as Rahab approached the grand house where her sister lived. She spoke to the servant guarding the door and he disappeared inside the wall. Lights were lit about the city and stars appeared in the darkening sky, and still Rahab stood outside the gate. The sudden reappearance of the servant startled her and she gasped and missed his words. Assuming he had bid her enter, she started forward, but he stepped aside to bar the door. He looked severely at her and intoned gruffly, "The lady does not wish to be disturbed."

Rahab turned and walked swiftly away. When she reached her own house she latched the door and threw herself upon a couch, sobbing. Her sister's scorn would rob herself and her family of safety. Rahab felt helpless. Her heart full of trouble, she rose with weary steps to her rooftop and looked across the river to the Hebrew campfires flickering beyond and the red glow of the pillar of fire rising in the midst.

Rahab had prayed much in her short years to her gods. But those prayers had been recitations of a form that she had learned. She wished to pray to the Lord God of the Hebrews. But what form was followed when one spoke to Him? She wished for Salmon's presence again, so that he could explain to her if and how a person could pray to the Lord. But Salmon was there, across the river somewhere. So Rahab looked up into the star clustered sky and spoke.

"Lord God of the Hebrews, I do not know the proper way to pray to You. You know my heart, please accept this feeble prayer. I thank You, Lord, that You have shown Your mercy unto me, one so unworthy." Rahab was glad to say the words, to thank the Lord. Her heart was warmed and she knew that He listened to her and that He did not laugh at her prayer. So she continued. "Oh, Lord God, You have given me the promise that my family will be safe if they will come to my house. I thank You for your mercy shown to them, also. But, Lord, my father and mother and my sister will not heed. I cannot do more than I have done. But I want them to live." Rahab knew that the great God, Who had flung the stars into the night sky, could bring her family to her house to safety. She knew that she must trust Him to do so.

Chapter 2

Delivered

On the third day after Rahab had visited her family, she awakened to a strange new sound. She dressed rapidly and went to her rooftop. A most amazing sight met her eyes. The Jordan River, swollen past its banks, had ceased to flow toward the great salt sea. But the waters coursing from the Sea of Chinnereth above continued as usual. And there, before Rahab's eyes, the water was piling up as a mountain, as if held back by an unseen wall.

The great camp of the Hebrews was no longer. All tents were gone and the people, by thousands, were lined up along the river's edge. In the midst of the dry river bed stood two men in blue robes, holding poles from which hung a draped object. Rahab watched with awe as the people stepped down the riverbank, into the dry bottom, and walked across to the other side. There they continued to file along, following the pillar of cloud, to the plains of Jericho.[7]

Rahab remembered the story Zaphnath had told her, and suddenly she wanted to see him, to tell him everything that had happened to her, to ask him to come to safety, too. She hurried through the morning streets until she knocked at his door in the high wall. It was early, and it was several moments before Zaphnath opened his door to her.

Rahab's manner was remarkably changed from her previous visit. Zaphnath smiled and offered her a seat on the wooden bench. But Rahab was too excited to sit. She took Zaphnath's gnarled hands in her own soft ones and said, "Zaphnath, they are crossing the river! I watched them from my roof on the wall. Two men in blue are bearing a draped box in

---

[7]Joshua 3:16

the midst of the dry river bed, and the Hebrew people are crossing over on foot. Oh, Zaphnath, it is just like the story you told me of the Hebrews when they fled from Pharaoh and crossed over the Red Sea!" She stopped breathlessly and watched the smile fade from Zaphnath's worn face. He shook his snowy head and said sadly,

"Yes, child, it is like that day. But that day they left us after great destruction. Today they come here to destroy us. No one can stand before their God."

"Oh, Zaphnath, the most wondrous thing has happened to me! I have come to trust in the God of the Hebrews, and He has promised to save me alive and all who will be with me in my house when the Hebrews take the city! Zaphnath, you must come to my house. You will be safe there. It is true, yes, really true. Please, Zaphnath, you are the dearest friend I know. Come to my house and be safe!"

Zaphnath continued to shake his head through her recitation and when she was done. He spoke slowly, sadly, "No, child, no. The God of the Hebrews was my ruin, and He shall not be my salvation."

"Zaphnath, you believe in the reality of the Lord. I know that you do. For years you have talked to me of the God of the Hebrews. I know He is real. He is my Lord. He has promised to save anyone alive who will be with me in my house. Please, Zaphnath. Once before He was your ruin, yes. Please let Him save you, now!" Fear clutched at Rahab's crying heart. Her friend must come to safety. He of all she knew did believe in the God in Whom she trusted.

But Zaphnath continued to shake his old head. He sat heavily upon his bench and with his eyes closed he began to hum his song. Rahab left him quietly.

The buzz in the city was that the Hebrews, by magic, were creating an illusion; that the water was not indeed piled as a mountain, but only appeared to be. But those who saw it with their own eyes could only believe what they saw.

Rahab returned to her roof and watched the continuing train of Hebrews flowing across the Jordan River. At long last they were all passed over. Rahab watched as twelve men reentered the river bed and from there carried out twelve large stones. She watched as a man piled up twelve huge stones beside the men in blue. Finally the men with the draped box, too, came up out of the river bed. Suddenly, as though a wall had been removed, the mountain of water plummeted down, raising a wide curtain of spray and mist, lapping fiercely against the riverbanks, deepening the river bed and carrying an abundance of sediments with it as it once again rushed on toward the salt sea.[8]

The King of Jericho did indeed seal the city. No one could pass out or in through the giant, barred gates. Soldiers guarded everywhere, looking for strangers, nervous, short-tempered. But for her trips to the market for food, Rahab spent most of her days on her roof, watching the new Hebrew camp in the distance.

Rahab watched in the morning as the people left their tents to roam about, gathering something from the ground.[9] Rahab wondered at them. What could they find upon the ground to gather each morning?

On the fifth morning Rahab could see from her distant viewpoint that grain was brought from somewhere into the Hebrew camp and the Hebrews feasted upon it. The next morning, the sixth of their new camp, the people once again went out to gather from the ground, as usual. They ran about, like ants scurrying about a broken anthill.[10]

As each day succeeded into the next with no move from the Hebrew camp, some hearts dared to hope. But Rahab knew.

---

[8]Joshua 4:18

[9]Exodus 16:4

[10]Joshua 5:12

She had been told that the end would come. Each day she prayed again to the Lord, in simple words from her soul, that her family and her dear Zaphnath would come to her house for safety.

This morning Rahab knew something was afoot in the Hebrew camp. Rahab watched from her vantage point as the people formed into an ordered line and began a slow but steady approach to the city of Jericho.

"They are coming," Rahab told herself. "They are coming and not one of my family has come to safety. I must compel them."

Rahab hurried through the crowded streets. People surged back and forth wildly, fearful, crazed. In great haste she spoke to her parents and her brother. They listened. They looked worried. Yet, they did not believe that safety was to be found at Rahab's house on the wall.

Then she approached her sister's house. The guard looked at her severely and seemed reluctant to announce her. But as he finally opened the door, Rahab pushed past him and ran through the garden and into the house. Her sister, Rebah, looked up from her stitchery, startled, as Rahab ran to her. When the guard appeared, apologetic, Rebah dismissed him.

"I know you do not wish to see me, Rebah," Rahab spoke. "But the Hebrews are marching toward the city, now, as I speak. It has been shown me that there will be safety for all who will come to my house. Please, Rebah, come, you and your family. You will be safe there."

Rebah quietly laid aside her handwork and looked at Rahab. There were tears coursing down her cheeks, and a surge of tenderness compelled Rahab to take her sister into her arms. As they wept together, Rebah explained between her sobs that Damion had come to her and told her Rahab's story. But Rebah's husband had made her promise not to listen to him, just as her husband had made her promise so many times not to see her sister. Rahab suddenly understood her sister's former attitude toward her. She pulled back gently to look at Rebah and said, "But you must come, it is true. Your husband must come, and your children. Please, Rebah."

"I must please my husband," was the reply.

"But you will all die!"

"Perhaps, although my husband believes as does our king that Jericho can stand up to an attack by the Hebrews." Rebah looked sadly at Rahab and said quietly, "Thank you. You must go now."

Before returning to her own house Rahab went to plead again with Zaphnath, but to no avail. The old man only shook his head and relapsed into his song.

When Rahab finally returned to her rooftop, the Hebrew soldiers were very close. She could hear the loud, clear blasts of the trumpets which were carried at the front of the marching soldiers. She checked to see that her cord of scarlet was intact and then sat beside the window to wait.

Confusion filled her. She had been so certain that the Lord would bring her family to her for safety. Why should He promise to save them when it was not in her power to bring them here? Tears could not come, so she watched with dry eyes as the Hebrew troops marched silently up to the Jericho wall, not far from her house.

They did not attempt to break through the mighty gates. They did not shoot arrows or spears or attempt to climb the towering wall. Indeed they did nothing but turn and continue their march along the wall, the only sound the blasting of the trumpets and the tramping of their feet. Rahab watched until the entire file of soldiers had marched out of her view around the wall.

A hush hung over the city. People crowded the rooftops to watch with growing apprehension. What were they doing? Why?

"Is Salmon marching there with the Hebrew troops?" Rahab wondered. And then she prayed, "Lord, I must trust You.

What else can I do? I do believe that You will keep Your Word."

Rahab was laying her head on her arms against the window sill when she heard the faint drumming of marching feet again and the blare of trumpets. She looked along the wall toward the sound and saw that the Hebrew troops had entirely compassed the city and were now coming to her part of the wall. She watched their silent treading until they were beneath her very house and she was looking down upon their heads. And still they marched on. Then, curiously, they veered away and filed back toward the camp at Gilgal.

Great relief flooded the city as Rahab walked again through the crowded streets. She heard the conversation around her in victorious and taunting tones.

"They searched us over and went away! They see that there is no hope for them to conquer us! The feeble Hebrews and their God have fled the mighty gods of Jericho!"

People feasted and rejoiced in their hope. Rahab did not wish to remain home. She could not, would not be there for the temple guard, should they seek to call her to the temple. So she wandered through the streets, wondering. She still believed what had been told her by Salmon. Yet, in the face of today's occurrence, she could only wonder.

The city had almost stilled itself when Rahab finally sought her bed. But she continued to lay awake, her mind a whirl of confusion. She could not sleep. So she arose and mounted to her rooftop, from where she watched the lights flicker far away in the Hebrew camp. The tower of fire reflected in her eyes.

The words came with difficulty, but she finally prayed, "Lord, of course You know why they came today and merely marched around the walls. I do not. Calm my heart, oh Lord, and let me not doubt You. I believe what You have revealed to me. I thank you that hope remains for my family. Bring them to me, Lord."

Rahab stood in the cooling breeze awhile longer and then returned to her bed. Why was it that she found so much comfort and relief when she talked to the Lord? He had never once answered her prayer with audible words. And yet she always felt the answer in her heart.

To the great dismay of all in the city of Jericho, the Hebrew soldiers reappeared the next day to encircle the city once more with constant rhythm in their march and yet without uttering a word. Once more they turned from the city and marched back to camp.

The aftermath this second day was not the jubilant triumph of the day before. Worry once again creased the brows of many. The king met with his counsellors to wonder at the Hebrew strategy, and with the priests of Baal and Ashteroth to divine the spiritual significance.

Rahab's wonder grew as she watched the soldiers tramp by below her on the second day. Surely the Hebrews had a great plan from the Lord. She must trust and wait. But what of her loved ones? She was sure after the first day that they all scorned her warning. But now, after a second day of silent march around the city, perhaps her family would listen.

Rahab hurried to talk with her parents. Her father looked older and her mother wore a haggard expression quite foreign to her. Rahab's father paced back and forth as he spoke, "The king has assured us that they can have no power against us. He believes that they wish to weaken us by fear, and that is why they come and strangely march around. We must not succumb to the fear they wish to impose upon us."

"Father," Rahab said tenderly, "They do have a plan, I believe it. And their God will eventually give them the city." Rahab knew her next words would cut to her father's very soul, but she must speak. "Father, I have come to trust the Lord God of the Hebrews. He has shown me His mercy. That is how I know that I will be safe when the Hebrews attack, and that is how you, too, can find safety. Yes, now they are merely compassing the city. But the strike will come. And Father, Mother, you must come now to my house."

Anger colored her father's face as he glared at her. "You! A temple harlot to our great gods! And you would turn from them to another God of Whom you do not know?"

"But Father, I do know the Lord. He is real to me. I believe in Him. I trust in Him."

Her father pointed to the door and simply said, "Go."

When the strange tramping of the Hebrew soldiers commenced on the third day, the king called all of his wise men and counsellors, together with the priests of the gods, to discuss what must be done. As the wise men emerged from their solemn consultations, the citizens of the great city Jericho crowded around the raised platform where the king and the chief of the priests stood. Rahab's house on the wall was in close proximity to the temple of Baal. She stood on her rooftop, watching the scene in the temple court below her.

"My good people," shouted the king, "we have taken counsel with the wisest of men and we now know what our gods would have us to do. Our revered high priest will now explain." The king waved his richly robed arm toward the priest, who bowed low and turned toward the expectant crowd.

The priest stood in silence for a full minute while the crowd hushed to utter silence. He then spoke slowly and deliberately.

"Our great gods, Baal and Ashteroth, have spoken and shown their desire. They will that our enemies be defeated and depart from our fair city. But we must pay the price they demand." The high priest paused and let the people ponder his words before he continued. "We have daily, yes hourly offered sacrifices before our gods at this temple. But now our great gods have required the gift of ten children, five males and five females, all under one year of age. Those given freely as gifts to our gods will ensure our deliverance from our enemies."

The hushed crowd stood motionless. The priest stood

erect and silent, serenely surveying the quiet crowd. A sudden wail pierced the quiet, and as the people stood and watched, a man walked forward, carrying a child in his arms. A weeping woman followed him, clutching and pleading, but he ignored her lament and walked to the high priest, extending his arms, raising the child aloft.

The high priest took the child and held him forth for the crowd to see. "Here," intoned the priest, "is a loyal citizen of our great city, and a devout follower of our gods." He paused, scanning the crowd. He then continued, "But this glorious sacrifice is meaningless unless there are others who will show their devotion. The gods have required ten children."

Minutes ticked by. Then Rahab watched sadly as one after another the fathers carried their children forward to the priest, mothers weeping and clinging. Suddenly her heart sank within her and she gasped with horror as she watched her sister's husband descend the platform and take his youngest child from Rebah's arms. He turned and walked back toward the priest. Rebah followed him, imploring, beseeching him, her cries carrying to Rahab's rooftop, and yet he continued his march ahead. At the platform he reached his arms toward the high priest, but the priest waved him away, speaking to the watching crowd.

"Our great gods are pleased. The sum has been reached. Ten gifts to our gods have been given."

Rahab released a long sigh that she had held while watching the scene unfold below. She watched as Rebah clutched her child in her arms and ran back along the street toward her home.

"Oh, Lord!" Rahab prayed. "You spared my sister's child from sacrifice to Baal. Will you let him die a sacrifice to a Hebrew sword? I must trust that you will not."

The horror of this third day unfolded with such dreadful intensity that the Hebrew troops marching round the city were all but forgotten, although the cause for all the dread. One thousand candles were lighted in a circle about the large, raised, circular stone altar on which the giant images of the gods Baal and Ashteroth stood. The interior of the images served as a furnace, fueled and heated to tremendous extremes. And then, as the devout began to chant, slowly at first and then more rapidly and loudly, until the sounds blended with the screams of suffering and anguish, the gifts to the gods were bound and one at a time were placed upon the outstretched hands of the images, from which they tumbled downward along the searing arms into the flames.

Men and women screamed and groaned. Some swooned and fell to the pavement. Frenzied devout gnashed themselves with knives while their blood spurted upon fellow worshippers and flowed to the gutters.

In the midst of the hideous ceremony a loud thumping sounded at the door. Fear clutched at Rahab's heart as she went to the door. Was this the time?

"What do you want?" she asked.

"Temple guard," came the hoarse whispered reply. "You are summoned to the temple."

Rahab had feared such a call. The temple harlots were an important part of intercession to the great gods. Great sums of money were added to the coffers of the temple through their merchandise. Yet Rahab could never again be a part of temple worship. With her heart she served the Lord, God of heaven and earth. What could she do?

So standing at her door, as the guard pounded impatiently, Rahab prayed, "Lord, deliver me!" Then she simply said, "I will not come! Go away."

The temple guard was confused.

"Are you ill?" he asked.

"I will not come!" was her answer.

The temple guard turned, undecided, and looked about. Finally he moved away, back toward the temple.

Rahab fell upon a couch and cried in relief and gratitude to the Lord.

When Rahab returned to her roof the ceremony had ended. She watched the people shuffle along the dusty streets, wordlessly, stepping over the unconscious bodies strewn in their way. An acrid odor wafted to Rahab's rooftop and with a heavy heart she thought of the infants who had died. And yet, she knew that many more infants would die when the Hebrews attacked. She could not save them all. But her sister's children, Damion's children. She could save them. They had but to come to her house.

Rahab walked out through the quiet homegoers and sought her sister's home. The guard was nowhere to be seen, so Rahab opened the gate and entered. She found Rebah with her three children in the courtyard. Rebah was clutching them all to her, crying uncontrolled. Rebah's husband stood watching her, helpless. He glanced at Rahab as she approached, but said nothing. The horrors his family had experienced far outweighed his scorn for Rahab.

Rahab spoke gently to her sister. "Rebah, I thank my Lord that your child was spared. But even the sacrifices given to Baal and Ashteroth today will not deter the plan of the Lord, the God of the Hebrews. You must come to my house. Don't you see how urgent it is?" Rebah continued to weep with her children, so Rahab turned to her brother-in-law. "I now belong to the Lord, the God of the Hebrews, Who made the heaven and the earth. He has promised to spare my life from the Hebrew onslaught and the lives of all who will come go my house. Please, I beg you, come."

Rebah's husband looked sadly at Rahab. He had been willing to make the ultimate sacrifice to save the city from the Hebrews. Rahab understood such devotion, although misdirected. He only looked away and hung his head in defeat.

"What can I do? What can I say? It is true! You must come to my house!" Rahab found herself shouting. Her brother in law looked up again and said hoarsely,

"Leave us."

Rahab left Rebah's house sorrowfully and ran along the street to Damion's home. Inside she found her brother and his wife in hushed conversation, their children grasped protectively in their arms.

"Dear Damion!" Rahab cried. "Do not think that the high priest is done asking for gifts to appease the wrath of the gods. But, alas, although they escape the dreaded flames, your children will be killed when the Hebrews take the city. Please, Damion, and my dear sister in law, come to my house for safety. It is sure, for the Lord has promised safety there."

Damion and his wife both rose to their feet. Damion spoke with emotion, "Rahab, my wife and I have just discussed your offer of safety. We may be fools, but we have decided to come."

Rahab's utter grief was transformed to joy. She seized her bother and cried against him with relief. "Thank the Lord!" she repeated over and over. Then she turned to her sister in law and said, "I will help you gather whatever you want to bring along. Only let's hurry!"

Rahab stood atop her roof and breathed in the cool evening air, a welcome relief from the oppressive streets below. Damion's children played hide and seek in her stalks of flax. Damion and his wife mounted the steps and joined Rahab at the battlement.

"When will they attack?" Damion's wife asked softly, looking across the miles to the Hebrew camp.

"I don't know," Rahab replied. "I only know that they will come, and now you will be safe because you have come to my house." Rahab turned to embrace Damion and his wife. "I'm so thankful to my Lord that you have come."

Damion looked from the rooftop toward the streets of Jericho and said sadly, "But what of our parents? And Rebah?"

Rahab closed her eyes and said in hushed tones, "I pray that the Lord will bring them here."

Damion's oldest child came asking,"What is the red rope

hanging out your window, Aunt Rahab?"

Rahab led the family to the room with the window wall and showed them the cord of scarlet. "This is a token. It is this scarlet cord hanging out the window which is surety of our safety." She looked at the children and said firmly, "It must remain here, in the window. Do you understand? It is very important."

"We understand," answered the oldest child. Rahab smiled and gathered them into her arms. What lay ahead for these dear children? She praised the Lord in her heart that they would live.

As the Hebrew soldiers began their march on the fourth day, the high priest of the gods began his petition for gifts once more, offerings of children. The quota this day was fifty. Cries and shrieks rose with the chants from the temple court below. Damion and his wife entertained their children in the room by the scarlet cord, to be ready, and also to be as far as they could from the dreadful sounds.

Rahab stood aloft and peered into the turmoil of the temple area, but she did not see Rebah or her husband. Rahab prayed again that the Lord would bring them to her house.

Day five brought a demand for one hundred sacrifices. It was clear that those who would willingly offer had already done so, for the soldiers went from house to house, exacting the gifts from the wretched parents. Rahab could hear their screams and the rough whipping of the soldiers. She heard the drone of chanting from the temple area and knew that the gifts to Baal and Ashteroth were being rolled down those terrible ramps into the flames.

An urgent pounding sounded at the door. Damion and his family huddled in the window room. Rahab spoke through the door with caution, "What do you want?" She feared a verbal battle with the temple guard, and maybe a priest. Perhaps they could force their way in and physically coerce her to go to the temple. Or perhaps they knew of Damion's presence and were come to take his child.

But a frightened voice answered her, "Open quickly, it is Rebah."

Rahab swung open the door and swept Rebah's family inside. The sisters embraced in tears and Rebah's husband explained, "At first I felt it was my duty to Baal to offer our son. But as I see repeated sacrifices and still the Hebrews march around us, I decided we should come. I am not willing to offer my child." He paused and looked at Rahab hopefully. "I am willing, however, that all my children should live."

"You did truly mean for us to come, didn't you?" implored Rebah.

"I'm so happy that you've come," Rahab assured her and then turned and led them up to the window room.

"See who has come!" she announced to Damion's family with joy.

While the children played quiet games the adults talked about the uncertain future. The others could not understand Rahab's faith that they were now all safe in her house, but the very surety of her confidence gave them courage and hope.

"When will the attack come?" came the familiar question from Rebah's husband.

"I don't know when, I only know that it will come," was all that Rahab could answer.

As day six dawned, and with it came the tramping of the Hebrew feet from Gilgal, Rahab knew she must try again to persuade her parents to come to her house. One hundred days may pass with the silent treading about the walls of Jericho, but Rahab knew that the day would come when the Lord would give the city to the Hebrews. On that day her parents must be safe in her house.

Rahab watched the Hebrew troops as they rounded the wall as far as she could see. Then she hurried to her father's house, wrapped closely in her veils so that none could recognize her. Fear clutched the city in an horrible grasp and sorrow flowed through every street of the city. The city was sealed from within, but terror besieged each heart. Hope for deliverance by the hand of their gods had fled from the breasts of most.

Rahab's parents received her passively, her father's bold impudence faded.

"Father, Mother," she pleaded, "Damion and Rebah and theirs have come to safety to my house. I know that the Hebrews are making a strange offensive against the city. Perhaps their strategy is to afflict fear, Father," she conceded. "But that is not all that they will do. Someday they will not merely encompass the city without assault. And I know that the Lord, the God of the Hebrews, will give them the city." Rahab paused, seeking a reason plausible to her parents. "My brother and sister are there. Their children are there. Father and Mother, even if there be no safety in my house, we will all be together. Please come."

Rahab's father offered no excuse but his stubbornness. He had been raised a worshipper of the gods. All his life he had devoutly sought to please Baal and Ashteroth. He could not change now.

On her homeward way, she found herself at Zaphnath's door. She knocked and prayed. When the old man opened the door, Rahab clutched him dearly and besought him tearfully, "Please, dear friend! The Hebrews will not march about the city wall forever. Please come to my house for safety. My brother and my sister have come. Please, Zaphnath, you have been my dearest friend. I cannot bear to let you die when there is sanctuary. Please come with me, now."

Zaphnath patted her back tenderly, and with a broken voice refused her offer. "Rahab, my child, you have been such a dear friend to this old man. You have listened to my endless prattle about Egypt, I know, I know. And, yes, my child, I do believe that there is safety at your house, yes, yes, I do, I do." Zaphnath was nodding his head and Rahab dared to hope. But he continued, "But the safety is not for me. No, not for me.

Asta met the wrath of this mighty God. I have had forty years to remember, yes, to remember. I think it is time, now, for me to face His fierceness."

Rahab clung to him, sobbing and pleading. Finally Zaphnath pulled her to his door and said kindly, "Go, child, go to your house and be safe."

"No! You must come, too!" She clung more tightly, but his aged hands released her grasp and pushed her gently through the doorway.

"Go now, child, go." Zaphnath closed and latched his door. Rahab fell against it, anguished.

As the sixth day closed Rahab stood again on her rooftop watching the distant campfires flicker. She wished so that she could talk with Salmon again. Perhaps he could explain what was happening. But maybe even the Hebrew soldiers were in obscurity about the battle plans. Her only peace was found in prayer and faith in what God had promised her.

The Hebrew soldiers began their customary march in silence before the sun had fully risen on the seventh day. This change in procedure alarmed the king and chief priest. But the tension mounted as the Hebrew soldiers came full circle and did not veer toward Gilgal as each day before, but began a second circle of the city. Vendors barred their doors. Residents of the great city cowered behind doors latched and bolted. The king of Jericho paced his palace, wringing his hands and imploring his gods to strike the enemy dead as they marched. Yet the tramping outside the wall continued. The priests conferred in anxious tones, but could bring no relief to the king.

Upon conclusion of the second revolution and without a word, the Hebrew soldiers began to circle the city a third time. A hush descended heavily upon the city. Even the children sensed the awful fear of their elders and were quiet.

When the Hebrews began the fourth time to encircle the city, the king called all his counsellors and priests to the palace. The soldiers sought Rebah's husband at their abandoned home only briefly, for they feared to roam the silent streets of Jericho. At last the high priest concluded that a continual sacrifice should be offered to Baal. He realized, however, that the gifts to Baal must be drawn from older children, now. The tense and terrified soldiers went ruthlessly through the city gathering the precious gifts for Baal. Some resisted and were lost to sacrifice as they fell to a soldier's blows or sword.

The horrid lament of the city continued in the monotonous chant of the priests and a few devout as the rites to Baal commenced and continued through the long, toilsome day.

The intensity quickened as the Hebrew soldiers rounded the walls and began the fifth compass of the city. The frenzied faithful of Baal and Ashteroth slashed themselves and wailed in agony to their gods. Some swooned away to die as their life drained slowly from them in a warm, red stream. Oppressed beyond control, some of the devout flung themselves against the searing idols and began to climb aloft, only to fall away in death. A horrible stench filled the pungent air and settled into every home, every corner of the city.

Rahab and her loved ones gathered close in the window room. They, too, were silent. But for a tiny niece who asked for food, even the children sat in silence.

A short while after the Hebrew soldiers had passed beneath the window for the sixth time and began a seventh circle, a loud knocking was heard at the door below.

"Ignore it," counselled Damion. "It could well be the guard or a priest summoning you away to the rituals."

"Or it could be our parents," answered Rahab, who left the room and descended the stairs. Damion sadly watched her go.

"What do you want?" Rahab asked at the door.

"Open, Daughter," her father's voice cracked in fear.

Rahab shouted gladly and threw open the door to find her parents, quaking with terror, tears streaming down their ashen faces. She pulled them in and secured the door, throwing her arms around them raptly. Her parents had come. Praise be to the Lord! He had been faithful, after all! Then, shouting to her brother and sister, she led her parents to the window room.

"Wouldn't it be better to stay in the lower room?" her mother suggested as they mounted the stairs.

Rahab could not answer for the rush of loved ones upon her parents as they were welcomed into the room. They sat in a close circle and spoke tender words of love and courage to one another.

"Mother," Rahab finally interrupted from the window, where she held forth the scarlet cord, "this cord of scarlet is our surety. We must remain here. We will be safe. I know it because I trust the Lord. He has brought you here and we will now all be safe."

"Rahab, my dear daughter," said Rahab's father, "I cannot understand your devotion to this foreign God. But there is no hope in sight, even to me, a faithful worshipper of our gods. I cannot trust in this God as you do, but I rest in your trust of Him."

The day was far advanced as the Hebrew soldiers completed the seventh compass of the city of Jericho. They had just passed beneath the window in the wall when a sudden blast of trumpets startled the small assemblage in Rahab's house. They clung closer together as a loud shout accompanied the trumpets and rose in a deafening crescendo.

And then was the beginning of the end of Jericho. The walls of the city, which had withstood valiant attacks in the city's long, illustrious history, trembled violently. Then, with an ear-splitting crack and groan, the entire length and height of the mighty walls plunged to the earth, splintering, fragmenting to dust, and exposing the now vulnerable city within. All of the wall fell, that is, but the small portion in which the house of

Rahab the harlot was situated. That element alone stood firm.[11]

With the miraculous felling of the wall came the Hebrew soldiers, each one straight ahead, into the city. Rahab's family embraced fervently, with eyes closed, but with ears hearing the devastation of the city.

Rahab's awed heart could barely contain the wonder of the moment. Her house had indeed stood, while the wall of the city had fallen. But her heart found grief, also, as she remembered her dear Zaphnath who, believing in the power of the Lord, would not come to refuge and would soon meet the sword of a Hebrew soldier. She cried silently, encircled by her loved ones' arms. She praised God for their safety. But no comfort could soothe the pain of her grief for Zaphnath.

Rahab jumped with the fright of a hand clasping her shoulder and a voice behind her saying, "Rahab, we have come for you and your family. Hold hands tightly and follow us." Rahab turned to see towering above her huddled family the two young spies whom she had sheltered that night which now seemed so long ago. Rahab spoke to her family and they quickly rose to their feet and clasped hands, following close behind the tall soldier. Salmon led them with long strides from the room and down the stairway, the little ones' feet pounding rapidly against the stones. Enan followed the train and kept the file moving swiftly. As they emerged from the house into the street, stifling smoke choked them. Salmon reached for Rahab's hand and began to run through the burning streets, over the crumbled dust that had been the wall, and out across the plain toward the Hebrew camp.

When Rahab's lungs were close to bursting, and she wondered that her parents could run so far, so fast, and also the little ones, Salmon slowed and stopped.

Rahab's family collapsed together in the lush grass to

---

[11]Joshua 6:20-22

weep and wonder at their escape. But Rahab stood, wrapping her veils around her, and watched the flames reach to the sky as the sun began to sink into the west. Salmon stood beside her, breathing heavily. They stood together, thus, as the darkness gathered around them, and witnessed the demise of Jericho.

Chapter 3

Decision

Rahab awoke to savory smells of food cooking over morning fires. She sat up on the mat on which she had been sleeping and rubbed her eyes with her fingers. She was alive. Her family were alive. Jericho had died.

Mixed with remembrances of terror and devastation, of flight and escape, were memories of a strong hand that had held hers as she ran from the city, of a gentle voice that had soothed her fears, of a kind man who had brought her family here, to this tent, and offered them a place to sleep. Salmon. His brown eyes had looked at her and his strong hand had held hers through her dreams when she had finally drifted into sleep after many hours.

Rahab shook her head and rose to her feet. She must forget Salmon's eyes and strong hands. She must forget Salmon. The man may have a wife. Yet, if not, there was no hope that she, a temple harlot, could ever have the love of such a man.

Rahab quietly left the tent, where her family yet slept. The sun was dazzling and at first blinded her. She shaded her eyes and looked about her. A sea of tents was about her. They were low and sprawling, made from the skins of animals stretched over poles. Many were dyed bright colors making the camp cheerful and bright. Women were bending over the fires as children ran and played games. Groups of men were discussing, probably the fall of Jericho. Rahab stepped away from the tent and noticed the eyes of several women suddenly directed her way. She felt uneasy beneath their stares, but smiled shyly at them. None smiled back. Most turned back to their tasks. But one young woman, wearing a beautiful shade of green, continued to gaze at her. As Rahab continued to walk, the young woman's eyes narrowed to slits. Even after Rahab had left her far behind she could feel the piercing blue eyes watching her.

The Hebrew camp seemed to reach into the distance

endlessly. There must be multiplied thousands of them, perhaps millions! And yet their camp seemed ordered and organized. Rahab turned and started back toward the tent where she had slept. Her eye caught sight of the charred remains of the great city of Jericho, still smoldering in the distance, and a sob caught in her throat. Zaphnath! Gone! Rahab hurried into the tent and wept silently upon her mat.

Presently a woman's voice called at the doorway of the tent, "Are you awake? I have prepared some food if you wish to eat."

Rahab dried her tears and went back outside. A slight woman, perhaps in her thirties, was stirring a pot over a fire. She looked up when Rahab emerged and smiled kindly.

"I am Salmon's sister, Maachah. You must be Rahab. We are so thankful to you for helping Salmon and Enan when they were spying in the city. Please sit, there." Maachah motioned toward a thick mat on the grass and Rahab lowered herself onto it.

"Are your family still sleeping?" Maachah asked, serving some thick porridge into a dish.

"Yes," answered Rahab. "They are exhausted from last night." Rahab looked tenderly toward the tent where her family slept. "I thank the Lord that they are safe." She took the dish from Maachah, thanking her, and began to eat slowly.

"Salmon has told us of your faith in the Lord. It's wonderful, isn't it, that a heathen woman such as yourself can find the mercy of God?"

"Yes," answered Rahab, "it is wonderful." Yes, she thought to herself, she must be a heathen woman. Or she had been. And the great God of the Hebrews had shown her His mercy.

"My husband has told me this morning that the battle was a complete success. Wasn't that such a marvelous thing that the Lord did! We could see from here when the walls of the city just crumbled to dust and fell to the ground. My husband said that not one soldier was even injured!" Maachah stopped suddenly as she saw a look of grief pass over Rahab's face. She went quickly to Rahab's side and took her hands gently. "I'm sorry. I should not be talking so. Jasper says that I talk too much. You must have lost people that you loved in Jericho. Please forgive my tongue." Maachah's cheeks had reddened and she looked intently into Rahab's eyes.

"You are forgiven." Rahab tried to smile. "There was one friend, an old man. But he refused the offer of safety." Rahab's voice broke and she said no more. She tried, but she could eat no more. So, thanking Maachah, she rose to her feet.

Just then a large, square man approached and spoke to Maachah. Maachah said something to him quietly. He looked at Rahab and smiled. "Welcome," he said with warmth in his voice. "You saved our little brother, and we are grateful." Maachah stepped forward and introduced her husband, Jasper.

A small child with touselled hair emerged from the tent rubbing her eyes. She looked about her, dismayed, and then caught sight of Rahab. Her little feet carried her quickly to Rahab's side where she buried her face in Rahab's veils.

"Hello, little one, are you hungry?" Maachah asked kindly.

The little girl peeked from behind the veils with big eyes, but said noting.

"She doesn't understand the Egyptian tongue," Rahab explained. I learned the language from an old man from Egypt." Rahab's voice trailed off sadly.

"Ask her if she is hungry," Maachah said gently.

Soon all of Rahab's family were eating breakfast, talking quietly among themselves. Rahab interpreted for Maachah, who was full of questions for her guests. Soon Jasper put his large hand on her shoulder and said, "We should let our guests eat in peace, should we not?" So Maachah turned back to her cooking.

But she soon forgot Jasper's reprimand and said to Rahab, "It is so fun to cook! I hope everything tastes right. I've had very little practice cooking such food."

"What food are you accustomed to cooking?" Rahab asked.

"Oh, we gathered the manna everyday, you know, and ate it. We baked it or boiled it or ate it plain. It tasted like honey wafers. All of my life I have eaten manna everyday, that and quail, and very little else." Maachah sighed and then quickly added, "It was so wondrous, of course, that the Lord supplied us with manna, else we had starved, so many of us, you know."

"What is manna?" asked Rahab.

Maachah laughed liltingly and said,"That is what it means, 'What is it?' My mother said it was corn from heaven, angels' food.[12] It was small and white. Every morning we found it on the ground and gathered it. Those who gathered too much and those who gathered too little always had just enough when it was measured. And after the sun was hot, it melted from the ground! If we left any of it until the next day it bred worms and stank, except on the sixth day, when we gathered twice as much. That was because that on the seventh day, there was no manna on the ground in the morning. And the manna we gathered double on the sixth day never spoiled, but was ever fresh on the seventh day."[13]

"How marvelous!" said Rahab. "I believe I saw the Hebrews gathering manna in the morning, for several days. But why was there none on the seventh day? And why do you cook other food, now?"

"Oh, the seventh day is the Sabbath, you know, the day of rest. That is the day that we may do no work at all."[14] Maachah answered. "And when we began to eat the corn of the

---

[12]Psalm 78:24,25

[13]Exodus 16:16-24

[14]Exodus 20:8-11

land, the manna ceased."

As she was talking with Maachah, Rahab looked up to see Salmon approach. Maachah smiled at him and said, "Salmon, little brother! Would you care to eat?"

Salmon smiled warmly down at his sister and shook his head, "Thank you, but I have no time to eat, now. Joshua wishes to speak with Rahab and her family. I must take them to see him now."

Rahab explained to her family and they followed in a tight group as Salmon led the way. As they walked between the tents Rahab saw the young woman in green, staring coldly. Rahab looked away uneasily.

After what seemed a long walk, the family saw an amazing sight. Inside a curtained court was a tent. Rich blue, scarlet, and purple curtains draped a glittering gold, silver, and bronze frame. Atop this tent rested the pillar of cloud that Rahab had seen in the distance, rising up toward the heavens. As they approached, Salmon explained to Rahab that this was the Tabernacle, the center of worship and communion with the Lord. The Lord Himself dwelt here, in the Holy Place, on the mercy seat above the Ark of the Covenant. It sounded very mysterious to Rahab, and her heart raced with excitement at the thought!

A man stepped out from a group by the gate of the court. He was old, perhaps the age of Zaphnath, but he was still a strong soldier. This was the great leader, Joshua.

Salmon spoke to Joshua in a tongue that Rahab did not know. Joshua stepped toward Rahab and she fell at his feet in obeisance. But Joshua reached down and lifted her to her feet with strong hands, saying in Egyptian, "No, my daughter, do not prostrate yourself. It is the Lord Who has saved you alive and your family, because of your faith in His almighty power. Now, because of your kindness that you showed to the two spies, I offer you a home with us, within the tribes of Israel."

"You are kind, sir," answered Rahab. "I will speak with my family."

Rahab relayed the message to her parents, her brother, and her sister. Her father was the first to answer. "The God of the Hebrews has indeed saved our lives from the destruction of Jericho. But this God has not my faith and trust. I will not stay here, with His people."

Rebah's husband spoke as Rahab's father ended, "We, too, must not stay here with these people. I am grateful for deliverance, but we will not dwell with them."

Damion faltered, undecided. He looked long at his wife and children, his father and mother, and then said to Rahab, "I believe that the God of the Hebrews is a great God, worthy of worship. But I must go with my father." He put his arm around his wife's shoulders and she sadly nodded approval.

Rahab returned to Joshua blinking back her tears. "My family thanks you for your kind and generous offer, sir, but they wish to depart and make a life for themselves." She swallowed, closing her eyes. She loved her family. She knew her next words would separate her from them forever. But she knew she must say them. "I, sir, desire to accept your kind offer and remain here with the people of God."[15]

"You are welcome," Joshua nodded toward Rahab. "And we will supply your family with all that they will need, tents, clothing, dishes for cooking. Because they are your family, we assure them safety from our army wherever they may dwell."

Rahab started to bow before Joshua, but caught herself and merely nodded. "Thank you for your kindness," she said.

Rahab translated throughout the day as her family were given the things promised by Joshua. When all was packed and ready for travel the sun was sinking into the west, so Rahab's family remained in the Hebrew camp for the night. They sat in a tight circle to eat the evening meal, talking of precious times they had known. But there was no laughter.

---

[15]Joshua 6:25

The women had led secure lives in stone houses, cared for by servants. They must now sleep in tents and live in the countryside. But the treasure of life seemed of more value to them, now, than the pleasures of life had before.

They talked late into the night, while the campfires blazed around them. Maachah and Jasper retired to their tent. Salmon returned and went to his bed. And still Rahab's family talked on. The children fell asleep against their mothers and were carried to their beds.

Rahab's father tried to persuade her to leave with them, for she was not one of the Hebrews. But, although her father's pleadings pulled at her heart, she told him that she must remain with those whose lives were directed by the Lord Whom she had come to trust.

After very little sleep, Rahab's family rose with the dawn, and departed toward the south. With eyes cried dry of all tears Rahab watched them until they disappeared into the horizon. "Help them, Lord," she whispered. "They do not trust in You, although I think my brother may be near it. Please keep them safe. And someday, Lord, may they put their trust in You."

Rahab turned and walked slowly back into the camp of the Hebrews. This was now her home. The Lord held her future in His hands. She must only trust Him.

Maachah was very kind, trying hard not to say too much. She let Rahab be alone with her thoughts most of the day. When it was time to prepare the evening meal, Rahab joined her to help.

"Are you alright, Rahab?" she asked gently.

"Yes, thank you, Maachah. I have only praise in my heart that my family lives, even though they have departed. God has spared me the pain of their deaths. I am happy."

Maachah smiled and showed Rahab how to knead the fine flour and form flat cakes which she laid carefully over a stone pulled from the embers of the fire. Rahab was glad for the work to occupy her hands and attention.

As the sun began to set Jasper and Salmon returned to the tent site. They sat upon mats by the fire, talking together in excited tones. As the women brought their food they looked up and Jasper explained.

"Salmon has been commissioned by our great leader, Joshua, to spy out the city of Ai. He and Enan will leave tonight, under cover of darkness. The Lord has given us such a wondrous victory at Jericho, that Joshua wishes to waste no time in continuing to take the land for the Lord."

Rahab sat quietly, in the shadows away from the fire. Salmon had come as a spy to her city, and that was her means of salvation. Now he was to spy out Ai. A strange fear invaded her heart, yet she knew that the Lord would protect him. He served the great God as a spy, and the Lord would hold him in His hands.

When darkness had come in full Enan came to their tent site. Salmon kissed his sister and embraced his brother in law. But before he joined Enan he turned to Rahab with his calm brown eyes.

"I wonder if the Lord has prepared so miraculous an escape for us from Ai as He did from Jericho." A smile stroked the corners of his lips.

A pang touched Rahab's heart. She wished to be the only such one in Salmon's life. But that was a foolish wish, she knew. He could care nothing for her, surely, and it was selfish to desire that no one in Ai should be spared. So she smiled back into his eyes bravely and said, "I pray that the Lord will guide you and keep you in safety."

The night was long and sleepless for Rahab. Following the sleepless nights before she should have slept soundly, but her thoughts were with a tall, handsome soldier, as he spied a hostile city.

The campsite was humming when Rahab awakened late. She found Salmon sitting by the fire, talking with Jasper and eating. She remained in the background, but crept close to listen.

She was disappointed when she heard the two men conversing in the strange tongue of the Hebrews.

Maachah rounded the corner of the tent, her familiar smile in place, and handed Rahab some beautifully woven garments.

"Please have these, Rahab," she said. "They were my mother's and I have saved them for someone special."

Rahab looked with surprise into Maachah's eyes. There was no taunting there. A warm sensation filled Rahab. Maachah had said that she was someone special. She dabbed quickly at the tears that welled unbidden to her eyes and took the lovely garments into her arms.

"Oh, Maachah, they are beautiful! But they look new. Perhaps..."

"My mother wore them through all of her years of wandering in the wilderness. Please take them." Maachah looked sincerely into Rahab's eyes. Then she saw Rahab's puzzled expression and she laughed her ready laugh. "Oh, you are wondering how so new garments may have been worn for years. God wondrously kept our clothes and our sandals, too, you know, from wearing out in the wilderness.[16] They are a miracle of God."

Maachah's laughter relaxed Rahab, and her last statement made the clothes even more beautiful. So, thanking Maachah abundantly, Rahab went to her tent to put them on.

Rahab liked the feel of the fine material from which the pale blue garment was made. It smelled fresh and good. And Rahab felt like another woman when she had slipped from the vestments of harlotry into a Hebrew woman's dress. And, indeed, she knew that she was another woman from the one who had employed those vestments. She straightened her thick black hair with a comb of ivory.

---

[16]Deuteronomy 8:4

When Rahab stepped from the tent she felt Salmon's eyes turned toward her. She blushed and slowly spiraled for Maachah to examine her.

"That dress was just made for you!" Maachah exulted. "The shade of it brings out the roses in your cheeks."

Rahab smiled and thanked her, knowing full well that it was Maachah's brother who had brought the color to her face.

Salmon rose to his feet and watched Rahab approach. His face was expressionless, but his brown eyes danced.

"You look well rested," he said, the corners of his mouth beginning to smile.

Rahab remembered that Salmon had had no sleep at all during the night. She remembered, too, his weighty business, and asked, "How went your business last night?"

Salmon folded his arms across his chest and looked sternly at her. "We were in grave danger, all the night," he intoned with a deep voice. "The Lord cared for us, of course, but He sent us no angel this time to deliver us." Salmon ended with a broad smile. Rahab blushed deeply, uncertain how to react to being called an angel. But Salmon continued, "The great general, Joshua, has already been told, of course. The city of Ai is much smaller than Jericho, and Enan and I have determined that it may well be taken with two or three thousand men, and that there is no need for all the people to go up to this battle."[17]

Salmon went to his bed, but the soldiers of Israel were mustered to prepare for the battle. The ones chosen for Ai jostled each other with good humor as they stood in their ranks until the great leader, Joshua, appeared before them. Then they stood straight and still to hear their orders.

"Our two faithful spies," Joshua's voice boomed so that the farthest soldier could hear him, "have decided that we few here," Joshua let his arm sweep before him toward the soldiers

---

[17]Joshua 7:3

standing at attention, "are sufficient to take the city of Ai, for they are but few." The old warrior surveyed his ranks and then added lightly, "Let us be on our way so that you may return in time to sup upon the good meal your wife will prepare while you are gone."

A cheer rose from the ranks and they marched in step out of the camp behind their general.

Rahab kept busy all the day helping Maachah and learning the ways of the Hebrews. She decided that she must also learn the language of the Hebrews, so Maachah patiently taught her, and she practiced speaking Hebrew, to Maachah's constant delight and laughter. As she worked, though her hands were busy, her mind was free to remember Salmon's eyes when he saw her in Hebrew dress, his smile when he talked with her of Ai, and what he had called her, an angel.

Jasper was a bother to his wife, getting in the way all day and complaining that he should be with the ranks gone to Ai. Salmon arose while the sun was still high in the sky and tried to occupy Jasper with conversation. There was a sudden commotion at the far edge of the camp, and Jasper and Salmon ran to hear the news, sure that it must be the victors home from the battle.

But when the two men returned to the campsite it was not with joy. Salmon sat by the fire wordlessly, absently tossing fragments of grass into the flames. Jasper spoke quietly to Maachah and Rahab.

"Something went wrong. The enemy chased our army and thirty-six of our soldiers fell before their swords. Joshua is even now with the elders at the Tabernacle. They have rent their clothes and put dust upon their heads, and are entreating the Lord for the cause of the defeat."[18] Jasper paused and looked

---

[18]Joshua 7:6

toward Salmon. "And our little brother feels responsible for the deaths of the thirty-six men, for it was he and Enan who told Joshua that so few soldiers were needed."

Rahab wished to go to Salmon's side and comfort him. Very thoughts of him had comforted her in the long days of waiting in Jericho. But she could not. It was not her place. So she must stand by and only watch his lonely torture.

The atmosphere in the Hebrew camp strangely reminded Rahab of the city of Jericho when they lived in fear of the Hebrew troops marching about the city. The hearts of the people of the great God had melted and there was confusion and fear in the camp.

No one felt like eating the meal that Maachah and Rahab had prepared. They sat around the fire quietly. Rahab wished so that there was something to say to Salmon to ease the pain in his heart.

When a messenger ran past their tents proclaiming a meeting, the women followed the men to the Tabernacle. A great multitude of people, men, women, and children had gathered and were standing in silence, waiting. The voice of Joshua boomed forth, loudly, clearly.

"Sanctify yourselves for tomorrow, for the Lord God of Israel has said that there is an accursed thing in the midst of you, O Israel. You cannot stand before your enemies until you take away the accursed thing from among you."[19]

The multitude stirred and whispers swept through the ranks. What accursed thing had been done?

Joshua continued, "In the morning you shall be brought according to your tribes, and the tribe which the Lord takes shall come according to families. The family which the Lord shall take shall come by households. And the household which the Lord shall take shall come man by man.." Joshua paused and then

---

[19]Joshua 7:13

went on. "It shall be that the man that is taken with the accursed thing shall be burnt with fire, he and all that he has, because he has transgressed the covenant of the Lord, and because he has wrought folly in Israel."

The people of Israel went slowly back to their tents, talking in quiet tones, questioning, wondering.

When they had returned to the tent site, Rahab asked Maachah, "How does one sanctify oneself for tomorrow?"

"We must set ourselves apart unto the Lord. We must confess all sin we can think of that we have committed against Him. We must pray and think of His Word. We must cleanse our minds of all thoughts that are not pleasing to Him," explained Maachah.

So Rahab went to her tent and began to pray. She had never confessed her sin to the Lord, and now it seemed an impossible task. But she truly wished to sanctify herself so that she could not be a cause of hindrance to the working of God in the camp of Israel. Rahab did not know much of God's Word. She knew only those things that had been told her by Salmon. But she thought on that wondrous promise that the Lord had made to her, and of His marvelous fulfillment of that promise. And then she wondered at her thoughts. Was it wrong of her to think fond thoughts of Salmon? Was it wrong to be pleased by his smiling glances and his very words? She knew she had no hope of ever owning his love. So Rahab asked the Lord to guide her thoughts, to help her only think those things that would please Him. Rahab did not know if she had truly sanctified herself unto the Lord the way it was to be done. But she knew that all was confessed to Him, and she felt clean and new.

They rose very early in the morning and gathered to Joshua. The people grouped in their tribes and passed before Joshua and the elders. The tribe of Judah was taken, and Rahab learned with awe that Jasper and Salmon were of the tribe of Judah. Relief flooded through Rahab, washing away her tenseness, when the family of the Zarhites was taken, and Jasper and Salmon returned to stand by the women. Maachah grasped Jasper's arm tightly and leaned against him. From the family of the Zarhites, the household of Zabdi was taken, and when the household passed by, man by man, Achan the son of Carmi was taken.

The immense assembly stood in absolute silence as Joshua spoke to Achan, "My son, give, I pray you, glory to the Lord God of Israel, and make confession unto Him, and tell me now what you have done and do not hide it from me."

Achan fell to his knees before Joshua and cried out, "Indeed I have sinned against the Lord God of Israel, and this is what I have done. When I saw among the spoils of Jericho a good Babylonian garment and two hundred shekels of silver and a wedge of gold worth fifty shekels, I coveted them and took them. Behold, they are hid in the earth in the middle of my tent, and the silver under it."

Joshua called Salmon and Enan to him and sent them to search Achan's tent. Rahab trembled as she stood amongst the multitude of Israel. Salmon and Enan returned shortly, carrying the offenses, and laid them before Joshua.

What happened then amazed Rahab and imprinted deeply upon her mind an impression of the great God of the Hebrews. The entire family of Achan was taken to the valley of Achor, his wife and his children. All of his belongings, his tent and his animals, were also taken. The offenses taken from the city of Jericho were laid by Achan and his family.

Joshua spoke sadly in the hearing of the tribes of Israel, "Why have you troubled us? The Lord shall trouble you this day."

Then, as Rahab watched in horror, men, women, and children, lifted stones from the ground and threw them at Achan and his family. Rahab looked away as those she had come to love, Jasper and Maachah and Salmon began throwing the stones, also. When a great heap of stones had been formed,

Joshua burned the entire heap.[20] As Rahab watched the smoke ascend into the twilight, she knew that what had taken place was ever so different from the sacrifices of Jericho to the god Baal. This was not a sacrifice to appease an angry deity. This was the hand of God in judgement against disobedience to His Word.

As they walked back to the tent site, tired and hungry, Salmon fell into step beside Rahab, so she spoke to him, "Why was it sin for Achan to take the garments, silver and gold from Jericho?"

Salmon continued to look straight ahead as he walked along, but answered her quietly, "Before we entered Jericho the Lord told Joshua that the city was accursed to the Lord and everything in it, except you, Rahab, and all that were with you in the house, because you hid Enan and me when we spied the city. All the silver and gold and vessels of brass and iron were consecrated to the Lord and were to go into the treasury of the Lord."

Rahab looked intently at Salmon as he strode along and said, "Then the defeat at Ai had nothing at all to do with you, Salmon."

Only then did Salmon look at Rahab and he smiled his gratitude for her comfort. "I have confessed every sin to the Lord, and have offered a sacrifice to Him at the Tabernacle.[21] I now know that He does not hold me responsible." Salmon stopped suddenly and Rahab almost stumbled trying to stop also. He reached out a strong hand to catch her and then, still holding her arm, he looked into her eyes and said, "Do you understand why we stoned Achan and his family?"

Rahab looked away from his intense eyes and said,"Not fully. But I supposed as I saw it happen that the Lord must hate

---

[20]Joshua 7:16-26

[21]Leviticus 4:27-35

disobedience to His Word terribly."

Salmon smiled at her and she looked back into his warm brown eyes. "That is exactly the reason." He sounded pleased with her answer. "God is holy, and He hates sin. God loves us and we need only fear if we disobey Him.[22] He will punish sin."

Salmon's words could have been fearful, but they were not. Rahab knew this great God of Whom Salmon spoke. She did not know Him well. She had not known Him long. But she was glad to learn more about Him. Salmon had said that God loved her. She wanted only to please this wonderful Lord.

As soon as they had eaten, a messenger came to call Salmon away. He had been chosen to go with those who would lay ambush for Ai according to the plan which the Lord had given to Joshua. Rahab dared to say to Salmon after his parting words to his sister and Jasper, "I pray that you will be safe. The battle is the Lord's this time." Salmon smiled and then disappeared into the night with Enan at his side.

Early in the morning Joshua numbered the soldiers and marched toward Ai. Rahab wondered, as did all the camp of Israel, what great plan the Lord had given to Joshua. The day wore on slowly, Maachah wondering after her husband, and Rahab wondering after the tall handsome Salmon. Night came and yet the troops of Israel had not returned. Maachah and Rahab sat together by the fire, trying not to worry, assuring each other of the leading of the Lord.

When full dark had come on the second day, the troops of Israel finally returned, tired, hungry, but happy and excited. Jasper and Salmon sat at the fireside, eating, and talking about the battle of the day. Jasper patted the mat beside him and invited his wife to sit and hear the story. Salmon smiled at Rahab and motioned for her to join them. So she sat upon a mat by the fireside and listened to Jasper and Salmon relating the excitement

---

[22]Matthew 10:28

of the battle.

Salmon told how the troops that had marched away at dark had laid in wait all night between Bethel and Ai on the west side of Ai. The troops with Joshua had camped on the north side of Ai, with a valley between them and the city. Joshua led them in the night into the valley, and when the King of Ai arose early in the morning, he came out against Israel to battle on the plain. Joshua led the Hebrew troops away as if they were being beaten again before Ai, and the king of Ai called every man out of the city to pursue them. They left the city open and unprotected and those in ambush rushed into the city and took it, and burned it with fire. After the city was set afire and the men of Ai saw what had happened, the Hebrew soldiers advanced against the men of Ai from the city and they were trapped in the midst and God gave the Hebrews a great victory.[23]

Rahab did enjoy the story, but she enjoyed most the light in Salmon's brown eyes, the lilt in his excited voice, the animation of his strong body as he talked. He was smeared with mud and caked with dust. His hair was tousled and his beard soiled. But to Rahab, the man sitting by the fire telling his tale enthusiastically was the most handsome sight that she had ever seen.

Amidst all the excitement of the battles life still carried on in the camp of Israel. Meals were cooked, tents were cleaned, and water was carried. As Rahab busied herself learning the life in the camp, she would on occasion cross paths with the young woman with the sharp blue eyes. Always Rahab felt uncomfortable beneath her steady gaze. Rahab wanted to know the reason, but she could not ask the young woman, so she went about her duties carrying the question in her heart.

Then came the observance of Rahab's first Sabbath. The women had prepared the day before every item of food that

---

[23]Joshua 8:1-29

would be needed. No work was to be done on the Sabbath, not even picking up sticks or starting the fire. The small family sat quietly or talked of the wonders that the Lord had performed. Jasper turned to Rahab and explained to her that the purpose of the Sabbath was for man to have a day of complete rest, one day a week. Jasper told Rahab how that the Lord had created the entire heavens and the earth and all that are contained therein by His Word alone, in six days, and then He had rested on the seventh day. That is why the seventh day is the day of rest.[24]

That day Rahab learned that there was a daily sacrifice offered to the Lord as a burnt offering. In the morning a lamb was offered, and in the evening a lamb was offered. But on the Sabbath day, two lambs were offered to the Lord besides the continual burnt offering of every day.[25]

Several days later, Joshua, called an assembly of the camp away to Mount Ebal and Mount Gerizim to the north. All were to attend, the stranger as well as the Hebrew, so Rahab travelled with Jasper, Maachah and Salmon. Upon Mount Ebal Joshua had built an altar unto the Lord God of Israel and had plastered it. Rahab watched as burnt offerings and peace offerings of cattle and sheep were offered upon it. She did not understand all that happened, but as she watched Salmon's face, she knew this was of great importance, and had been commanded of the Lord.

Joshua then wrote upon the stones a copy of the law of Moses, as the multitude looked on. Salmon promised to tell Rahab later what the law of Moses said. Rahab watched as the men in blue carried the draped box on poles, which Salmon told her was the Ark of the Testimony, and the people were divided into two sections, one toward Mount Gerizim and one toward Mount Ebal.

---

[24]Genesis 2:1-3

[25]Numbers 28:3,4,9,10

Salmon explained that the men in blue were the Levites, chosen of God to bear the Ark of the Testimony, which signified the very presence of the Lord. Rahab's heart thumped in excitement. She felt so very near to the Lord Whom she loved.

Rahab stood with the tribe of Judah upon mount Gerizim. When all were in place the Levites said to the people in a loud voice, "Cursed is the man that shall make any graven or molten image, an abomination unto the Lord, the work of the hands of the craftsman, and puts in it into a secret place."

Rahab had listened intently, trying hard to understand her strange new language, but was startled when the throng of people around her answered as one, "Amen."

The Levites spoke again, their voices ringing out, "Cursed is he that sets light by his father or his mother." Salmon, at Rahab's side, translated into Egyptian for her to better understand.

Again the people answered,"Amen." Rahab looked at Salmon and he smiled slightly and nodded.

So, after the Levites said, "Cursed is he that removes his neighbour's landmark," Rahab joined with the people to say,

"Amen."

The Levites continued, "Cursed is he that makes the blind to wander out of the way."

And the people said, "Amen."

"Cursed is he that perverts the judgement of the stranger, fatherless, and widow." Salmon looked at Rahab and smiled as the Levites mentioned the stranger.

Rahab smiled back and joined the, "Amen."

The Levites continued with curses for lying with those of one's own family, for smiting one's neighbour secretly, and for taking a reward to slay an innocent person. To each one the people answered, "Amen."

At last the Levites said, "Cursed is he that does not confirm all the words of this law to do them."

As she said, "Amen," Rahab was awed. The Lord God

of the Hebrews indeed hated sin, and had cursed many matters which had been a part of daily life in Jericho.

Then the Levites, in voices still loud and clear, began to list the wonders that the Lord would perform for His people if they would hearken diligently to His voice and observe all His commandments. They would be blessed in the city and in the field. Their children would be blessed, their crops, their cattle and sheep. They would be blessed coming in and going out. The Lord would cause their enemies that would rise up against them to be smitten before their faces. The Lord would establish them a holy people unto Himself if they would keep the commandments of the Lord and walk in His ways.

Rahab was utterly thrilled. Such wondrous promises! And she, who had seen the working of the hand of God, knew He was able to perform all He promised. Rahab smiled happily at Salmon with flushed cheeks and he returned her smile.

But then the Levites continued with heavy words. They said that if the people would not hearken to the voice of the Lord their God to observe to do all His commandments and His statutes which He commanded, that these curses would overtake them: they would be cursed in the city and in the field, their children and crops, cattle and sheep would be cursed, they would be cursed coming in and going out. The Lord would send vexation and rebuke in all that they attempted to do until they were destroyed and had perished, because of the wickedness of their doings in forsaking the Lord God. They would have pestilence and consumption with a fever and extreme burning and with the sword and blasting and mildew. God would not give them rain and their enemies would overtake them and kill their children and wives. They would be scattered among the nations and they would find no ease.

Rahab was disturbed by these words. Why would a people who knew the great God of heaven and earth ever turn from Him? She could not imagine it.

Joshua himself then stood and read the most wondrous

words that Rahab had ever heard.[26] As he read, Salmon told Rahab that they were the very words of God, the book of the law, which God had given to Moses, a great leader before Joshua, and he had written down. As Rahab listened, she wept and laughed and wondered at the greatness of this God Whom she had come to know.

---

[26]Joshua 8:30-35; Deuteronomy 27:9-28:68

Chapter 4

Love

Each day taught Rahab more of the ways of the Hebrew people and their language. Each day she also learned more about the God of the Hebrews.

Rahab tried the Hebrew language on everyone she met and was improving quickly. Salmon would laugh at her mispronunciations, but he praised her, too, for her progress. One day when Salmon was walking with Rahab, carrying a load of grain for meals, Rahab relapsed into Egyptian and asked, "Is there a reason that Joshua alone is an old man and everyone else is much younger?"

"There is a reason," Salmon answered. "When my people left Egypt forty years ago, the Lord led them to the Promised Land, here, in Canaan. Moses, the leader at that time, sent Joshua and eleven other men to spy out the land."

"Joshua was a spy like you!" Rahab interrupted.

"Yes, he was a spy. And only he and one other man, Caleb, brought back a good report to Moses. The other ten men said that the cities were too strong and the people too mighty to overtake. The people complained to Moses that they and their children would all be killed. So the Lord sentenced the people of Israel to wander in the wilderness forty years until all of the people twenty years or older had died. We who have come to the promised land are their children. The oldest among us are fifty-nine years of age. Except Joshua and Caleb. The Lord allowed them to enter the land with us because they gave a good report and trusted in the Lord."[27]

"Your parents, did they die in the wilderness, too?" asked Rahab gently.

---

[27]Numbers 14:29,30

"Yes. I was born in the wilderness and have lived all my life in the tents of my family." Salmon paused and looked out at the mountains in the distance, past the fertile valley of the Jordan River. "I thank the Lord that I am among those who have finally come to this land, promised to our fathers for generations."

As Rahab and Salmon neared the tent site they passed a woman bending over a fire. She stood as they passed and looked at Rahab with the familiar glare. Rahab looked away and began walking faster.

"Why the hurry?" asked Salmon, quickening to keep pace with her.

"That woman. She always looks at me so strangely. She makes me feel so uncomfortable." There, she had told someone. Would Salmon think her foolish?

"Do you know that woman?" Salmon asked.

"No," she admitted, "I do not even know her name."

"She is Miriam, a cousin of mine. You are a curiosity, you know, being a survivor of Jericho. Perhaps you should try to speak to her someday."

That was a practical answer. Rahab should have expected as much from a man. He could not understand how she felt. But perhaps she should follow his suggestion. Yes, she would try to speak to the woman in green, someday.

Each day Salmon left the tent site to report to Joshua for duty. When he returned he usually brought with him food that was handed out to all. Jasper was assigned to work units and was gone most of the day as well. So Maachah and Rahab were together much of the time. Rahab learned that Maachah and Jasper had been married seven years and had not as yet had a child. It was the yearning of Maachah's heart to be a mother.

"Oh, Maachah, I hope that the Lord will soon bless you with a child. I do not know what yearnings I have, anymore, since the Lord has taken me from Jericho." Rahab paused and watched Maachah, but her expression had not changed. "But children can never be a part of my life."

"Of course they can!" exclaimed Maachah. "And why should they not be? You are young and attractive and should soon have a husband."

"I?" Rahab asked, shocked. "I don't think any man would be my husband."

"I know one who would be," Maachah said with a tease in her voice. "My little brother is very fond of you."

Rahab flushed and turned her face away. Surely Maachah could not truly believe that Salmon could ever want her. She searched for words but could find nothing to say.

"In fact, I think he is in love with you," Maachah said decisively.

"Oh, no, Maachah. He cannot be. He must not be." Rahab said with a sob.

"And why not, my dear? Of all the women I know well in the camp I would say that you love most the things of God."

Rahab looked at Maachah thoughtfully. Maachah must know what she was, what she had been. Her very garments she had worn into the camp published it. Yet, this fact did not seem to affect Maachah's opinion that Salmon could love her. But Rahab knew it would matter. So she said, "Maachah, thank you for your confidence in me. But please, let's not talk of this again. Please."

Maachah saw that Rahab was serious about it, so she assented and tried hard not to mention it again.

When Salmon and Jasper returned to the tents that evening they were full of talk about the ambassadors that had come that day to Joshua. Around the fire as they ate their meal they told the women.

"Some men came from a far country," explained Jasper. "They were sent by their king to make a league with the Israelites because they heard of the name of the Lord our God and the fame of Him and all that He did in Egypt and to the two kings of the Amorites beyond Jordan."

"How does Joshua know that they are come from a far

country, and not from a city near to us?" Maachah asked.

"They left their land with fresh bread and new wine. Their provisions are now dry and mouldy and their bottles broken. Even their clothes and shoes are old and worn. Joshua has made peace with them and a league."

Rahab asked, "Does the Lord allow His people to make a league with the people of the land?"

Salmon answered her, "These people are from a country far away. We are not to make a league with any of the inhabitants of the land of Canaan, but the Lord has commanded us to drive them out of the land."

The visitors from the far land were the talk of the camp as Rahab and her family had been after the fall of Jericho. Salmon and Jasper talked often of them.

When the visitors had been in the camp for two days, Salmon was once again helping Rahab carry food to their tent site. As they walked along Rahab tried hard not to think about Maachah's words, but she could not help herself. The very nearness of Salmon always quickened her pulse. His easy voice and warm brown eyes were engaging. There was no man but Salmon. Yet, a friend he may be, a husband never. She must be content to share his friendship.

"Enan and I are to spy again, tonight." Salmon told her mysteriously.

"Where?" she asked.

"It is a secret mission for the great leader, Joshua. I will leave tonight at dark."

Rahab smiled, but her heart would ache while Salmon was out of the camp at night spying the land.

Late on the following day, Salmon and Enan returned. Salmon went directly to report to Joshua. When he returned to the tent site he spoke with Jasper and the two of them left. When they came back the two women were anxious to know what had happened.

Salmon looked very grave. There was not laughter in his

voice as he said, "The visitors in the camp are from Gibeon. They are our neighbors. Gibeon is a great city, one of the royal cities, and the men of Gibeon are mighty. They deceived us because they knew that the Lord God had given us the land and they were afraid for their lives."

"What can we do?" Maachah asked.

"We can do nothing. We sware an oath to them in the name of the Lord and we may not touch them. However, Joshua and the elders have determined to make them hewers of wood and drawers of water for the congregation and for the altar of the Lord."[28]

"Why did the Lord allow them to deceive Joshua?" Rahab asked meekly.

Salmon looked down sadly. "It was because His people did not ask counsel at the mouth of the Lord."

Rahab walked slowly along the brimming bank of the river, stepping between the trees. The sunlight sparkled on the ripples as it flowed steadily toward the salt sea. Rahab sat down on a rock and trailed one foot in the cold waters. She looked around her at the beauty of the Jordan valley and the mountains beyond. She felt the thrill of being alive. She drew in a long breath of the sweet, fresh air and exulted in her life. She knew the Lord, the Creator of all that she beheld. He held her in His Almighty hands. She had prayed often in the days since the demise of Jericho. But there was one prayer she had not dared to pray. Sitting by the river's edge she began to speak to her Lord.

"Oh Lord, You have been so good to me. I deserve nothing but your wrath, yet you have given me life and liberty from the bondage I knew. And You have let me have Salmon as a friend. I care for him. You know it, Lord. I do not expect anything more than his friendship. But please guard my heart

---

[28]Joshua 9:8-27

from loving him too much, and please let my love never show to him. I treasure him as a friend."

She let the tears flow unchecked down her cheeks. This love had brought so much pain and yet she would gladly endure the anguish forever just to be near Salmon.

Rahab walked slowly toward the tent site, deeply in thought about Salmon. Someone spoke sharply, bringing her out of her contemplation. She looked up and was eye to eye with Miriam. Miriam's blue eyes and full lips smirked at Rahab.

"Well, Harlot, I want to speak on behalf of the good women of Israel. We do not want you here. We do not want you around our men." Miriam glanced briefly toward the ruins of Jericho, far in the distance, and added, "You should have been destroyed there. You are soiling our camp with your presence."

Rahab did not look away from Miriam. Her cheeks burned hot and anger boiled in her heart. She had never truly hated anyone, but hatred stirred in her toward the woman standing before her. She did not know what to say. She feared that if she attempted an answer she might show herself a fool before the smirking Miriam. So without a word, she stepped gingerly around Miriam and walked swiftly away.

Only when she had gone several steps did the tears come. The worst pain was that what Miriam had said was true. She was a harlot. She did not belong with God's people. The kindness of Maachah and Jasper and Salmon was a mystery. Perhaps Miriam's reaction was how most people felt.

Rahab returned to the camp to hear excited voices. She knew she dared not share her grief with anyone, so she dried her tears and tried to look normal. She entered the tent site to find Salmon, looking very agitated. He gave her a brief smile and then continued his conversation with Jasper and Maachah, "Because these five kings and their armies have camped by Gibeon the men of Gibeon have sent to Joshua for help. They asked us to come up quickly and save them, and help them. We must help, for we have made a league with them. You and I must report immediately, Jasper, for Joshua will lead the troops away and go up to Gibeon tonight."

Jasper kissed his wife and left her wiping her tears. Salmon embraced his sister and then smiled weakly at Rahab. "Pray for this mission. Pray for me." Before Rahab could really answer him, he had slipped away with Jasper.

"A woman's life is one of waiting, wondering when her man will return," Maachah told Rahab in the morning. I know that Jasper is in the Lord's hands, but I cannot forget Ai. If there were to be sin in the camp again..." Her voice trailed off and Rahab took her hands gently.

"I cannot fully understand your feelings, Maachah. But I know that the Lord will take care of Jasper. And Salmon." Rahab said.

"Rahab, you do know how I feel. I think you feel that way about my little brother, don't you?"

Rahab wanted to remind Maachah of her promise not to speak of this, but she knew Maachah was right.

To fill the empty hours Maachah brought forth fine linen and threads of beautiful hues and slowly, patiently, she taught Rahab to carefully guide the threaded needle through the fabric to form lovely patterns. Rahab admired the linen and told Maachah that she for years had woven linen and that this was the finest she had seen. Maachah smiled and told her that it was woven by the very ones whom God had chosen to weave the lovely curtains of the Tabernacle and the court. Rahab was impressed. Maachah, too, was impressed to learn that Rahab knew the trade of weaving linen from the flax plant.

"Perhaps you can come by some flax and weave linen for sale," suggested Maachah. "Now that we have arrived in the Promised Land, the Lord will expect us to make our own clothing."

"Oh, yes," exclaimed Rahab. "I would like very much to do something to make my way among the Hebrews. I cannot weave any such linen as this, though." She held up the cloth on which she stitched.

"Cloth will be needed and I am sure that the linen you weave will be just what we need. The man who wove this is no longer living. When Jasper returns I will ask him to look for flax for you."

Upon the mention of Jasper's name, both women fell silent, thinking of the two men who were gone to fight against the five kings who had attacked Gibeon.

When their fingers were at last stiff and weary from embroidery the two women walked to draw water from the river and, perching the clay jugs gingerly upon their heads, they carefully walked back toward the tent site. Suddenly, Maachah stopped and put her jug down. She shaded her eyes and looked toward the sun, still high in the sky.

"Doesn't it feel to you that it should be the evening hour, and time to prepare supper for the men, who might soon return?" she asked.

Rahab looked at her quizzically. Then she, too, lowered her water jug, shaded her eyes and looked toward the sun. "Yes," she answered uncertainly, "It does seem that the sun should be farther to the west than it is. Oh, well. We are waiting. That must be why the day seems so long."

Maachah looked at Rahab and smiled. "So, we are waiting. Do you admit that you wait for my little brother to return from battle?" She kept smiling at Rahab, who colored brightly.

"Please, Maachah, you have promised not to talk about it!" Rahab said.

"I thought that I had promised not to talk to you about Salmon's love for you. I am now speaking about your love for him. You do love him, don't you? I can see it in your eyes each time you look at him, you know, and I can hear it in your voice when you speak to him." Maachah still smiled, but spoke kindly.

Rahab did not want to answer her. Yes, yes, she loved

Salmon. But it just could not be! Perhaps she should soon leave the tent site of Jasper and live in another part of the camp. The camp was large. She could live where she would not see Salmon every day, where she would not hear his voice. But she could not stop thinking of him. What could she do?

Rahab remained still, with her head bent low. Maachah put her arm around Rahab's shoulder and held her for several moments, wordlessly. Finally she spoke. "I can see that it really does pain you when I speak about Salmon loving you and you loving him. I don't understand why. But I will try, very hard, not to speak of it again."

The women returned to the campsite and tried to busy themselves with small tasks. When they tired of that they sat together and looked toward the north, from whence the army of Israel would return. Finally Maachah stood to her feet and shook her skirts impatiently. "Rahab, something is wrong!" she exclaimed in irritation. "The sun has not moved at all since we carried the water from the river, you know, yet hours have passed. At least, they must have passed." She stopped, looking northward in confusion. Then she quickly went to the fire and stirred the embers to a bright glow. "Let us prepare supper. I know that the sun is still high in the sky, and I do not understand. But I know that it is time to begin supper."

As the women began their cooking task, they saw several other women approaching their tent site. The women wore astonished expressions and were talking rapidly among themselves. A tall woman with a thin face spoke to Maachah.

"What do you think is happening? Why is this day wearing on so long? What could be the matter?"

As soon as the woman stopped talking the rapid conversation resumed among the women. Maachah smiled at the tall woman and tried to sound encouraging.

"Well, I don't know what's happening. Surely there is a reason. The Lord knows." She paused and looked at the anxious group gathered before her. They had come to her for comfort, so she tried to counsel wisely. "We are preparing supper. Although the sun is high, when our men return they will be hungry you know. Perhaps you should go busy yourselves also, to prepare for your men."

The women looked at each other thoughtfully. Maachah's counsel seemed wise to them. So, grateful for something to keep them busy, for awhile at least, they thanked Maachah and hurried off to their fires.

Rahab worked the soft dough with her fingers to form the flat cakes of bread. As she worked she remembered Maachah's words. She had said "our men" will return hungry. Yes, they were Maachah's men. But she had included Rahab. Rahab savored the words and let herself dream of Salmon being "her man." The dream was sweet, but the bitter hurt in her heart reminded her that it could never be.

The strange day waxed longer and longer. The food that the women prepared laid in readiness beneath the high, bright sun. Weariness crept over the women and they sat, propped against the tent poles and talked quietly. Finally sleep overtook them and they leaned against each other and had the rest of unconsciousness. After several hours, Maachah awoke suddenly and shook Rahab.

"Rahab, wake up! The sun is finally setting in the west!" she exulted.

Rahab awoke and together they watched the lovely shades of pink and purple fade to gray. Then, a shout was heard in the camp. The men had returned!

Maachah and Rahab hurried through the camp toward the north. They pushed through the throng of people waiting to greet the soldiers. Joshua led his troops at a slow but steady march into the camp. He turned to them and praised the great God of heaven and earth Who had so marvelously shown His power that day. Then he dismissed his men and turned homeward.

Maachah tried to look over the crowd before her to find Jasper. He found her first, and sweeping her into his arms, he kissed her and held her close. Then, with Maachah leaning on his arm, he walked to his tent site.

Rahab watched their reunion happily. She was startled to find Salmon standing at her side, weary, dirty, but so handsome that she wished so that she could embrace him in love as Maachah had Jasper. But she was happy just to have him near. They walked back to the tent site together. Salmon seemed extremely happy, but too tired to talk about the battle of the long, long day.

When the men had eaten, they sat by the flickering fire and quietly talked to the women of the miracle of that wondrous day. Joshua, their great leader, had stood on the battlefield in the sight of all Israel, and had commanded the sun and the moon to stand still. And the Lord had hearkened unto his voice and held the sun and the moon in their place until the battle had been won.[29]

Maachah told of their amazement at the long day. Rahab told how the women had come to Maachah for comfort and how she had counselled them and told them that the Lord knew what was happening. Jasper smiled proudly at his little wife. But Salmon's warm brown eyes stayed on Rahab's face. She looked at him and he held her gaze. She could not look away, nor did she wish to. He smiled at her and her heart was warmed. Rahab finally pulled her eyes away, closing them and biting her lip. The familiar ache returned to her heart. She must not see Salmon look at her thus. It made the hurt burn more deeply because she knew that she loved him, and she feared that Maachah was right and that he loved her, too. But it could never be.

Jasper and Maachah excused themselves and left the fireside. Rahab and Salmon sat together by the fire. Salmon sat

---

[29]Joshua 10:12-14

holding his dish in his hand, looking at Rahab.

Do you wish more?" she asked him, reaching for the dish and starting to rise.

"No. Please stay here." He continued to look at her in the firelight and she warmed beneath his gaze. "Today, on this long, long day, I once stood atop a hill while in pursuit of the enemy, and viewed this land, this land flowing with milk and honey." He paused for a moment and then continued in a soft voice, "And I thought of you."

Rahab's cheeks burned, and she wished to look away, but his intense brown eyes held hers to his. He continued, "I have wandered in the wilderness all of my life. But now that the Lord has brought us to the Promised Land, I desire to have a piece of the Lord's earth to call my own. I desire to farm that land and watch the rich earth bring forth the green blade and the grain. I desire to graze my own sheep and cattle on that land." He paused again, and Rahab was startled as he reached out and took her hand gently in his own. "And I desire to raise my children on that land, with you as their mother." Rahab gasped slightly and felt weak. If she had been standing she surely would have fallen to the ground. Then he said, "Rahab, I wish to take you as my wife. Will you have me as your husband?" Salmon's warm brown eyes searched hers for an answer.

Panic seized her. This was her dearest dream, and yet she knew it could never be. She pulled her hand away, and rising quickly to her feet she gave a weak cry and escaped into the darkness. She ran heedlessly, passing tents where men and their families sat sharing a meal and the wonders of the day past. Tears blurred her vision and she stumbled over a tent stake and tumbled to the ground, bruising her legs and hands and scraping her face against a rope. She sat where she landed and sobbed into her arms, which were wrapped around her knees.

Strong hands grasped her shoulders and lifted her to her feet. Her chin was pulled gently but firmly to face her into the sorrowful eyes of Salmon. He stood looking at her thus for a moment and then, leading her by the arm, guided her past the tents to the outer edge of the camp. They passed a sentry, who let them go at a word from Salmon. Salmon led Rahab to a large, flat rock and sat her upon it.

"Why did you run away? You have hurt yourself," Salmon's voice became tender as he noticed the blood on her face.

Rahab felt as though her world, which only a few moments ago had been so beautiful, was now crashing down about her. She looked into Salmon's sad eyes and tried to talk through her tears.

"I cannot be your wife. Such a man as you must have a wife who... I cannot be any man's wife." Rahab closed her eyes against the pain in Salmon's eyes and sobbed hopelessly.

Salmon held her shoulders and shook her gently. "Rahab, look at me." She opened her swollen eyes. "If you do not wish to be my wife I understand. I cannot expect you to return the love I feel for you. But, please, do not weep so." He looked helplessly at her.

He loved her. Salmon loved her. And oh, how she loved him! But she could never be the wife of a man like Salmon. Why must he torture her this way, to suggest that she would not wish to be his wife. Rahab swallowed hard and wiped her streaming eyes on her dress.

"Salmon, it isn't that I don't wish to be your wife." She swallowed again, searching for the words to say. "But I am a harlot. I cannot be your wife. You cannot have a harlot to wife. The good women of Israel despise my presence. I soil the very camp of Israel." The truth of the words stabbed her crying heart with searing pain.

Salmon remained still, holding her shoulders and looking into her eyes. But tears began to well in his brown eyes and spill over onto his tanned cheeks. He looked at her for a long time. When he finally spoke it was with a hoarse whisper.

"Are you a harlot, Rahab?"

Her eyes widened and she answered him sharply, accusingly, "Surely you knew that when you first saw me. I wore the attire of a harlot."

Salmon continued to gaze into her eyes and repeated softly, "Are you a harlot, Rahab?"

Confusion swept over her at his question. Why did he ask her? What was she to answer?

"You are not a woman of Jericho. You dwell among God's people. You do not worship gods of stone or wood. You worship the Lord of the heaven and earth, the God of the Hebrews." Salmon's voice had softened, and his words carried love to her ears. "Are you a harlot, Rahab?"

She knew then what he was asking. She understood. So she answered him, "I once was."

"Are you a harlot, Rahab?" Salmon repeated the question again.

"So many men..." Rahab stopped when Salmon shook his head, and again asked,

"Are you a harlot, Rahab?"

Rahab sat in the cool darkness, following the long, long day, feeling Salmon's strong hands gripping her shoulders. Was she a harlot? No. She was a woman, snatched from the debris of Jericho, changed not only in garb but in heart as well. No. She was not a harlot.

Looking straight into those deep brown eyes, Rahab simply answered, "No."

Salmon's grip on her shoulders lessened and his face relaxed. He smiled weakly and said, "You may not care for me, Rahab. But please understand that you can be the wife to any man. You are a woman who loves and serves the true God. Do you understand?"

Rahab placed her hands upon his. "But I do care for you, Salmon."

Hope illumined his eyes. He took a deep breath and then he asked, "Will you be my wife?"

The dark night was suddenly bright with stars around her as Rahab smiled as well. She looked at the man who loved her, who wanted her to be his wife, the man who believed that she was not a harlot, and she answered, "Yes."

Chapter 5

Adversary

Rahab had been rejoicing in life itself since her rescue from Jericho. But when she awoke on the next morning, everything shone. The sun was brilliant, the flowers gorgeous. Her heart sang and she had a hope for the days ahead that she had not dared to dream. Maachah could sense her joy and cornered her to find the reason. Rahab tried hard to behave normally, but the great happiness inside her glowed from her and she could not keep herself from telling Maachah everything.

Maachah was delighted over Rahab's news. "There, I told you that my little brother was in love with you, didn't I?" She seemed very pleased with herself for having known. Rahab enjoyed the thought that Maachah and she would be sisters.

When Salmon emerged from his tent he smiled broadly at Rahab and Maachah. Rahab blushed and suddenly felt shy. Salmon loved her. She would be his wife. Salmon sat by the fire and Rahab brought him a bowl of the breakfast that Maachah had prepared. Then she sat by his side and watched him eat.

"Well, is this yesterday, today, or tomorrow!" Jasper's voice boomed as he emerged from his tent. Everyone laughed at his joke and he joined the two at the fireside.

As Maachah handed Jasper his breakfast she said, "Salmon and Rahab look especially well this morning don't they?"

Jasper looked at Salmon and Rahab and then at Maachah with a questioning look. Maachah just smiled and waved her hand toward Salmon. Jasper looked back at Salmon with a question. Salmon laughed and said, "Rahab had consented to honor me by becoming my wife."

Jasper jumped up and began thumping Salmon's back and congratulating him. Then he looked at Rahab and with a tease in his voice said, "Maachah and I are so grateful that you came along to save our little brother from a life of bachelorhood. He needs someone to take care of him besides us." Jasper ended with a laugh.

Rahab was glad that Jasper and Maachah would now be her family. And she would have a lifetime with Salmon!

When the merry breakfast had ended the two men reported to Joshua. Maachah and Rahab were cleaning the tent site when they returned. Salmon invited Rahab for a walk with him and Maachah waved her away. So Rahab and Salmon walked together slowly, away from the tents, to the river's edge.

They sat upon two rocks, side by side, with the morning sun upon their faces and the ripple of the river passing by them. Salmon took Rahab's hand in his and raised it to his lips, brushing his lips softly over her knuckles. "Are you happy?" he asked, looking into her eyes with his warm brown ones.

"I have never been so happy!" she answered him. She reached out a hand and touched his soft brown beard. "I love you, Salmon." The words felt warm and good. She had wanted to say them for so long, and now she could, for she would be his wife.

"You have made me very happy, Rahab," Salmon said softly.

They sat together listening to the river and talking together in the warm sun. Salmon talked again of his plans to acquire land and to farm. His excitement pleased her and she knew that she would rather do nothing else in life than be at Salmon's side as he farmed his land.

When Salmon and Rahab entered the tent site, Jasper approached quickly and pulled Salmon aside. He explained something in muted tones and when Salmon returned to Rahab his countenance had changed. He frowned and took her hands in his.

"What is it?" Rahab asked, concerned.

"Joshua has called an assembly of the troops. It has been reported to him that the five kings have hid themselves in a cave at Makkedah. We are to gather provisions for a long campaign against these kings and their cities." Salmon looked sadly at Rahab. "I'm very sorry to leave you."

"Oh, Salmon, I'm very sorry to let you go, but I know that you must go. I will pray for you every moment. When will you return?" Rahab's exquisite joy was fading and in its place a dull ache was growing.

"We will return when the conquests have ended." Salmon paused, looking thoughtful. "If we married, now, I would not need to go."

Rahab looked into his eyes, puzzled.

"The law of the Lord says that when a man marries a wife he may have one year free from war to stay home and comfort his wife,"[30] Salmon told her.

Rahab watched Salmon's eyes and she knew that although he loved her and wanted to marry her, he was a soldier in the army of the God of Israel, and he must go. So she smiled and shook her head, saying, "Oh, Salmon, I could not possibly be ready to marry you quickly. I must have a dress, you know."

Salmon softly rubbed his thumb against her cheek and smiled. "Thank you, Rahab," he said. Rahab loved him all the more.

The camp of Israel was a buzz of activity as men packed food, blankets and water into bundles to carry on the long march ahead. Families spoke tender words and promises amidst the bustle, and by nightfall, when the men went to sleep in their own tents for one last time, all was in readiness.

Salmon and Jasper knew that they could not stay sitting by the fire late, for the next day promised to be a tiring one, as well as the days beyond. Salmon and Rahab spoke tender words of love and hope and promised to implore God's watchcare for the other every day.

When Salmon and Jasper marched away with the troops

---

[30]Deuteronomy 24:5

the next morning, Rahab and Maachah stood, arm in arm, sharing the pain of parting. The men had marched away before. But this time they knew that it would be a long time before they would see those two men that they loved, again.

Long, weary day moved into long, weary day, as Maachah and Rahab began the wait. Some men stayed in the camp, to guard it from intruders, to gather food, to care for the women. Some were newly married and had remained according to the law of God, as Salmon had told it to her. But the man Rahab loved was marching to battle, following the great leader, Joshua, and in the hand of God.

One morning Rahab awoke to the sound of rain pattering against the tent. She wrapped a cloak around her and went outside. Maachah emerged from her tent just as she did, and they scurried together to tuck away anything they did not want wet. They ate a cold breakfast and then sat in the doorway of Rahab's tent and watched the rain fall in steady rhythm. They talked and laughed and enjoyed the diversion from the everyday tasks which had become a burden in the absence of the men.

In the early evening the rain abated and the sun began to shine again, in the west. Suddenly a rainbow appeared, arching from horizon to horizon, and the two women exclaimed at its beauty.

"Do you know the story of the rainbow?" asked Maachah.

"No, I don't think so. Tell me." Rahab smiled at the prospect of a story.

"It is written in the first book of Moses, in the law of God. The whole earth was wicked and the Lord sent a flood that reached higher than the mountains to cover the entire earth. But one man, named Noah, found grace in God's eyes, and the Lord told him to build an ark, a large boat, you know, to save himself and his family alive, as well as two of every air breathing animal on the earth. So when the flood came, they were safe inside, for forty days while the rains came, and one hundred-fifty days while the waters were abating. Finally the ark came to rest again upon the earth, and Noah and his family, and the animals, left the ark and began to replenish the earth. Noah offered a sacrifice of thanksgiving to the Lord, and the Lord put His bow in the sky. He told Noah that it was a sign of a promise that He would never again destroy the earth with a flood. When we see the rainbow, we can remember His promise."[31]

Rahab loved the story of the rainbow. Never again would she see one after the rain without thinking of this day, with Maachah telling her the story from the book of God.

One day Maachah came to the tent site carrying a large bundle of flax stalks. She proudly dropped them before Rahab and said, "I found some flax so that you may weave your linen! We can get all you need, when you run out of this." She ended triumphantly, smiling at Rahab. Rahab thanked her friend and began immediately on the job of changing the rough, course stalks of flax to soft, beautiful cloth. She was glad for this way to keep busy. The days passed by much more quickly when she was busy all the day with her work. And as the fine linen was produced, customers flocked to their tent site to buy it. Rahab and Maachah gathered the coins and jewels used in trade and hid them away beneath the tents.

Days passed into weeks and still the camp of Israel waited for the troops to return. Messengers ran to the camp occasionally with news of the triumphant victories which the Lord gave to His army. When they came, everyone gathered to hear the news and to joy in the fact that no soldier of Israel had died. After resting in the news delivered from the troops, going on alone was easier for awhile.

When the army of Israel had been gone to battle for two months, Rahab awakened to hear violent retching outside her tent. She found Maachah doubled over, heaving with an empty

---

[31]Genesis 9:13-15

stomach. Rahab waited until Maachah had stilled and then led her carefully to a mat and seated her.

"Oh, Maachah," she said, very concerned, "you are ill! You must rest today, and I will keep away all customers for linen, and I will care for you."

Maachah smiled weakly, her face pale. "Oh, Rahab, I am sick because I am carrying Jasper's child!" The effort of speech seemed to exhaust her, and she leaned back against the tent, smiling in content.

Rahab gasped in joy and hugged Maachah hard. A baby! The Lord had heard Maachah's prayer and had given her a child! "Maachah, how wonderful! I will need to care for you far longer than today. Oh, what fun it will be to have a baby! And Jasper, he will be so pleased."

Maachah's coming child made the days exciting, which had been drear and dull. Maachah's sickness soon passed and then she glowed with health and happiness. Everyone she met joined in her joy over her baby. She wished so that she could tell Jasper, but it would be such a pleasant surprise for him when he returned.

Rahab walked along the dusty path from the river, thinking how a good rain would be so welcome. She smiled to herself as she remembered her first rain in the Hebrew camp and the story of the rainbow. She was unconscious of the woman who had fallen into step beside her until a sharp voice brought her to awareness.

"Well, Harlot, I see that you are still with us, polluting the camp of Israel." Miriam squinted at Rahab and thrust her chin forward. When Rahab saw who it was she continued to walk, eyes ahead. Miriam kept close beside her and continued. "Do not think that we, the good women of Israel, did not notice how you were at the side of one of our good men, Salmon, each time you had a chance. And we have heard that you have enticed him and he has asked you to be his wife. Hah! There are women in this camp who are worthy of that man's love. Who are you that you think you can have such a man? Who do you think you are, Harlot?" Miriam ended cruelly.

Rahab stopped and faced Miriam. Anger boiled in her breast with pain and shame. Salmon had suggested that she talk with Miriam. But Miriam had twice now spoken to her contemptuously. How could she speak well to her? What could she answer a woman of Israel who rightfully called her, "Harlot"? She could never give to Miriam the explanation Salmon had given to her. Perhaps that excuse only had merit in Salmon's heart because he loved her. Miriam certainly did not love her, nor she Miriam. So, for lack of suitable words, Rahab wordlessly turned back down the dusty path.

Rahab stumbled into the camp through her tears. Placing the waterpot down quickly, she ran to her tent and fell in sobs upon her mat. Maachah, who heard her sobs, asked gently at her door, "Rahab, dear, whatever is wrong?"

Rahab invited her in, and she sat beside Rahab on the mat. Rahab looked at her through her tears and said, "Maachah, you could never understand what I am going through because you are pure and good. I was a temple harlot in the city of Jericho. Since I was very young I was dedicated to the service of the gods of Jericho as a harlot." Rahab watched Maachah's face as she sobbed out her story. Maachah did not look shocked nor abhorred. Rahab continued, "There is a woman in the camp who has twice now let me know that my presence here is not appreciated by the good women of Israel. She spoke to me on the way from the river and told me that I do not deserve Salmon's love. Oh, Maachah, I fear that she is trying to be cruel to me, but she is right! Salmon convinced me that I am no longer a harlot. That is true. But I still cannot deserve his love." Rahab ended with a sob.

Maachah put her arms around Rahab in comfort and gently spoke, soft tears in her eyes as well, "Rahab, when my little brother returned from spying out Jericho, he was so excited to tell us of a young woman who had been a temple harlot, bound by the cruel religion of Jericho, who had put her trust in the true and living God. He was so happy to be able to go to your house on the night of the attack upon Jericho, and rescue you and your family from the city. Salmon has ever spoken of you to us as a woman whom the Lord has changed so miraculously. Salmon has all his life been taught the truth of the Word of God and His worship. But you turned from a pagan worship to serve the Lord. Salmon admires you for that. And he has mentioned to us his admiration at your choice to let your family leave without you and to stay here with the people of God. Rahab, we are called the people of God. But many here are that in name only, you know, with little or no personal trust in the Lord Himself. But you, dear Rahab, truly trust in the Lord. My little brother can see that in your life and that is what impresses him most. You said that Salmon convinced you that you are no longer a harlot. That is true, Rahab. You are not. I have ever thought of you, since I first met you, as a heroine of the Lord. And as to deserving the love of a man, I don't suppose any of us do. That is just one of God's great blessings upon us."

Rahab's tears had ceased to flow and the hard knot of pain had eased in her heart. "Thank You, Lord," she prayed silently, "thank You for Maachah's friendship and kindness. I needed her just now."

As Maachah began to swell from her child the excitement grew as well. Rahab wove with extra care soft linen to sew into tiny clothes for the newcomer. Maachah wove a beautiful basket with handles on the sides in which to lay her child to sleep. Such beautiful plans were made and the hours passed with pleasure, from day to day.

On the tenth day of the seventh month was the Day of Atonement. Maachah, large with child, and Rahab walked slowly to the Tabernacle. Because of the press of people, little could actually be seen, so Maachah explained the ceremony taking place for Rahab.

"The high priest, Eleazar, will offer a bullock as a sin

offering for himself and make an atonement for himself and his family. He will then take a censer full of burning coals from the altar and put incense upon the coals before the Lord and a cloud of incense shall cover the mercy seat that is upon the ark of the covenant. Then he will sprinkle the blood of the bullock with his finger upon the mercy seat toward the east and before the mercy seat seven times. He will then take two goats and present them before the Lord at the door of the Tabernacle. He will cast lots, and the goat upon which the Lord's lot falls will be offered to the Lord. Eleazar will kill the goat of the sin offering for the people and bring the blood within the vail and sprinkle it also upon the mercy seat and before the mercy seat."

"This shall make an atonement for the holy place because of all the sins of the children of Israel. He will put the blood of the bullock and the goat on the horns of the altar and sprinkle the blood upon it with his finger seven times to cleanse and hallow the altar from the uncleanness of the children of Israel."

"When he finishes reconciling the holy place and the altar, he will lay both hands upon the head of the live goat, and confess over him all the iniquities of the children of Israel, and all their transgressions and all their sins, putting them upon the head of the goat. Then he will send the goat away into the wilderness by the hand of a man and the goat will bear upon him all the iniquities of the people into an uninhabited land. There he will be released."

"When this has been accomplished one shall carry the carcasses of both the bullock and the goat whose blood was shed outside the camp and shall burn with fire their skins and flesh. In this way shall our sins be atoned."[32]

As the day approached for Maachah's deliverance of her child, worry began to crease her face. "I do wish for Jasper to be here for the birth of his child," she told Rahab. But the messages

---

[32]Leviticus 16:5-28

which came to the camp from the army of Israel placed them far away, busily engaged in taking the land for the Lord. Rahab was concerned for Maachah's health as the day approached.

"Rahab, I have prayed so that Jasper could be here. But I am just one small woman of Israel. I suppose that the battles of the Lord are much more important that one baby. Oh, Rahab, I want my husband to be near me. I want him to see his child and share with me in the birth of our firstborn."

Rahab wished so that she had words to comfort Maachah, but she did not.

For weeks Maachah had talked to Rahab of the coming feast of Passover. It was the talk of everyone that they met. The women would chat about Passover when they met at the river to fill their waterpots. They would gather in groups at each other's tents and discuss Passover as they worked stitching or weaving.

Maachah explained Passover to Rahab. "When the children of Israel were in bondage in Egypt," she said, "God sent plagues upon the Egyptians to show them His power and to convince Pharaoh, the king of Egypt, to let His people go and leave the land of Egypt. All of the plagues were terrifying, but Pharaoh's heart was hardened and he refused to let the Hebrews go. So finally, God sent the tenth and worst plague. He sent His death angel to pass over Egypt and to kill the firstborn in each home. Only those who obeyed God's commandment were spared. God told the people to kill a lamb and put the blood on the two side posts and on the upper door post of the house. The Lord said that the blood would be a token upon the houses and when He saw the blood, He passed over and did not destroy the firstborn in that house."[33]

Maachah paused in her recitation when she saw the tears begin to stream down Rahab's face. She took Rahab's hand and gently asked, "Whatever is the matter, dear? What have I said to

[33]Exodus 12:21-23

upset you so?"

Rahab wiped at her tears and answered with difficulty, "I had a dear friend in Jericho, an old man named Zaphnath, whom I loved dearly. He lived in Egypt at the time when God sent the plagues upon Egypt. His wife was hit in the head by an immense hailstone and died. His only son died on the night that you speak of. Zaphnath believed in the reality of the God of the Hebrews, but he would not come to safety at my house." Rahab ended with a sob and closed her eyes tightly.

Maachah put her arm around Rahab's trembling shoulders and said, "I remember you mentioned your friend when we first met. Rahab, the plagues of Egypt were a horrible thing indeed for the Egyptians. The death of the firstborn was terrific beyond compare. But do you see, dear friend, that amidst the horror, there was safety and deliverance in the blood? The Lord has told us that it is the blood that makes an atonement for our souls,[34] and it was the blood that bought our deliverance from Egypt."

Maachah said no more until Rahab had ceased weeping. Then she continued to explain the Passover. "The Lord told us that every year in the month Abib, on the tenth day of the month, we are to select an unblemished lamb, a male of the first year. We are to separate it from the flock and keep it until the fourteenth day. That day is the Lord's Passover. That evening we are to kill the lamb and roast it with fire and eat it with unleavened bread and bitter herbs. This will remind us of the lambs that were slain in Egypt, whose blood on the two side posts and the upper door post spared the lives of the firstborn within, when the death angel passed over. All leaven must be removed from our households and we are to eat unleavened bread for seven days following the Passover. This is the feast of unleavened bread. It is called the bread of affliction to remind us all the days of our life of the day that we came out of Egypt. On

---

[34]Leviticus 17:11

the fifteenth day is a holy convocation and we are to do no work at all except what we must do to serve food. Also, on the twenty-first day is a holy convocation, and we may do no work. Each of those seven days a lamb shall be offered in an offering made by fire unto the Lord by the priest at the Tabernacle.

When Maachah had finished her narrative Rahab had calmed completely. She was a woman of Israel, now, because she believed in the God of the Hebrews, the Creator of heaven and earth. She wanted very much to observe the Passover and be a part in remembering God's great deliverance of the children of Israel from bondage in Egypt.

So, when the month of Abib came, Maachah carefully chose and purchased an unblemished lamb and brought it to the tent site on the tenth day. She and Rahab removed all leaven from their tents. On the fourteenth day, which was the Passover day, Miriam came.

"Maachah, dear," she said, quite purposely not looking toward Rahab, "you know, don't you, that God has forbidden a foreigner to eat of the Passover. I do hope you have told that woman, and are not planning to disobey the Lord." Miriam still looked only at Maachah. Rahab felt her cheeks begin to burn, and a knot of anger grew within her.

Maachah only smiled at Miriam and answered, "Thank you for your concern, Miriam. But the Lord also said that if a stranger sojourns among us and will keep the Passover unto the Lord according to the ordinance of the Passover and according to the manner of it then he shall do it. We are to have one ordinance, both for the stranger and ourselves.[35] Rahab will be keeping the Lord's Passover with me." Maachah still smiled as she ended, but the tone of her voice was firm, challenging any objection.

Miriam smiled faintly and said, "Well, you will do as you

---

[35] Deuteronomy 16:11

will do. I only wanted you to be aware of God's Law." Only then did she look at Rahab, with a withering glance, as she turned to leave.

That evening Maachah roasted the lamb, careful not to break any of the bones. Because there was far too much lamb for two women to eat, several other women who were alone and childless joined Maachah and Rahab at the tent site, to eat the Passover meal. At the close of the meal, all remains of the lamb were thoroughly burned in the fire.[36]

For the next seven days, Rahab and Maachah baked and ate unleavened bread each day. They joined the multitude each day to stand outside the court of the Tabernacle as the priest offered the lamb in sacrifice reminding God's people of the lambs which were slain and the blood which delivered God's people from Egypt.

One Sabbath afternoon as they sat in the sunshine resting, Rahab looked at the beautiful dress which Maachah's mother had worn and asked, "Why do all of the Hebrew clothing, of men and women, have a fringe at the bottom and a ribbon of blue around the hem, whatever the color of the garment?"

Maachah smiled, leaning against a tent pole with her hand on her swollen belly. "The fringe and ribbon of blue are so that when we look at them we will remember all the commandments of the Lord, and do them, and not seek after our own hearts and eyes but be holy unto our God."[37]

Rahab fingered the blue ribbon and considered Maachah's words silently for several minutes. Then she spoke softly and said, "Tell me about your mother and father, Maachah."

Maachah's eyes misted and closed. In almost a whisper she said, "My mother's hands were always busy doing good for us and for others. She listened when I needed to talk and she

---

[36]Exodus 12:3-10

[37]Numbers 15:38-40

always had a wise word for me. Three babies were born to her which died soon after birth. Yet she never let her grief for them destroy her care for us. She taught me how to be a wife and mother." Maachah paused. Then she opened her eyes and looked at Rahab. "She loved me. I knew that. Even when I disobeyed or lost my temper or was in some other way unpleasant my mother loved me. She disciplined me when I needed it, but even then I knew that she loved me. I only hope that I can be the kind of wife and mother that she was. I miss her very much and I would like so to share the joy of my coming child with her."

"My father was tall and strong. Salmon is very much like he was. He was the prince of the tribe of Judah under Moses' leadership[38] and was always very busy with the affairs of governing. But he always had time for us. He was very wise and taught us the Word of God faithfully. He loved us, too. It hurt Salmon and me to know that our parents must die within the forty years of wandering. But it was God's will, and everyone lost parents in the wilderness. We are thankful for the years we had with our parents to love and teach us." Maachah suddenly smiled at Rahab and added much lighter, "And we are thankful to be able to enter into the Promised Land. Our lives have been lived looking forward to this. And what a joy that my child will be born here!"

Early on the morning after the Sabbath, Rahab was wakened by Maachah. "Rahab, I have been labouring for several hours, now, and I wish you to call the midwife for me, now, please."

Rahab jumped up quickly and dressed. She hurried out into the still morning air and found the tent of the midwife. Waking her from a sound sleep, Rahab led her to Maachah's tent.

Rahab had never before witnessed the birth of a child.

---

[38]Numbers 2:3

She watched the agony and suffering of Maachah transform to joy and tender love as she brought forth a son, and cradled him in her arms.

"He is so beautiful!" Maachah exclaimed repeatedly as Rahab agreed. Rahab took a turn holding the tiny child and felt a wonder that she had never before known.

While Maachah's small son was attempting his first meal, Maachah looked sadly at Rahab and said, "My dear Jasper has a son and he does not even know. He did not know that we were expecting a child."

Rahab heard the loud blast signalling a messenger from the troops was in the camp. She excused herself from Maachah to go hear the news and bring it back to her.

When she reached the familiar throng waiting to hear the news, her heart quickened and thankfulness swept over her. There, on the platform raised for the messenger, stood Jasper, loudly announcing to the eager listeners the position and victories of God's army. When he was done, he was immediately thronged by those who would seek personal news of their loved ones. He tried to give each one a word of encouragement. Finally the crowds thinned and Rahab was able to approach him.

"Jasper!" she exclaimed, clasping his hands and smiling broadly.

"Hello, Rahab." Jasper looked about, expectantly. "Where is Maachah?"

"She is at the tent site. Come quickly to see her." Rahab pulled him toward the tents.

"Why did she not come to hear the news? Is she ill?" Jasper's voice was edged with concern.

"Well, she is in bed. But, come, she will be so pleased to see you!"

Rahab ran ahead of Jasper when they neared the tent. She stuck her head into the doorway, and just before Jasper reached her, she said to Maachah, "I have brought you the best news from the army!"

Jasper pushed through the door past her, concerned for his bedridden wife. Then he stopped, at first confused. But as the reality of the scene which met his eyes dawned upon him, that he was a father, and that the tiny child clutched to Maachah's breast was his son, he fell in joyful tears to his knees beside his wife. Rahab left the tent and closed the door flap behind her.

Jasper stayed as long as possible with his little family, enjoying each moment thoroughly. On the eighth day, the baby was circumcised and given the name Jared. Rahab was touched by the simple ceremony and the meaning of it as explained by Jasper. The Lord had given this sign to His people as a token of the covenant between Him and them.[39] When forty days had passed for Maachah's purification, Jasper bought a lamb of the first year and a young pigeon, and taking his family with him, went to the Tabernacle.

At the Tabernacle, the lamb for a burnt offering, and the pigeon for a sin offering, were given to the priest of God. Rahab stood apart and watched through the doorway into the court of the Tabernacle as the offerings were sacrificed to the Lord, according to the law of Moses.[40] Maachah had told her that this offering would cleanse her from the issue of her blood. Rahab did not understand, but she stood in awe and watched the wonderful ceremony proceed. This was what the Lord had commanded, and it was beautiful.

The day that Jasper returned to the army was a sad one indeed for the little family. He knew that his tiny son would grow much before he could hold him again. But the battle for the Lord must be fought, and Jasper was thankful that the Lord had brought him home to be there with his wife and son.

Before he left, Rahab told Jasper messages of love to share with Salmon. Jasper had told her everything he could think

---

[39]Genesis 17:10-12

[40]Leviticus 12:2-8

of about Salmon's comings and goings, and Rahab had tried hard not to interrupt his happy family attentions.

When the two women were once again alone, with the little Jared, Maachah settled into the role of mother, and Rahab returned to making linen. The joys of raising a baby kept each day alive with pleasure and enjoyment, and little Jared seemed to grow so quickly.

On a bright, sun-drenched morning Rahab walked out of the camp to sit upon the rock where she and Salmon had first declared their love for one another. She had now been in the camp of Israel for almost two years. Although she slept in a tent instead of a grand house on the wall, she slept now with a clean heart and free mind. She lived among the people of God, people to whom He had made such wonderful promises, and to whom He had shown Himself in such wondrous power. She loved a great and mighty man of God. And he loved her and had asked her to become his wife. And she would be. The long months of Salmon's absence had been a test of endurance, but the very thoughts of him, of his warm brown eyes and his confidence in her as a woman who trusted the Lord, made her love for him grow daily. Each day she prayed for his safety and his soon return. Perhaps his duties of soldiering and conquering the cities for the Lord brought some distasteful assignment to his hands, and she prayed for strength to carry him through.

Rahab knew that unfinished tasks lay waiting at the tent site, but the dearness of the spot and the warmth of her memories bade her stay awhile longer. She raised her eyes to survey the horizon and was alarmed to see dust rising high in a billowing cloud which seemed to advance upon the camp of Israel. Forgetting her desire to remain there, Rahab ran quickly into the camp and found Maachah sitting beside Jared on a blanket spread in the sun.

As always, Rahab stopped to speak words of love to Jared, and then she turned to Maachah and told her of the cloud of dust she had seen.

The two women heard a loud tumult in the camp and a runner passed them, shouting, "The army of Israel has returned!"

Maachah snatched Jared from the blanket where he sat cooing and ran with Rahab toward the shouts. There, the soldiers who had fought to win the land for so many months fell from their file to search for wives and children. Joyous reunions all about them made the two women all the more impatient to find Jasper and Salmon. Little Jared, confused by the tumult, began to wail loudly. Finally, Rahab pulled Maachah aside and said, "Perhaps we should wait over here and let Salmon and Jasper find us. There are so many thousands in this multitude."

So the two women stood, watching the crowd slowly thin as families walked together back to their tents. Then they heard a welcome voice shouting above the din, "Maachah! Rahab! Over here."

They saw Jasper and Salmon approaching together, first walking and then breaking into a run. Jasper embraced his wife and little son with joy, laughing and talking happily.

Salmon went straight to Rahab. He took her hands and smiled into her eyes with his warm brown ones that she had missed so much. Then, letting go her hands, he took her into his arms and held her close to him, burying his bearded face in her long, dark hair.

When he released her from his strong grasp, he simply said, "Rahab, my Rahab." The weariness of the long months past melted away with his words, and Rahab felt that she would burst with her happiness.

Around the fire the two men talked of the long months behind them, of the battles and the conquests. The cities lay barren of all human life, yet ready to be occupied by the people of Israel. Fields lay ready to be tended, houses to be cleaned and lived in, shops to be taken over and used. The men talked with excitement of the wonders of the land of Canaan, its beauty and richness.

Salmon, who was holding Rahab close to his side, with

his arm around her, said, "The land is rich beyond comparison. My heart yearns to till that land."

"When will the people of Israel move into the cities?" asked Maachah.

"The Lord will direct Joshua into dividing the land to the tribes of Israel," answered Jasper. "But the whole land is not yet taken."

Rahab leaned toward Jasper, foreboding in her voice, and asked, "Do you mean that you will return to fight, again?"

Salmon pulled her closer, trying to comfort her. "Yes," he said, "we will have to return. But for now, while we're here, let's not think about that time. Today is important. Let's live today." Salmon ended, looking into Rahab's eyes with love. Yes, it would do no good to worry about a departure again in the future. She would try not to think of it. She would enjoy Salmon's presence while she could.

In the evening, as the glow of the sky began to fade and the stars appeared, Rahab and Salmon walked hand in hand outside the camp to the flat rock. They sat together and watched the gathering dusk. Rahab was so happy to have Salmon home, that she could scarcely contain her joy.

"If I had not had you to come home to, I don't know if I could have endured the months of fighting and taking the land for the Lord," Salmon told her tenderly. "The Lord was so good, and took care of us in the fighting. God met our needs for food and shelter and strength for the battle. But I thank Him so that He cared for my heart, as well, and gave you to me to think and dream about."

Rahab smiled at Salmon through the fading light and said, "Life is now a beautiful thing to me, Salmon, since I was rescued from Jericho. But I didn't dare to dream that I could ever be as happy as I am since God gave me your love."

"Rahab, I want to make you my wife, now. But I feel it is my duty as a soldier to remain with the army of Israel until all the land is taken for the Lord." Salmon explained.

"Salmon, I have no desire greater than to become your wife, now. But I understand. I will wait for you, Salmon, if I must wait all my life."

They remained silent several moments, looking into each other's eyes as the dark descended. Then Salmon drew her gently into his arms and kissed her. The memory of his kiss stayed with her after they had returned to the tent site and after Rahab had gone to her bed, and was fresh in her mind when she awoke in the morning.

Salmon was happy to see that Rahab had kept busy with weaving and was impressed with the fine soft linen that she made. Maachah and Rahab brought out the coins and jewels and spread them before the men.

"Have you earned all of this from selling your linen?" Salmon asked as he hefted a stack of gold coins.

"Yes," Rahab answered him, her cheeks coloring. She was gladdened to please him.

A normal routine soon settled upon the little family in the tent site. The fellowship at meals was even livelier with the small Jared who at first crawled and then began to toddle. The women kept busy with baby and linen through the days as the men reported to Joshua to fulfill their duties.

One day as Rahab walked along the well-worn path toward home from the river, she heard the dreaded voice of Miriam speaking. "Well, Harlot, I see that you still hold Salmon in your evil grasp. Do you realize who he is? He is the son of a prince of Israel. And who are you? We know, don't we, Harlot? And still you plan to marry a man whose shoes you are unworthy to touch. What do you say for yourself, Harlot?"

Rahab's greatest desire was to spit in Miriam's face and run. But anger boiled in her heart and rage brought bitter words to her lips. "If you are an example of a good woman of Israel, then Salmon would be desperate, indeed, to find a wife among you. I would be pleased if you would not waste my time to speak to me again." Rahab turned and tried to walk away slowly, but the water in the jug upon her head sloshed and spilled upon her shoulders and hair and tears coursed from her eyes.

When she reached the tent site she quickly lowered her waterpot and entered her tent avoiding Maachah's greeting. Sitting cross legged upon her mat she wept tears of self pity and anger until she had no more tears. Then she sat silently, wondering again if all that Miriam said was true.

"Maachah, has Rahab returned, yet, from the river?" Rahab heard Salmon's voice outside her tent.

Ashamed at her red and swollen eyes and trembling voice, she called out, "I am here, Salmon."

Salmon detected the tremor in her voice and asked, "Is all well with you, Rahab?"

Rahab wanted to assure him that it was, but she must be truthful with him, so she answered, "No, it's not."

Salmon's voice conveyed his concern as he bade her, "Come out, please, Rahab. Let's walk."

Slowly Rahab emerged from the tent. Maachah busied herself with Jared and Rahab blessed her in her heart that she did not look her way. Salmon caught her hand and led her away from the tent site.

They walked in silence for awhile and finally Salmon squeezed her hand and asked, "Can you tell me what troubles you, Rahab?"

Rahab sniffed and said in a soft voice, "Miriam spoke with me today. She was hateful to me, Salmon, as she has been before, while you were away. Before, I merely walked away, with no answer to her. But today I was so angry with her." She stopped walking and looked into his eyes. "She is so hateful to me, Salmon. So I said something hateful back to her."

Salmon stood looking into her eyes with his brown ones, which were not now warm, but blazed with fire instead. But when he spoke his voice was calm and gentle as always. "Miriam is wrong to be hateful, of course. Whatever her reason she is wrong. But you are not responsible for Miriam's behavior. You are responsible only for your own. Rahab, there may always be people who will dislike or misunderstand you. The important thing is your attitude toward them, how you react. God loves us although we sin against Him and disobey Him. We surely can love those who treat us unfairly."

"Love her?" Rahab asked incredulously.

The warmth had returned to Salmon's eyes as he took both her hands in his. With tenderness in his voice he said, "In the Law of God, He said, 'You shall not avenge nor bear any grudge against the children of your people, but you shall love your neighbour as yourself: I am the Lord.'"[41]

Rahab fell into Salmon's arms, weeping again, and saying, "Oh, Salmon, I am so sinful! How can I ever please God? And you, how can I ever be worthy to be your wife?"

Salmon let Rahab weep against him for awhile, stroking her long ebony hair with his strong hand. Then he pulled her face to look at him and said, "We don't live without sin, Rahab, not anyone. But God is merciful to us and forgives when we repent of our sin. Do you remember the sacrifice of the Day of Atonement?" Rahab nodded. "The blood makes atonement for the sin of the people. But it's when one truly repents and asks forgiveness that the blood is applied. We please God when we confess our sin." Salmon then smiled at Rahab and added, "You please me just by being you. I love you." Salmon drew Rahab back into his arms and kissed her tears away.

When Rahab was again alone, she poured her heart out to her God in prayer. She did not understand the ways of this wondrous God Whom she had come to know, but she asked Him to help her in some way to love Miriam. It would be impossible for her to love her of herself. The love must be given her from God.

Several weeks after the return of the soldiers, there was

---

[41]Leviticus 19:18

tension around the fire at the evening meal. Salmon and Enan were to depart at dark to investigate the trouble brewing to the north. Scouts had reported the movement of troops from several cities to the waters of Merom.[42] The little family feared that that time had come when Salmon and Jasper would need to return with the armies of Israel to the conquest of the land. After the meal, they all clasped hands and Jasper led in prayer.

"Our great and loving Lord, we beseech Your care upon Salmon as he gathers information for Joshua where our enemies are come together. And if this be the signal for us to return to the battle for You, please keep us and these our loved ones in your care and bring us soon together again to praise Your name."

Before slipping away into the darkness with Enan, Salmon held Rahab close and whispered, "Keep me in your prayers, my love."

As on other nights when Salmon spied for the great general, Joshua, Rahab could not sleep. She sat in her tent doorway and watched the stars twinkle above her, praying for the safety of Salmon and Enan. Sleep finally overtook her as the stars began to fade and pink lined the eastern horizon.

Rahab was startled awake by the brush of a beard on her face and a soft kiss on her cheek. She found herself still sitting in her doorway and Salmon kneeling before her.

"Salmon," she said, putting her arms around his neck. He lifted her to her feet and kissed her.

Then he said, "Rahab, the king of Hazor has gathered the troops from several neighboring cities to fight against Israel. Joshua has ordered the troops of all the tribes of Israel to report this morning. We will continue the battle until the land has been won for the Lord."

Rahab saw how tired Salmon looked after his long night's work, and touching his cheek softly said, "But you have had no

---

[42]Joshua 11:5-7

rest. Must you report with the others this morning?"

"I must go with them to win the land. The Lord will give me the strength I need." Salmon gathered her into his arms again and spoke into her hair, "I felt your prayers for me last night. Let me feel your prayers for me everyday, Rahab. When I return I will make you my wife." He looked into her eyes and smiled slightly. "Will you have time to make a wedding dress?"

Rahab smiled back at him, remembering a time long ago, and nodded. "Yes, I will have it ready when you return to me."

After a final kiss Salmon lifted his pack and walked quickly away from her. Rahab wiped the tears from her eyes and picked Jared up into her empty arms. The little boy was pulling his mother's skirt and crying, but Maachah was lost in the parting embrace of her husband.

When the troops of Israel had once again marched from the camp an awkward silence hung in the air. With great effort Maachah and Rahab resumed the duties of everyday life. But in Rahab's heart a new emotion began to blossom. When Salmon returned this time, the wars would be finished and she could become his wife.

Chapter 6

Marriage

Rahab poked her finger with her needle and stuck it into her mouth. Then she waited while her finger dried before returning to the soft, fine linen which lay in a large heap in her lap. She had taken the greatest care to weave this linen, for it was to be her wedding garment. With small, even stitches, Rahab sewed the dress which she would wear when she became Salmon's wife.

For so many months Rahab had desired to begin sewing her dress, but would not. She busied herself instead with duties in the tent site and helped and played with Jared. But when the messenger had come and announced that the army of Israel had done its final conquest and would soon begin the long trek home, Rahab wove the special linen and began to sew.

Rahab paused again from her work to rest her eyes. She scanned the horizon before her and took in the beauty of this land in which she had lived all her life. Rich foliage carpeted the valleys and crept up the hills beneath tall trees, blending as one in their abundance. Frequent rains and a climate peculiar to this spot of God's earth alone bore fruits of every kind. Misted mountains rose on the horizon, laden with forests and beasts of the field. But for Rahab life had truly begun when she had met the God of the Hebrews. And the beauty of this land meant much more to her now, for she would be the wife of a man who would till the earth and bring forth the fruits of the land.

Rahab had come to feel at home in the camp of Israel. It had been nearly five years that she had lived among the Hebrews. In her heart she was a Hebrew, also. And soon she would be the wife of a Hebrew man.

Jared was a constant source of delight in the lives of the two waiting women. At three years of age he already bore the large hands and broad face of his father. His endless chatter amazed the women and his easy retention of the things he was taught was a joy. On strong little legs he followed his mother and ceaselessly ran about the tent site from morning to evening. Rahab let him "help" her sometimes as she wove her linen, and his small fingers were often burned as he helped Maachah cook. The burning desire of his childish life was for the return of his father, whom he hardly remembered but for the constant loving narratives by his mother.

When the troops of Israel finally returned to the camp at Gilgal they did not all return together, marching, as before. They came in clusters, leading donkeys and camels laden with riches taken from the enemies. They led herds of cattle and flocks of sheep. Wagons filled with wondrous wares were driven slowly into the camp.

Laughter filled the air. Every soldier returned a rich man, with gold and goods. Wives and children greeted the returning men and went happily to their tents to plan the coming days, when they would leave their tents and move into the vacant cities of Canaan.

Rahab had prayed for Salmon every day and dreamed of him every night for the months, and indeed the years, of their separation. But when her eyes again beheld him at his return from the conquest of Canaan he was far more handsome than her memories served her. His warm brown eyes smiled at her in love, his strong, tanned arms embraced her, and with his soft brown beard tickling her face his lips greeted her with a promise to never leave her again.

Jasper could not seem to get enough of his little son. He hung on each word of childish prattle as if on words of greatness. He could not contain his joy and his loud laughter rang out clearly throughout each day, and into each night, as he exulted in his son.

Salmon, too, was overjoyed at his small nephew's growth and attainments. He often promised Rahab many such sons when they were one and had a home in this wondrous land flowing with milk and honey.

Salmon and Rahab went to their flat rock to speak of their plans for the future. Salmon's voice betrayed a note of sadness as he spoke of the peoples of the land who still dwelt in their cities.

"Didn't you drive out all the heathen?" Rahab asked him.

"No, there are five lords of the Philistines and all the Canaanites, Sidonians, and Hivites which dwell in Mount Lebanon," was Salmon's answer.[43]

"But why should any of the heathen remain?" asked Rahab.

"The Lord will yet drive them out from before His people," Salmon told her. "We may inhabit the cities, now, and the Lord will continue to drive out our enemies. We must not intermarry with these people, and we may not serve their gods." Salmon paused and a sadness swept over his handsome face. "But the Lord told Moses before his death that the people will turn to other gods, the gods of the strangers of this land, and will forsake the Lord and break His covenant with them."[44]

"But why would anyone forsake the Lord and turn to the gods of this land?" Rahab asked in wonder. "I served the gods of this land in their horror and fear. Now I serve the Lord of heaven Who loves me. I would never turn from Him to idols again."

Salmon smiled and reached his rough hand to hold her chin, saying, "I am happy to hear you say those words, although I know you never would. But there are many here who are called by God's name but do not love and trust Him."

Early one morning, not long after the arrival of the Hebrew army, the awaited miracle began. Jasper and Salmon had explained to Rahab what the Law of the Lord says

---

[43]Judges 3:3,4

[44]Deuteronomy 31:16-18

concerning the marriage of a Hebrew man to a captive woman. Although Rahab was not a captive, she was a woman of the land of Canaan, and must observe the commandments of the Law.

Maachah first cut Rahab's long raven locks and then carefully shaved her head. Rahab watched as the strands of hair fell to the floor of her tent and wept silently. How Salmon admired her hair! And now it was gone. Then Maachah helped her to closely pare her nails. Although Rahab's parents had escaped the wrath of God, still she must bewail them for thirty days. And then, after one month, she could become Salmon's wife.[45]

During the days of her humbling, Rahab remained within her tent as much as possible, praying for her family instead of bewailing them, remembering again the mercy of God in her life.

Although Rahab separated herself in her tent, she could hear the conversations in the tent site. One evening, near the end of her first week, she heard Salmon explaining to Maachah, "The lot for the tribe of Judah was cast first. But before it was cast, the leaders of our tribe, together with Caleb, the prince of our tribe, went to speak with Joshua. Caleb reminded Joshua that forty five years ago, when they two alone brought a good report of the land, our past great leader, Moses, sware that the land which they spied, where Hebron is, would be Caleb's and his family's for ever, because he had wholly followed the Lord.[46] Caleb is eighty-five years old, but he asked for the mountain in which the Anakims, a race of giants,[47] dwell. Caleb trusts the Lord to be with him and to help him drive them out of the

---

[45]Deuteronomy 21:10-13

[46]Numbers 14:24

[47]Numbers 13:33

mountain.[48] So, because Hebron was given to Caleb, the lot of the tribe of Judah is the land surrounding Hebron." Rahab heard a tenderness enter Salmon's voice as he continued, "The very hill upon which I stood and surveyed that land is in the lot of Judah, the very land I described to Rahab. The Lord has given me my desire, to the very piece of land for which I longed."

Two and one half tribes had chosen to take the lands to the east of the river. Although their lands had been conquered at the very start, and their families already occupied the cities, the men had remained with the troops of Israel in taking the entire Promised Land for the Lord.[49]

Tents which had stood in one spot for five years were taken down. Belongings were packed and placed in carts or hefted onto strong backs. Farewells were said and well-wishing could be heard about the camp. The lots had been cast by Joshua and Eleazar the priest for Judah and the children of Joseph, the tribe of Ephraim and the half tribe of Manasseh. Slowly the migration began toward the new homes in the Promised Land.

The tents in Jasper's tent site remained as they were. The family would remain until Rahab's thirty days were accomplished. Then they would go to the lot of Judah, to find their new homes and begin their new lives.

The days of Rahab's waiting were nearly at a close, when she heard a familiar voice outside the tent. "Well, Maachah, I see that you are not yet packing to leave." It was Miriam.

"We will wait until Rahab's thirty days have expired and she may be wed to my brother. Then we will depart for our new homes." Maachah answered.

"So Salmon will really marry her?" It was a question, but Miriam did not wait for an answer. "And where do you plan to settle?"

---

[48]Joshua 14:12

[49]Joshua 1:12-15

Maachah answered her cautiously, "We will make our new homes in Bethlehem."

A peal of laughter which disgusted Rahab was followed by these words which sounded so terrible to her, "Bethlehem! Why my family is also going to Bethlehem! So I guess that this is not goodbye, but only farewell until we meet again."

Rahab sat alone in her tent and felt a weight descend upon her heart. She had secretly been anticipating the move to Bethlehem as a reprieve from Miriam's presence. "Why, Lord, why must she go to Bethlehem?" Rahab implored. "Surely there are so many places within Judah she could have gone. What purpose is there for her to be where she can torment me?" Then Rahab remembered her former prayer, that the Lord would help her to love Miriam. That prayer had not yet been answered. Maybe, because she had not yet learned to love Miriam, she must be punished with her constant presence. "Lord, please forgive me. Salmon has told me that my attitude toward Miriam is what matters to You. You know my attitude toward Miriam. Make it to be what it should be, that I may please You."

On the last day of her separation, Rahab emerged from the tent and helped Maachah prepare the food for the marriage feast. Her hair had begun to grow, but she kept her head bound closely with a veil. Luscious foods of many kinds were prepared. Jasper and Salmon brought fresh fruits and vegetables from the richness surrounding the camp, and Rahab herself kneaded the dough for the bread. She went to bed that night tired, happy, and with a knot of excitement in her stomach.

When Rahab awoke in the morning, she spent some time in prayer. Then, after washing herself thoroughly with warm water that Maachah handed into her tent, she dressed in her lovely wedding dress. She longed for her long dark tresses to lay against the soft white of her dress, but pushed the thought from her mind. She was to become Salmon's wife, today. Her hair would grow again. But today, as she was, she must be beautiful for Salmon.

Maachah had roasted a bullock and two lambs from the herd which Jasper had taken from the conquest. Wondrous aromas wafted through the tent site. Jared ran about excitedly.

Near midmorning the guests to the wedding feast began to arrive. Many of their friends had already departed the camp, but there was a large number of guests gathered when Rahab emerged from the tent. She smiled at Salmon and he smiled back with his brown eyes. Together they walked to the wedding mat and sat, side by side. The guests then seated themselves around the couple. Maachah, aided by several other women, served the food and drink. Rahab sat beside Salmon, unable to eat the delicious food for the excitement within her breast. Friendly conversation and warm congratulations flowed around her. Today Rahab would become a Hebrew woman. Today Rahab became Salmon's wife.

Suddenly the comfort of the moment was shattered by a harsh voice speaking to Salmon. Rahab looked up startled to see Miriam, whom she had believed to have already departed the camp.

"My dear Salmon," Miriam said, a sweet smile on her face, "I have long admired you and your gallant feats for Israel. I only hope that your gallantry at Jericho has not brought destruction upon you."

Rahab heard Miriam's awful words and waited. She dared not even look at Salmon. But when he answered, his voice was calm and kind, "Thank you for attending our marriage feast, Miriam. I am glad to see that you are still among us, and able to attend." He paused and smiled right into the eyes of the hateful woman. Rahab watched the hard lines of Miriam's face soften as Salmon continued.

"I can never thank the Lord enough that He put Rahab there, in Jericho, to save our lives as we spied. I thank God for His wondrous mercy toward Rahab, in sparing her life and allowing her to learn of His love. I am blessed, indeed, to have her as my wife."

With the scorn entirely melted from her face, Miriam walked away to take a seat. Rahab sat in amazement at what Salmon had done. He had really done what he had told her to do. He had answered Miriam in love and kindness instead of returning her hatred, and therefore her hate had not hurt him. Rahab knew that Salmon truly loved Miriam, in spite of herself. Such love was foreign to Rahab. Such love was her desire.

The feast continued throughout the day, with guests appearing and leaving as the hours passed. As the day began to wane, Jasper seated himself beside Salmon and Rahab, holding Jared on his lap. Jasper looked at Rahab and said, "From the beginning, before ever sin had entered the world, the Lord meant for man and woman to live together in love. When God had made the first man, Adam, from the dust of the ground, and then his wife, Eve, from Adam's rib, Adam said, 'This is now bone of my bones and flesh of my flesh. She shall be called Woman, because she was taken out of Man.' And the Lord said, 'Therefore shall a man leave his father and his mother, and shall cleave unto his wife, and they shall be one flesh.'[50] Welcome to our family, Rahab."

Rahab considered the beautiful words of the Lord which Jasper had told her. She and Salmon were no longer to be two, but one flesh. The wonder of the moment impressed deeply upon Rahab's heart, and she knew she would cherish it in her memories.

With all the guests departed, Jasper helped Maachah to clean after the feast. Salmon lifted Rahab into his arms and carried her to the tent which was now theirs, to become his wife, one flesh together for life.

To be a man's wife was a wonder that Rahab had never imagined. Salmon made her laugh and enjoy each day. He was her friend, her lover, her husband. And as she lived each day

---

[50]Genesis 2:23,24

with him, she began to know that she had married a very wise man. And daily she felt that she knew Salmon's Lord better, for he talked of Him often.

The very day that all was packed for the move to Bethlehem, Salmon returned from Joshua to say that they would first go to Shiloh, where the whole congregation would assemble and set up the Tabernacle.

At Shiloh Rahab watched with awe as the Tabernacle, piece by piece, was set up. Here, in Shiloh, would be the permanent abode of the Tabernacle, and here was where Israel would come to offer sacrifices unto the Lord.

At Shiloh Joshua called to him the leaders of the seven tribes which had not as yet received their inheritance. Joshua told them to appoint three men from each tribe to spy out the remaining land and describe it in a book. The lots would then be cast there in Shiloh to divide the land to them. So the seven tribes camped in Shiloh to await their lands.[51]

Salmon could not stop thanking the Lord that the tribe of Judah had already been given their inheritance in the Promised Land. And when they departed from Shiloh, he could not hurry the little family along fast enough, as they travelled in caravan with others going to Bethlehem. When the day finally came that they approached near to Bethlehem, Salmon grabbed Rahab's hand and led her, running, to the crest of a hill.

"There!" Salmon exclaimed. "There is the land which I told you of. And it is ours, Rahab."

"But how do you know that it has not already been claimed by someone who arrived here before you?" she asked, out of breath from the quick run.

Salmon smiled at her, his brown eyes radiating his happiness. "Enan promised me to register this land in my name. He had his eye on another piece of land." Salmon looked at her

---

[51]Joshua 18:1-6

sidelong and said teasingly, "And Enan did not need to stay at Gilgal so long to be married."

Rahab smiled and Salmon caught her into his arms and kissed her. Then they returned to the caravan with which they travelled and soon they came to the stone buildings of the town of Bethlehem, high atop a hill. No strong wall circled the town, and Rahab expressed her concern. Salmon laughed and said, "The Lord will be our strong wall."

Houses large and small lined the streets of the town. Some had already been claimed and families were moving their scant belongings into them and claiming the contents thereof.

As Jasper and his family inspected a house, Salmon led Rahab away down the street to a solid square house on the outskirts of the town. "Here," he said, leading her inside. "I saw this house when we conquered Bethlehem and even then I could see you here, keeping this house, raising our children. This is the house to which I shall come home each night, to you." He smiled at her with his warm brown eyes and said, "Welcome home."

The outside appearance had hidden the charm of the house that Salmon had chosen for their home. But as they walked through the large, airy rooms and entered the bright courtyard, Rahab knew why Salmon had chosen this house. It already felt like home to her, although dust and dirt littered everything, and the flowers and vines of the courtyard were wild with lack of care.

"Oh, Salmon, it is wonderful. I am so happy with your choice." She hugged his tall frame and kissed his beard. "Now that I see this house, and I have seen your fields, I understand why you were so excited about this place, and why so impatient to get here."

Rahab and Salmon left some of their belongings in the lovely house to indicate their ownership, and sought Jasper's family. They found them in a cozy house on the main street of the town. Maachah excitedly showed Rahab from room to room, and although the house was dirty, as was Rahab's, Maachah could see nothing but the beauty. She wiped clean a bench in the courtyard, as overgrown as that of Rahab's new home, and they sat together.

"I am so happy, Rahab. I have lived all my days in the tents of my family and then Jasper's. This is my very first house, a real house. And it is so big, and so beautiful! Oh, won't it be fun to prepare meals in a house and not outside?" Maachah laughed with delight and Rahab joined in her laughter.

"I will miss you, Rahab," Maachah said, sobering suddenly.

"But I will live only on the other side of town. We can visit often, as often as we wish. We need not miss each other at all." Rahab answered, hugging her sister-in-law.

Little Jared ran through the house, up the stairs and then down, going in rapturous circles and whooping, "This is our house, this is our house!" Salmon and Jasper stood together and laughed at the child's delight at having a house to live in.

Salmon drew jug after jug of water from the well of Bethlehem and carried them to the new house while Rahab scrubbed until the walls and floors shone. Much of the furniture was good and could be used. Salmon tried his hand at carpentry and repaired some things, and soon the house was clean and neat, and looked like a real home. Salmon pulled weeds and trimmed vines and branches in the courtyard. He discovered two stone benches beneath the debris which he cleaned and placed beneath a shade tree. They went to bed at night in a bed of brass, for which Rahab planned to weave soft sheets and warm blankets.

Salmon went each morning to tend his herds and flocks, which were cared for by a hireling, and then returned to help Rahab. When the house was ready for living, Salmon purchased a plow from the new blacksmith in town and began to break his ground. He left each morning after breakfast and returned each night happy and tired.

At noontide each day Rahab carried a cool drink and something to eat down to the fields where Salmon laboured.

They sat together in the shade and ate and talked. Rahab knew that Salmon, who all his life had been a soldier and a spy, was now extremely content to be a farmer. And she was content to be a farmer's wife.

One day as Rahab returned to town from her lunch date with Salmon, she came face to face with Miriam. No words were spoken at first, but Rahab determined to be kind, so she said, "Hello, Miriam. I hope that you are getting settled well in Bethlehem."

"Hello," said Miriam, with deliberate pause. Then she added, "Harlot. I know that you are a good man's wife. But please know that does not make you a good woman. It is good for the town of Bethlehem to have your husband living here. It is tragic that we must have you with him." She ended with the familiar smirk across her face.

Rage welled up in Rahab's bosom. She had tried to speak in a friendly manner with Miriam, but it was clear that Miriam desired to carry on in her former manner. Forgetting her prayers for help and her resolve to try kindness, Rahab spoke, knowing even as she did that she would later regret it.

"Had I known that you would live here, I might have persuaded my husband to live elsewhere. You, Miriam, are the tragedy here. Are you so miserable that you must spread your shadows everywhere? I would be pleased if you would not try to neighbor with me." Rahab tossed her head, and her veil fell aside, revealing her short, waving hair.

Miriam suddenly burst forth with a peal of laughter and said, "Come now, Harlot, you are uncovering your secrets. But we here in Bethlehem know. And we burn with shame." She laughed again, loudly, as Rahab whirled, clutching her veil over her head, and ran home in tears.

For the first time since she and Salmon had married, Rahab felt again the dark knot of doubt. Was she indeed a blot to Salmon's name in the town of Bethlehem? And how could she live in such proximity to that woman? Life had been such a wonder, and now, once again, the blight of Miriam had entered. Rahab knew that she had failed. But she did not love Miriam. She could not. She would not. And never could she forgive Miriam for the suffering she caused.

When Rahab and Salmon next visited Jasper's family Rahab pulled Maachah aside and said, "Salmon knows of my difficulty with Miriam, but he has counselled me to use kindness towards her. I cannot, Maachah." Rahab's voice rose with her agitation and she continued. "Just this week Miriam once again showed me her scorn. And at first I was trying to be polite. But she is so hateful towards me that I get angry and say terrible things. What can I do?"

Maachah tried to calm Rahab and then said, "My dear sister, you are a far better woman than Miriam. Don't let her anger you. She must feel that she has won over you when you answer in wrath. I can only agree with my little brother. Try to only say pleasant things to her, even if she is tormenting you. At least she will not have the pleasure of angering you."

When Rahab was alone the next day, she went to her courtyard and fell contritely beside a stone bench. "Oh, Lord, forgive my anger. I cannot understand Miriam's bitterness toward me. And I cannot escape it. You have put us together in Bethlehem. So You must desire for me to learn to love the unlovely. I cannot, Lord. You must give me love for her. I have none of myself. I want to please You, Lord. And I do not want to harm my husband's name."

As Rahab returned to her duties in her new home, she felt that a great burden was lifted. She knew that she must face Miriam again, and possibly soon, but she also knew that the God of mercy would sustain her.

One morning as Rahab was busy at her loom, an eager knock sounded on her door. She answered and found Maachah, smiling as if with a secret. Rahab invited her in and little Jared ran ahead, to try Aunt Rahab's stairway. The two women sat in the shade of the courtyard.

"I know you are bursting to tell me something," said Rahab, "Tell."

Maachah's excitement bubbled out as she announced, "Jasper and I are expecting another child!" Rahab hugged her dearly and they chatted about the changes since Maachah's first pregnancy.

After the happy mother-to-be had led her little son away toward home, Rahab sat quietly for awhile. She and Salmon had been married, now, for two months, and she hoped to soon be carrying his child. She knew that it was still very soon, but she desired so much to give to him the children of which he had so often spoken to her.

Just as Salmon was putting out the lights one evening, a knock sounded at the door. He answered to find Enan, out of breath, standing outside. Pulling him inside, Salmon inquired at his urgency.

"Joshua has sent messengers to all the towns and cities. The children of Reuben and Gad and the half tribe of Manasseh have built a great altar by the Jordan River. All have been summoned to Shiloh to Joshua. We will go up against our brothers to war." Enan ended sadly and waited for Salmon.

"I must tell Rahab. I will join you shortly."

"Remember the law of the Lord," reminded Enan, "You are not to go to war, but to stay with your wife for one year."[52]

"You're right," said Salmon, "then I must let you go and fight alone. How will you ever get along without me at your side to keep an eye on you?"

Enan embraced Salmon saying, "I will miss you at my side. I thank the Lord that He has spared you the fight against our own brothers."

Maachah and Jared came that night to stay with Rahab and Salmon. Maachah wept against Rahab, more for the sinning

[52]Deuteronomy 24:5

tribes than for her husband's departure. "Why do they sin, knowing the wrath of God and His commandments?"

Rahab held her sister-in-law and could find no answer.

"Our people have ever been a people of little faith," Maachah told Rahab. "After they had seen the mighty works of God's hands when He brought the plagues down upon Egypt, and after the Red Sea opened before them and they walked across on dry land, they soon complained against Moses for the lack of water.[53] Then they complained for lust of the garlics and leeks of Egypt.[54] While Moses was on the mount receiving the very Law of God, written by the finger of God, the people turned to idolatry and gross sin.[55] Oh, Rahab, is there any hope for this people?"

Rahab tried to smile and said, "There must be Maachah, for the Lord Himself has chosen these people as His own. There must be hope for them."

Maachah sat up straight and said, "You're right. There is hope for these people because we serve a great God. But that is certainly the only reason."

Three long, fearful days passed until the soldiers from Bethlehem returned. Salmon, Rahab and Maachah ran to meet them as they approached town.

"Oh Jasper, I'm so glad to have you back!" Maachah exclaimed, embracing her husband. "We have been so confused by this, and so worried that you must fight against your own people."

Jasper smiled unexpectedly and kissed her. "Don't worry, little wife," he said calmly. "The Lord took care of everything."

As they sat together that evening, Jasper told the story of

---

[53]Exodus 17:1,2

[54]Numbers 11:5

[55]Exodus 32:1-6

Ed, the altar at the Jordan River. They had marched upon the Reubenites, Gadites and the half tribe of Manasseh, and Phinehas, the son of Eleazar the priest, had asked them why they rebelled against the Lord in building an altar instead of the altar of the Lord at Shiloh.

But the children of Reuben, Gad, and Manasseh had denied rebellion against the Lord. They avowed that the purpose of the altar was not for sacrifice, but for a witness between the tribes on both sides of the river. They said that they feared that in time to come the children of Israel might say that their children had no part in the Lord, because the Jordan River divided them. So they built the altar as a witness to the coming generations that they, too, worshipped God at His altar before the Tabernacle in Shiloh.[56]

"Was there any fighting?" Rahab asked.

"None at all," answered Salmon. "Phinehas was pleased with their answer and we marched home without a battle."

"God is so good!" exclaimed Maachah. "Even when all is dark from the human side, the Lord is still in control."

Salmon agreed and winked at Rahab, his brown eyes smiling.

"Yes, You are still in control, Lord," prayed Rahab silently, "even when the dark shadow of Miriam looms ahead."

After the years of living in the tents, life in the house in Bethlehem was a joy. Rahab enjoyed scrubbing and tidying her house. Sometimes she wondered about the woman who had kept this house before her, a woman who had died at the hands of the Hebrew army. Surely she had not known the great God of mercy. Rahab was saddened by the thought. She would touch a wall, a piece of furniture, and try to imagine another woman who had called this "home."

Salmon prepared a garden plot for Rahab in a corner of

---

[56]Joshua 22:10-34

his field. She had never been so close to the earth before, not even while living in the tent. She liked the feel of the cool, rich soil sifting through her fingers. And she learned to share a joy with Salmon, the joy of watching the tiny plants push their small green noses up through the soil toward the sun. Salmon carefully taught Rahab how to distinguish between her plants and the weeds. Yet, she sometimes, in her eagerness to pull out the weeds, also pulled a small, struggling vegetable. She discovered that once pulled, they could not be replanted, but would shrivel and die.

Enan would sometimes visit in their home for the evening meal. He lived alone in a house that was far too large for one man, but he liked the house and planned to fill it with a family.

Rahab's Bethlehem house had a beautifully polished table, with equally polished benches along the sides upon which to sit as one ate from the table.

One night Enan ate more quietly than usual. Both Rahab and Salmon noticed.

"Don't you like the food tonight?" Rahab asked with a tease in her voice as Enan pushed the food from side to side in his dish.

"It is very good." answered Enan, attempting to eat more enthusiastically.

"Is it that you don't feel quite well?" asked Salmon very seriously. Then he lightened as he added, "Perhaps in your heart?"

Enan looked at Salmon startled, and then smiled broadly. "It shows so well?"

"I remember when I first saw Rahab. You remember, don't you, how I couldn't eat well upon the mountains as we hid from the soldiers of Jericho?" Enan nodded at Salmon's question. "It was not from fear or weariness. It was from love, love for Rahab, that I couldn't eat. And will you tell us the girl who has captured your heart?"

Rahab leaned forward expectantly. She could not recall

ever seeing Enan with any of the young ladies in town, in particular. He was rather handsome, and quite famous, also, for his daring feats of spying. He owned large fields and flocks and herds, and of course his lovely house. So Rahab could imagine that many girls would be interested in him.

Enan leaned back smiling. He decided to prolong their inquisitiveness as long as possible, so he said, "I have really always imagined myself as a bachelor forever. I really can cook quite well, so why do I need a wife?" He smiled at Rahab and glanced at the untouched food in his dish. "I don't mind a disorderly house, and if ever I do, a servant would do well to straighten it." He paused, amused at their impatient expressions. "But when I acquired such a big house, with so many empty, hollow rooms, I decided that perhaps I should find a good woman to help me fill those rooms with children."

Salmon laughed as Enan finished and said, "Tell us her name, Enan."

Enan smiled a proud smile and continued his evasiveness, "She is by far the loveliest young woman in Bethlehem." He glanced at Rahab and quickly added, "Who is not married, that is. She is intelligent, can cook nicely, knows how to converse well, and is just the joy of my heart."

"Come, Enan," chided Rahab, "We want to know who she is!"

"Couldn't you guess from my description?" Enan laughed. "She is a relative of yours, Salmon, Miriam, the daughter of Abidan."

Rahab gasped and then covered her mouth quickly. Enan looked at her puzzled and then turned to Salmon as he smilingly said, "You are right, Enan, she is beautiful, if an old married man can judge beauty. I am happy for you."

Rahab rose from the table and quickly ascended the stairs to the bedroom and sat upon the bed. Enan was in love with Miriam, the woman who hated her intensely. How could that be? "Lord," she implored, "why did you let Enan fall in love with her?

He is Salmon's dearest friend. And she is my worst enemy! How can I bear this?"

After several minutes Rahab heard the door close downstairs and then Salmon's steps coming up the stairs. He entered the room and stood in the doorway, looking at Rahab with those brown eyes, which were now intense.

"Rahab," he said quietly, "Enan is in love with Miriam. You hurt him deeply tonight by leaving as you did. I think I do understand your problem with her. But Enan is my friend. I will not allow you to hurt him because of your differences with Miriam."

"My differences!" Rahab said, too loudly she knew, but this was all unfair. "It is Miriam who despises me. It is she who mistreats me!"

"Well that may be. But as long as Enan cares for her, and if he marries her, then for a lifetime, you must always treat her with the utmost respect and kindness, and never allow Enan to know that you have a problem with her."

"I think it will be obvious the first time that Enan sees Miriam and me together," Rahab said defensively.

"Good. Then Enan will be aware of it. But he will not be aware because of your behavior or speech. Do you understand, Rahab?"

Rahab felt the way she had as a child when her father had reprimanded her. This was all unfair to her. Salmon was being unreasonable. Her entire life would be unbearable if Enan truly did marry Miriam. She wanted to kick and scream and fight this terrible thing that was coming into her life. But Rahab loved Salmon. He was the dearest thing in life to her. She wanted more to please him than herself, didn't she? So she bravely looked into his severe brown eyes and said, "I understand. I will never say or do anything again that will show to Enan my real feelings about Miriam."

"Good," said Salmon, his brown eyes softening. "And I will continue to pray for you, that you will someday learn that real love does not depend upon the person loved, but upon the person loving. I pray that the Lord will show you this."

Salmon did not mention the affair of that fateful evening again. The next morning as he ate his breakfast he was his usual cheerful self. When he left to work his fields Rahab sat idly at her loom and let her mind wander to the times before in which Miriam had confronted her. What could she have said that would have changed anything? Really, she could not think of anything that would. Miriam hated her because of who she had been, and there were no words that could change that. Then she remembered the day of her wedding to Salmon, how that he had answered Miriam, and changed her demeanor completely, at least for the time. Was it possible that she, too, could say words as he had to change Miriam? She truly doubted it. But that was what Salmon wanted her to do. So Rahab prayed, "Oh Lord, You Who have shown Your mercy to me, when I am so unworthy, help me to show mercy to Miriam, although she does not seek it, for Salmon's sake. For Enan's sake." She paused in her prayer and then added with a choke, "For my sake."

A knock at the door brought Rahab to the end of her prayer. She went to answer the door anticipating Maachah's smile in greeting, but found a short, stooped man standing before her. He introduced himself as Arod, owner of a shop in town.

"I have heard that you weave exceptionally fine linen," Arod told her. "Would you be interested in selling linen to me, for my shop? Everyone is clamoring for new clothes these days, you see, and I would be willing to pay you well."

Rahab was startled by the suddenness of his suggestion. Yes, she would like very much to sell her linen. Weaving kept her hands busy when her housework was finished. And oh, it was fun to earn the gold coins.

"I would be pleased to sell you my linen," she told Arod, "but I will need to speak with my husband, first. I will stop by your shop and let you know the answer after I have discussed it with him."

Rahab was delighted when Salmon agreed to let her make linen to sell in Bethlehem. She hurried along the narrow street to the center of town, where shops lined the street. Upon inquiring, she found Arod's shop and entered. From the ceiling hung wares and goods of all descriptions. Merchandise lined the wall as well. Rahab had not as yet shopped here, and made a mental note to come here soon, to look at the wares.

A slender girl with light brown hair and tender green eyes asked her, "May I be of aid to you?" Rahab noticed the shy way in which she spoke.

"Yes, I have come to speak with Arod. Is he here?" Rahab asked.

"I will call him," the girl answered, and slid quickly out a back doorway.

As Rahab waited she heard a voice raised in anger coming from the back of the shop. The girl's soft answers were interrupted by sharp orders in a harsh voice.

When the girl returned, she lifted shy eyes to Rahab only long enough to say, "Arod will be here in a moment." She then slipped away to tend to business in the shop.

Rahab made her agreement with Arod for amounts and delivery dates and prices. Then, as she was ready to leave, she asked him, "Who is the girl who works here?"

Arod scowled and said, "Only a servant girl. Her name is Elshima. Why?"

"She seems to be a very nice girl," was all that Rahab answered, and bidding Arod, "Good day," she departed the shop.

Rahab went to Maachah's house, which was close to the shop, and told her of her exciting new venture. Maachah was pleased. Rahab noticed how tired Maachah looked as she carried her second child and asked, "Are you feeling well?"

"I feel alright, not sick, you know, but I am tired so much of the time," Maachah answered. "Not at all like the first time."

"Perhaps it is because the first time you didn't have a lively child to chase around. And you didn't have this large house to keep." Rahab thought for a moment and said, "Perhaps I could come and help you here a little each day. I could clean for you, grind your flour and bake your bread, and keep Jared busy so that you may rest a little."

"Oh, no, dear Rahab. You have a business now to attend to. I would not ask you to do such a thing. I will be alright. Jasper helps me with many things when he comes home in the evening."

Rahab did not like the thought of Maachah doing everything alone when she was so tired. But she was right, Rahab had now committed herself to deliver linen to Arod. Suddenly she saw in her mind the light brown hair and shy green eyes of Elshima.

"Maachah, I just today met a girl who I think could help you. It would be very good for her to be able to leave her present employment. Her name is Elshima, and she is the servant of Arod. If Jasper agrees that you could use some help, perhaps he could buy her services from Arod. I really do not know if he would be willing to let her go. I don't even know her. But I think it would be good for both you and her."

Maachah waved the idea aside, insisting that she was able to do everything alone. But Rahab did not give up. When she left Maachah's house she went to Salmon's field, which was quite a walk outside of Bethlehem. She found him toiling on a hillside to plow as far as possible up the side, before leaving the rest for the sheep to graze.

"Salmon!" she called, running to his side. He stopped and pulled the harness strap from his shoulder.

"Rahab, is something wrong?" he asked, wondering at her visit at this hour.

"No. But I need to talk with you," she answered.

Salmon walked with her to the shade of an old tree and they sat together.

"Salmon, Maachah is getting larger with child and the tasks of keeping house and keeping up with Jared are very tiring to her. I offered to help, Salmon, but today I arranged with Arod to deliver linen and Maachah will hear nothing of it." Rahab paused to catch her breath and continued, watching the question in Salmon's brown eyes. "Today at Arod's shop I met a servant girl named Elshima. She works for Arod, but he seems to be a rough taskmaster. I don't know her at all, but she seems to be a nice girl, and I think she may be a good help for Maachah. I suggested to Maachah that perhaps Arod would sell her service to Jasper. She just insisted that she was alright. But, maybe if you said something to Jasper..."

Rahab let her words trail away and Salmon smiled and said, "Are these the wiles of women? I have heard of them." He laughed aloud and said, "I will mention the matter to Jasper. But, Rahab, remember this. If Jasper decides that it's not for them, you shall not speak of it again. If you want to try to help her, you may, even if she protests. We don't want anything to happen to our dear Maachah."

To Rahab's delight Jasper liked the idea of someone to help Maachah. So he visited Arod and came home with the news that Maachah now had a servant girl to help her. Rahab helped Maachah prepare a room for Elshima's use.

When Elshima came with her few belongings, it was clear to all that she would fit in well with the family. She courteously bowed before the men and ladies and stood silently waiting. Jared took to her instantly and tried to lead her out to see the courtyard. Elshima smiled at the child and looked at Maachah, still standing silently.

"You may go outside with Jared," Maachah instructed her. She smiled and taking Jared's hand, walked to the courtyard with him. Rahab stayed awhile to help Maachah instruct Elshima, but found that she was not needed. Elshima listened intently to every instruction and then quietly set to work with efficient hands. Maachah expressed her relief at such good help to Rahab.

"Look how she takes to every task! Oh, Rahab, I was

upset at first to think of someone else in my house, doing my work. But I do think I will like Elshima. And I think I will enjoy the opportunity to go easier." She hugged Rahab and said, "Thank you, dear sister."

As the days passed, Maachah looked rested and happier. Rahab found herself so busy with her weaving that she was thankful for Elshima's presence, for she had little extra time to devote to Maachah.

One bright day that was fresh from a rain wash Rahab walked slowly home from the well with a jug of water balanced carefully on her head. There, in her path, stood Enan, and at his side stood Miriam. Rahab knew there was no escape, for they had seen her approaching.

Enan smiled and waved. "Rahab, come here," he invited. "I want you to meet my betrothed, Miriam."

Rahab approached and set her jug on the ground. She smiled at Enan and tried very hard to smile at Miriam, also. "Miriam and I have met," she said. "Hello, Miriam. Congratulations on your betrothal to Enan." She felt that was enough to say.

Miriam wore a gentle expression upon her face. Rahab had never noticed before, but Miriam was beautiful. Then Rahab saw the familiar gleam deep in her eyes as she spoke. "Hello, Rahab." It was the first time she had used Rahab's name. "Enan tells me that since he and your husband are best of friends you and I will be seeing much of each other in the days to come." Miriam smiled a lovely smile, but Rahab read an ugly message behind it.

Was it her imagination? Rahab knew that she expected the worst of Miriam. Maybe she was the sweet, wonderful woman Enan knew. Maybe the gleam in her eye meant nothing. But Rahab could not comment upon her statement. So she asked, "When will you be wed?"

Miriam and Enan looked at each other smiling. Enan answered, "We will wed as soon as the feast of harvest is completed."

As Rahab left them, she hoped for Enan's sake that the look of love she had seen in Miriam's eyes was genuine. After all, Miriam would marry Enan and should love him. How she felt about Rahab did not really matter.

Chapter 7

Antagonist

The summer was drawing to a close. Salmon hired several men to help him bring his crops in from the fields. He returned home each evening exhausted from the hard work, but happy. The dream of his years of wandering and soldiering was finally realized. Rahab enjoyed seeing how happy Salmon was from his work. She felt some of that same wonder as she harvested her garden and dried her vegetables.

Two young women were hired to help Rahab prepare the meals to take to the labourers in the fields of Salmon. Hot loaves of bread, parched grain, clusters of raisins, and cakes of figs were loaded into the wagon. Rahab accompanied the young women as they led the plodding oxen to the fields. The weary reapers sat beneath ancient olive trees and ate the meal slowly, engaging in friendly conversations.

The days began to shorten and the sun would set before the work was done each day. But Rahab was always glad when the Sabbath came. From sundown on the sixth day until sundown on the seventh day, she and Salmon would rest. They often visited with Jasper and Maachah.

Maachah was beginning to put on weight with her coming child, but looked rosy and happy, since Elshima had come to her home. Elshima quietly attended to her duties and entertained Jared easily. She was a welcome addition to the family. One Sabbath as Rahab and Salmon visited, Maachah pulled Rahab to the courtyard, where they sat in the late summer sunshine.

"Elshima is such a blessing," Maachah said. Then she sighed and added, "But I fear that we will someday lose her."

"Lose her?" Rahab looked at her friend puzzled. "Why should you lose her?"

"Well, she is a lovely young girl, you know, and has caught the eye of a young man who serves a neighbor of ours.

His name is Pagiel. She has not said anything to me about him, but I watch him when he comes near and speaks to her, and I fear she may be in love." Maachah paused and then went on, laughing lightly, "Well, I don't fear that she may be in love, you know, only that if she marries she will leave me."

"Oh, Maachah, I had so hoped that you would have Elshima's help until your baby is born, and as long after that as you deem necessary. Does this young man have the money to pay her price to Jasper?"

"I don't know. Secretly I hope he doesn't. But I do love Elshima, she is so dear. I do want her to be happy."

Rahab gathered much flax into Salmon's barn for weaving of linen through the winter months. She cleaned and oiled her spindle and loom, and laid them aside to rest for awhile, for she and Salmon would go together to Shiloh for the feasts of the seventh month.

Maachah would not go, because of the child she carried, so she promised to check on Rahab's house daily. Salmon brought out from storage the tent in which he and Rahab had lived when they were first married. Rahab gathered implements for cooking and blankets for sleeping.

On a bright morning Salmon and Rahab joined the throng of people, mostly men, but some with wives and children, walking from Bethlehem to Shiloh. With them came flocks of sheep and herds of cattle, freewill offerings of the men of Bethlehem for the sacrifices of the feast. They brought with them a tithe of their wine, grain, oil, and the firstborn of their sheep and cattle. As they travelled, they passed near Mount Moriah, upon the sides of which rested the city of Jerusalem, still inhabited by the Jebusites. The caravan stopped to buy fruits and drink from a well.

Salmon shaded his eyes and pointed up toward the highest peak. "There," he said, "is the mount upon which our father, Abraham, offered his only son, Isaac, as a sacrifice unto the Lord."

Salmon's words stunned Rahab. She shivered and looked into his serious brown eyes. "Your father, Abraham, offered his son unto the Lord?" She could not believe it. The God of the Hebrews hated the child sacrifices of the heathen. Salmon's eyes twinkled as he smiled and said, "The Lord told Abraham to bring his only son, Isaac, to this mountain and offer him unto the Lord. So Abraham obeyed, bringing Isaac, wood, and fire here to the mountain. As they travelled, Isaac asked his father where the lamb was for the offering, and Abraham answered him, 'My son, God will provide himself a lamb for a burnt offering.'"

"Didn't Isaac know that he was the sacrifice?" Rahab asked, awed by the story.

"No." answered Salmon. "When they arrived atop this mountain, Abraham built an altar and put the wood upon it. Then, although he was a very aged man and Isaac a strong youth, Abraham bound his son and laid him upon the altar." Salmon paused, watching the concern in Rahab's eyes. He did not know how his story brought to her mind the innocents of Jericho who had died in the flames of Baal and Ashteroth.

"Just as Abraham stretched forth his hand and took the knife to slit his son's throat, the angel of the Lord called out and stopped him. God said to him, 'Do not lay your hand upon the lad, nor do anything to him, for now I know that you fear God, seeing that you did not withhold your only son from me.' Then Abraham saw a ram caught in a thicket by the horns, and he offered the ram for a burnt offering to the Lord."[57]

Rahab relaxed and sighed in relief. "I knew that the Lord wouldn't require such a sacrifice."

Salmon put his arms around her and smiled into her eyes. "You are right, God despises the sacrifices of children that are made by the heathen. But, Rahab, the Lord has promised to send Someone to us, someday, Who will crush Satan's head and

---

[57]Genesis 22:2-14

deliver us from sin.[58] God teaches us that it is the blood that makes an atonement for our sins."[59]

Rahab looked at Salmon questioningly, "Do you mean that this promised One's blood will be shed?" Salmon only shrugged. Rahab persisted, "By whom? Surely God wouldn't allow Him to be sacrificed!"

Salmon smiled again and said, "Rahab, I don't understand, I only believe what God says."

When the Bethlehem caravan reached Shiloh, they found a multitude already camped on the hills and in the valley about the city. Salmon and Jasper pitched their tents and then went to talk with friends that they had not seen since the tribes had separated to inhabit the land.

The bustle of the tent city filled Rahab with memories of the five years that she had lived in the camp of Israel on the plains of Jericho. She paused to pray and thank the Lord again that she and Salmon now lived in the strong stone house in Bethlehem. Then she readied everything for the night and prepared a meal for the evening and the day following, which would be a holy convocation in which no work could be done.

Because Jasper had come without his family he ate the evening meal with Salmon and Rahab. Enan joined them as the sun sank into the west and the holy day began.

In the morning trumpets summoned everyone to the Tabernacle. There the priest, Eleazar, began the sacrifices to the Lord. On that day a series of sacrifices were offered to the Lord, of a bullock, a ram, and seven lambs, each accompanied by offerings of fine flour mingled with oil. The trumpets were blown throughout these sacrifices. Then a kid of the goats was

---

[58]Genesis 3:15

[59]Leviticus 17:11

sacrificed for a sin offering.[60]

When the first day had ended, as soon as the sun had set, merchants brought forth their wares and wound through the tents, hawking loudly. Rahab had brought linen to Shiloh to sell, but on this evening she and Salmon remained at their fire with friends, talking of the blessings which the Lord had given them.

On the following days, except the Sabbath day, Rahab sold her linen. Some customers came running to her, telling her how that they had missed such fine linen since they had left the camp at Gilgal. When her linen was gone, Rahab could only tell them that it was sold in Bethlehem, at Arod's shop. A few told her that it would be worth the trip to Bethlehem for such linen.

Rahab warmed beneath the praise, and wondered at God's mercy. She was a part of Israel, now, the wife of a Hebrew, and a weaver of fine Hebrew linen.

Salmon presented the tithe of all his increase before the Tabernacle, in the presence of Eleazar the priest, to the Levites. He explained to Rahab that when the Lord had divided the Promised Land to the tribes of Israel, He had given cities to the Levites, but no lands to farm. Their inheritance was the tithe, or tenth, of all the increase of the land. They in turn would tithe their receipts and give them to the priestly family. This was the plan of the Lord to provide for those who waited upon the Tabernacle and the service of the Lord.[61]

The tenth day of the month was once again a holy convocation. All were called to the Tabernacle by the blast of the trumpets. The priest, Eleazar, again offered the sacrifices of burnt offering to the Lord, as on the first day. Then the goat was offered for a sin offering, and the blood was sprinkled upon the altar seven times. Eleazar then put his hands upon the head of the live goat and confessed over him all the iniquities of the

---

[60]Numbers 29:1-5

[61]Numbers 18:20,21

children of Israel. A man was chosen to lead the goat away into the wilderness.[62]

The day was a sabbath of rest in which the people were to afflict their souls, in remembering their great sinfulness and the great mercies of God.

The fifteenth day of the month began the Feast of Tabernacles. Although they were dwelling in tents in Shiloh, Jasper, Enan and Salmon all went into the hills to gather the boughs of thick trees. With these they fashioned booths in which to dwell during the seven days of the feast.

The multitude of Israel gathered at the Tabernacle daily for the sacrifices. Each day fourteen lambs and two rams were offered to the Lord for a burnt offering. On the first day of the feast thirteen bullocks were offered. Each day the tally of bullocks decreased by one until seven were offered on the seventh day. A kid of the goats was also offered each day as a sin offering.

The eighth day was once again a holy convocation, with burnt offerings and a sin offering as on the first and tenth days of the month.[63]

When the evening of the twenty-second day came, the booths were dismantled and many were burned in the evening fires. Rahab packed and cleaned the tent site, desiring to leave behind no trace of their stay. In the morning Salmon and Rahab joined the caravan returning to Bethlehem.

The whole of the feasts unto the Lord during the seventh month had been wonderful to Rahab. Never had she seen such ceremony, and never had sacrifices had such meaning. As the blood flowed, she knew that it was the blood that atoned for her sins, which were many, and that she was forgiven, clean, pure.

When they finally came to the town of Bethlehem, weary

---

[62]Leviticus 16:9,10

[63]Numbers 29

from the days in Shiloh and the journey home, Maachah and Jared joyously greeted them, eager to hear every detail of the journey and feasts.

One day Salmon came home from his field, which he prepared for the planting of barley, and announced to Rahab, "Enan and Miriam will be wed in two weeks." He watched her closely, and she knew she must react correctly.

She carefully said, "Two weeks." Her mind sought wildly for words. "Enan must be very excited." She looked at Salmon, who watched her carefully with his deep brown eyes.

"He is looking forward to marriage with great anticipation," Salmon told her. "He has watched us together and told me that if he can be half as happy as I then he will be happier than he has ever imagined."

Thankful that Salmon had shifted the conversation to something more pleasant, Rahab grabbed him about the neck and kissed him, laughing. "And Enan cannot imagine the happiness you have given me!"

But Salmon suddenly sobered and looked at her severely. "Rahab," he said, and his tone sobered her as well, "Miriam's wedding is her day. Remember to keep it pleasant for her." Rahab wanted to remind Salmon that on her wedding day Miriam had come and tried to make it unpleasant. But the look in his eyes prevented her.

"Yes, Salmon," she answered lowly, still looking into his serious brown eyes. "I will only say that which is pleasant, or I shall say nothing at all." Salmon's features relaxed and he smiled. Then, catching her into his strong arms, he kissed her breathless.

The day of Miriam's wedding to Enan dawned bright and beautiful. It seemed to Rahab that God was smiling upon the marriage. Rahab would have had dark storm clouds to match Miriam's disposition. But she tried to shake the thought from her, remembering Salmon's stern warning about her behavior. Knowing that in her present state of mind she would most likely fail, Rahab cried out to her Heavenly Father for aid.

"Oh, Lord, you have seen each incidence of my life with Miriam. You have heard her hard words against me and you know that she hates me." Rahab paused, not desiring to speak frankly, but knowing that the Lord knew her heart, anyway. So she continued, "And you know that I hate her." There, she had admitted it to the Lord. "But Lord, I know that You love Miriam. You love me and I do not deserve the love of anyone, and especially not Your love. Salmon told me once that real love does not depend upon the person being loved, but upon the person loving. I do want to be able to love Miriam. But there is no love, anywhere, within me for Miriam. Give me love for her. And today, as we attend the wedding of Miriam and Enan, help my behavior and words to be in love, Your love. I cannot do it of myself. Thank You that You have ever taken care of me and my needs better than I could even ask."

Miriam's father had spread a sumptuous feast for the marriage of his daughter. Because Salmon was a dear friend of Enan he and Rahab were given seats of honor at the feast. Miriam blushed with pleasure as the guests approached and spoke with her and her groom. When Salmon and Rahab were seated near the bride and groom, Rahab watched Miriam, waiting to see the familiar cruel gleam in her eyes. But Miriam kept her radiant expression, hardly seeming to notice the new arrivals. Rahab noted that she wore a lovely dress and was decked with jewels and gold. Her loving glances toward her groom indicated to Rahab that love flowed between them. Rahab was glad of that. She did wish for Enan's happiness. As she sat at the feast, Rahab understood that that meant Miriam's happiness as well.

When a servant came, bearing a large jug and pouring wine to the guests, Miriam suddenly looked directly at Rahab. The familiar gleam appeared and she spoke, her voice soft and sweet. "Thank you, Salmon, dear, and your little wife, for coming to our wedding feast. I look forward to seeing much of you in the coming days. And years." The last two words sent a chill through Rahab. It sounded to her like a threat, a promise of suffering to come. Rahab did not feel the need to respond, since Miriam had addressed herself to Salmon.

"We are happy to be here," Salmon answered. "I have seen Enan in many circumstances through the years, good and bad. I enjoy seeing him so happy as you have made him today."

Rahab watched as Miriam blushed slightly beneath the praise. How was it that Salmon could say things just so, to please the hearer? "And we are looking forward to many good times in fellowship with you and Enan, are we not, Rahab?"

Rahab almost choked. Why must Salmon include her in this conversation? But she must answer, and correctly. So she looked at Miriam and actually smiled at her, saying, "Yes, Enan is very dear to us. He is part of our family. We are looking forward to you being part of our family, also."

At her words, Rahab saw a puzzled look replace the gleam in Miriam's eyes. Salmon continued to speak casually with Enan and Miriam. But Rahab sat in the crowded room and wondered at the grace of God that He had enabled her to say such words! And it was true. Enan was like family to them. His wife must become such, also. And to make it that way would be up to her.

Rahab anticipated the end of the feast and hoped that she had already said all that would be needed. But as the guests began to thin and Salmon announced to her that they would now go home, Enan and Miriam approached them. Enan embraced Salmon and thanked him, again, for coming. Miriam smiled sweetly and gave her thanks. Then she looked at Rahab, the puzzled look still in her eyes, and said, "Enan and I would like you and Salmon to come to our house to a meal next Sabbath. Will you?"

"We would be very pleased to come," answered Rahab, knowing that she need not consult Salmon on this decision. Then, because the Lord had blessed her so well this day with gracious speech, and because she had seen a question in Miriam's eyes, she added, "I hope that you and Enan will be very happy,

Miriam."

Miriam murmured gratitude, avoiding Rahab's eyes.

"You did very well," Salmon told her as they walked through the dark street to their home. "I think that Enan and Miriam will be happy together."

"The Lord was gracious and filled my mouth with proper words," Rahab told him. "I know now that it will be up to me to help Miriam be comfortable and happy when she's with us."

Salmon stopped and turned to her, seeking her eyes in the darkness. "Rahab, I think that the Lord may already be teaching you the truth of love."

"Miriam invited us to their home next Sabbath," Rahab told him.

"That will be a good test for you." Salmon held her in his arms in the darkness and kissed her. "Even those things in life which appear hopeless to us can be changed by the hand of the Lord. Miriam is not beyond hope."

Rahab prayed throughout the week as she wove her linen, ground her flour, baked her bread, and swept her floors. When the Sabbath day came, she and Salmon walked to Enan's house. They were graciously received by Enan's new wife.

Almost instantly Rahab found herself alone with Miriam, for the men had gone to sit and talk in the shade. Rahab had rehearsed some things that she could say to break the ice. Now was time for one of them.

"You have done some beautiful things with this house and have turned it into a lovely home," she said, trying hard to keep her voice even and low.

"Do you think so?" Miriam asked, glancing about her. But as her eyes came to meet Rahab's the familiar gleam brought foreboding. "Of course I do not ask counsel on decorating from a harlot." She bit off her words and remained silent, staring at Rahab.

Rahab had wondered what she would say if Miriam were to call her "Harlot" again. She had prayed for the right words, and now she spoke them slowly, "Miriam, you and I have been thrust together because our husbands are friends. We must make the best of it. We should both try to be as pleasant to each other as possible when we are together, for the sakes of our husbands. I don't want my husband to hear me say unkind words to you. It would hurt him. I fear, Miriam, that Enan would be wounded to hear you call me 'Harlot.' I am willing to try. Are you?"

Miriam smiled sweetly and said, "Why, Rahab, did I call you a harlot? I only said that I do not consult harlots for counsel." She narrowed her eyes and continued to stare at Rahab, leaving the full burden upon Rahab to speak.

Rahab stared back. Why was Miriam such a hateful person? Rahab thanked the Lord for His mercy to her. But perhaps Miriam was one of those of whom Salmon had spoken when he said that there were those in Israel, called by the name of the Lord, who did not really know and love the Lord. That was very likely Miriam's problem. Then, because she knew the Lord, she, Rahab, must try very hard to keep peace with Miriam. Pleasant words could not be so very hard to say.

"I hope we are agreed that we will speak pleasantly to each other for the sakes of our husbands," Rahab said. Then she added, softly, kindly, "Please, Miriam."

"Of course we shall ever speak pleasant things," Miriam answered her lightly. "However would we speak differently?"

Rahab helped Miriam carry the food, prepared the day before and arranged attractively upon trays, to the courtyard where the men sat. The remainder of the day was spent in talk, mostly between the two men, of the days gone past, and the blessings of the Lord. When the sun had set, Salmon and Rahab bid their hosts good night and walked home. Salmon must tend his animals before going to sleep.

As they walked, Salmon put his arm around Rahab's shoulders and squeezed her close to him. "How was it, today?" he asked gently.

"It went very well," Rahab said. "Miriam and I are

agreed to be pleasant."

"Good," was all that he said, but Rahab could feel his smile in the darkness.

Winter in the Bethlehem house was a very pleasant experience after the years in the tents. The thick stone walls blocked out the cold winds and Salmon and Rahab were snug inside. Salmon went to tend his business each day and came home ready for a warm meal and a seat before the warm hearth flames.

Rahab busied herself with her linen, but found time to visit with Maachah often. Together they made carefully embroidered clothing for the new baby. Maachah's ankles swelled easily, so she would stay off her feet as much as possible, while Elshima did the chores and looked after Jared. Maachah and Rahab revelled together in living in warm houses for the winter. Maachah would often tell Rahab stories of the wanderings of God's people in the wilderness. Rahab was amazed again how that a people who had seen the hand of God work so wondrously could so easily turn from Him.

Rahab had enjoyed the passage of the weeks without needing to see Miriam. But one morning Salmon announced, "I have invited Enan and Miriam next Sabbath." Rahab acknowledged his words and began to pray.

When the guests came on the Sabbath, Rahab felt ready for whatever Miriam may try. Miriam exuded friendliness and charm. They sat at the table and ate, Enan and Salmon carrying the conversation. After the meal, to Rahab's horror, the men went to Salmon's pens to see the sheep and cattle which would bear young when the spring came.

"Shall we sit here?" Rahab asked, offering Miriam a seat near the fire.

"We may as well," was Miriam's answer.

The two women sat wordlessly for several minutes.

Miriam broke the silence, saying, "Tell me," she paused and Rahab braced herself against the next word, but Miriam simply said, "Rahab, what was it like to live in Jericho, and serve those gods, what were they called?"

Rahab did not like Miriam's question, but she determined to answer with grace. "Salmon has told me that the Lord doesn't want His people to even mention the names of the gods of the heathen.[64] But, living in Jericho was a life of constant fear of offending the deities. To appease their wrath, human sacrifices were offered, babies, children." Rahab remembered the last horrible days in Jericho and shuddered, sorry that they had been brought to mind.

"What was it like for you, personally, Rahab?" Miriam asked, her voice liquid and pitiless.

"For me life was a constant endeavor to please my dreadful gods." Rahab answered. She looked directly into Miriam's scornful eyes. "I fully devoted myself to their service." Miriam snorted, but Rahab continued, "When the Hebrew soldiers surrounded the city, I knew that my life would soon end, and I feared greatly what that would mean, for I had no hope. But when Salmon and Enan came to my house on the wall, and Salmon told me of the mercy of the Lord, hope was born within me. Miriam, I know that I am unworthy of life itself, but God in His great mercy has rescued me from the cruel religion of Jericho and let me know Him. He has blessed me so wondrously with my husband. I can only thank Him for His love and mercy."

Miriam was silent. Rahab praised the Lord that He had given her gentle answers to Miriam's cruel questions. Finally Miriam spoke, "I have ever been a faithful Hebrew, observing each point of the law as well as any in Israel, and I don't say that I know the Lord. How can one know Him? He is God! How can you, who could well be an outcast in Israel, say that you know the Lord?"

"He has revealed Himself to me in His great mercy to me

---

[64]Exodus 23:13

in saving my life at Jericho, and in blessing me so these years since," Rahab answered carefully.

Miriam laughed and said, "And you think you know Him because of these things?" She laughed again as Enan and Salmon entered the room. Salmon smiled at Rahab, obviously pleased to hear Miriam laughing. Rahab smiled weakly. Now she knew. Miriam did not know the Lord, nor did she understand how one could know Him.

When their guests had departed, Salmon inquired as to how the time alone with Miriam had gone.

"The Lord truly gave me gracious answers," Rahab told him. Salmon smiled, pleased with her progress in her relationship with Miriam. "But Salmon, today Miriam told me that she doesn't know the Lord, nor does she understand how one can know Him. How can it be explained?"

Salmon frowned thoughtfully. "I guess all that one can do is to tell what the Lord means to him," he told her. "Knowing the Lord must be experienced to be understood."

As winter began to wane toward the spring, excitement filled many homes in Bethlehem. The return of the soldiers the spring before meant that many families were to be blessed with new babies. Maachah, Jasper, and Jared counted the days until their new family member would arrive. Rahab felt the strong pull upon her heart with the desire to bear a child for Salmon. Yet, after so many months of marriage, she was not yet with child.

A loud knocking sounded on the door late one evening. Salmon opened the door to find Jasper, out of breath and excited. "Maachah has sent me to call the midwife! And she wants Rahab to come, also."

Rahab hurried through the dark, frosty air to Maachah's home. She arrived before the midwife and found Maachah pacing the floor, breathing heavily. "Oh, Rahab!" Maachah cried as she entered. "I am so glad to have you here!" Rahab talked calmly and bathed Maachah's brow with a cool cloth, cringing through each birth pain.

The midwife arrived soon, bringing with her the birthing stool. Jasper was made to stay outside the room, pacing nervously across the floor. As the hours passed, Rahab knew that this was very different from Jared's birth. The midwife assured both women, however, that each birth was its own miracle, not to be compared with another.

As the day began to dawn, an exhausted Maachah brought forth her daughter. Jasper was finally permitted to see his wife. He approached the bed where she lay after her ordeal of the night and stopped short when he saw the tiny, frail child held to her bosom. He knelt at her side and kissed Maachah. Then, softly stroking the tiny fingers he said, "Her name is Jemimah."

"Your mother's name!" Maachah whispered. "I am pleased."

One day when the promise of spring whispered in the breeze, Rahab lowered her pot into the well of Bethlehem. As she drew it out full, she heard a voice beside her.

"Well, Rahab, how did you survive your winter in Bethlehem?" Rahab was astonished to hear such a pleasant greeting from Miriam. She sat her jug on the well's edge and answered, "Very well, thank you. And I am glad to feel spring in the air."

Miriam smiled. Then, with the familiar tinge of voice she said, "I have heard that your sister in law has been delivered of a daughter. Have you begotten a child for your husband, yet? Enan and I have been married but five months and I carry his child."

Rahab saw the proud, taunting look in Miriam's eyes. "I'm glad for you, Miriam. I'm sure that Enan is very happy," she heard herself say.

"Oh, he's extremely happy," said Miriam. "And is your husband as happy? Will you soon bear him a child?" she persisted.

Rahab lifted her jug to her head. Then, looking into

Miriam's eyes bravely, she said, "No," and started walking swiftly down the path toward her home.

Miriam trotted behind her to keep apace and said, "Well, Rahab, I've been thinking about it. It's my opinion that you may well be barren, as punishment from God for the life you lived in Jericho."

Rahab stopped and wheeled around, sloshing water from the jug. The old anger surged within her as she faced Miriam. "I don't care to hear your opinion, Miriam. We've agreed to speak pleasantly while our husbands are present. Let's agree not to speak at all if they are absent." With tears burning her eyes, Rahab turned and hurried along the path.

As she neared her home, shame overtook her. She had given Miriam the satisfaction of angering her. She, who knew the Lord, had spoken cruel words to Miriam. Now, when she must be with Miriam again, they both would know that although Miriam always said words to cut and hurt, Rahab had done her share, also. This would set her progress with Miriam back to the beginning. Oh, she did not wish to begin again.

That evening Rahab sat fingering the fringe of her gown absently. Finally she spoke. "Salmon." He lifted his brown eyes from the harness he was mending and looked into hers.

But she looked away and continued speaking. "I have been your wife for almost a year."

"Yes," Salmon said, with a smile in his voice.

"And I've not yet given you a child." She looked at him now and said, "I am not yet carrying your child. Salmon, could it be that I am barren; perhaps the Lord is punishing me for the life I lived before I knew Him?"

Salmon rose from his seat quickly, the harness clanging to the floor, and swept Rahab up into his arms. "Who told you that?" he asked, his voice etched with concern.

"Well, Miriam said..."

"Miriam." Salmon simply stated the name. Then, looking intently into Rahab's eyes with his brown ones he said, "Rahab, you know that for some reason Miriam delights in tormenting you. It's up to you to avoid being tormented. Don't let her words affect you." Then he pulled her close and stood holding her for several moments. Finally he said, "You are not barren. The Lord has promised to bless us.[65] He hasn't chosen to bless us with a child, yet, that's all." Salmon pulled her out at arms length and looked again into her eyes. "You are not barren. Do you understand?"

"But how can you know so surely?" she asked.

"I believe the promises of the Lord," he answered. "You believe them, too, Rahab. Don't doubt in this matter."

From that day Rahab and Salmon began to pray together for a child. It did not fully relieve Rahab's heart, but it did help her hope a little more.

This year the Feast of the Lord's Passover would be kept at Shiloh. Salmon and Rahab prepared for the trip and planned to again travel with a caravan from Bethlehem. Maachah would once again remain home and Jasper would accompany them. Enan also planned to travel with them. Rahab learned with relief that Miriam would stay home because of the child which she carried.

Rahab was once again taken by the grandeur of the sacrifices made unto the Lord God at Shiloh. They were bloody, indeed, and the blood of sheep and bullocks flowed freely throughout the days of the feast. But Salmon reminded her that the blood was necessary and was the Lord's will and desire, for it was the blood which atoned for the sin of the people. It was, he told her, a reminder to God's people that the Promised One would some day shed His blood to crush the head of Satan. Rahab could only watch with awe, knowing that her sin was atoned. It was a wondrous knowledge which brought peace. Rahab's heart all but burst with joy that she now knew the great

---

[65]Deuteronomy 7:14

God of heaven and earth and was no longer bound by sin.

On the day after the Sabbath which followed the Passover, Salmon took a sheaf of the firstfruits of his barley harvest to the priest at the Tabernacle. There Eleazar the priest waved the sheaf before the Lord. He then offered on the altar the lamb which Salmon had brought for a burnt offering. With the lamb was offered fine flour mixed with oil.[66]

As the caravan from Bethlehem wound its way home through the heavily wooded hills, they came to rest on the crest of a hill, near a grove of tall evergreen trees. Rahab leaned wearily back against a cool rock and shaded her eyes. Suddenly she sat up straight and gasped. Salmon followed her startled gaze toward an altar erected beneath the trees.

He went quickly to her side and asked quietly, "What, Rahab?"

"Oh, Salmon!" Rahab threw herself against him, trembling. She could barely speak, but managed to say, "It is an altar to..." She hesitated knowing the commandment of the Lord not to utter the name of pagan gods. She whispered hoarsely, " Baal. I served him beneath the green trees of groves such as this."[67]

Salmon held her, soothing her as one would a child. Then he left her side and spoke with Enan and Jasper. Together they approached the altar in the grove. The attention of all the pilgrims was drawn to them as they tied a strong rope around the altar and pulled. Several men joined them until the altar toppled and broke apart. Then, stone by stone, the men carried the broken altar to the steep descent of the hill and threw it all down the side, watching it tumble and shatter more.

When all trace of the altar was removed, a Levite travelling with them offered a prayer of thanks to the Lord that

---

[66]Leviticus 23:10-13

[67]Deuteronomy 12:2

He had destroyed such idolatry from the land. Rahab clung to Salmon, still trembling, and offering her prayer of thanks, perhaps the most sincere of all.

Rahab resumed the journey to Bethlehem in withdrawn silence. The harsh reminder of her life as a harlot overshadowed the wondrous Passover reminder of her deliverance from it. Salmon did not intrude into her silence until they had stopped to set up camp for the night. He lay on his back with his arms beneath his head and looked up through the open doorway into the starry night. Rahab closed her eyes but could not find sleep. Finally Salmon spoke.

"My desire is to shield you from anything that would hurt you, Rahab. I regret that I couldn't protect you today." Salmon turned onto his side and looked into Rahab's eyes, which were now open. "At the Passover feast we thought again of the mercy of God in atoning for our sin by the shed blood." He paused and then continued softly, "Rahab, the Lord delivered you from a life of pagan hopelessness. Today He gave to you a special and personal reminder that He loves you."

Rahab heard the love in Salmon's words. Yes, she should have expected Salmon to find God's goodness in what had happened today. And yes, indeed she had been reminded today of the terror from which she had been delivered. Yes, God did love her. The tight, frightful knot in her heart relaxed and warmth replaced it. Yes, God did love her, with a love that had delivered her from pagan darkness and had brought her into His wonderful light. She smiled at Salmon for the first time since the rest stop and reached a hand to touch his soft brown beard.

"Yes, Salmon," she answered him, happiness replacing the dread. "The Lord did give me a special reminder that He loves me. But how would I have known without you?" Salmon smiled back into her eyes and kissed her beneath the stars.

When Rahab found it necessary to entertain Miriam again, she prepared herself with much prayer. Miriam was beginning to show that she carried a child, and proudly flaunted herself before Rahab. Rahab found this day endurable as she sat silently listening to Miriam's prattle about her coming child and Enan's pride in soon becoming a father. She found that if she did not answer the pointed questions of Miriam she could not become upset and Miriam hardly seemed to notice her lack of response. When finally Enan and Miriam left to go to their own home, Rahab sighed with relief.

Salmon heard her sigh and caught her in his arms, smiling. "I heard the way she carried on today." His brown eyes twinkled. "And I heard your silence." He laughed aloud. "I think you're learning the way to handle her."

The second summer of their life in Bethlehem began with happy days and good memories made with Jasper and Maachah and their children. Rahab sighed again each time she must be with Miriam, but the strain of old had passed, and a new determination replaced it.

Sixty-six days after the birth of Jemimah, Jasper and Maachah went to the Tabernacle in Shiloh to offer a lamb as a burnt offering, and a young pigeon.[68]

Rahab accompanied Salmon to Shiloh for the feast of harvest, fifty days after his offering of the sheaf of the wave offering. He carried with him a basket containing the firstfruits of his wheat harvest and the fruits of the land.

The enjoyment of the tent city had worn off for Rahab, and she planned to merely endure the feast stay this time, looking forward to the return to Bethlehem. But when she watched Salmon offering his firstborn beasts and the firstfruits of his land, her heart warmed and she was glad that she had come.

Salmon stood before Eleazar the priest at the Tabernacle and said, "I profess this day to the Lord my God, that I have come into the country that the Lord sware to our Fathers to give us."

---

[68]Leviticus 12:5,6

Eleazar then took the basket and set it down before the altar of the Lord.

Rahab listened as Salmon recited, with great enthusiasm and expression. "My father was a Syrian, ready to perish; and he went to Egypt with a few and became there a great nation, mighty and populous. The Egyptians evil entreated us and afflicted us, and laid hard bondage on us. When we cried to the Lord God of our fathers, He heard our voice, and looked on our affliction, and our labour, and our oppression. Then the Lord brought us out of Egypt with a mighty hand and an outstretched arm, with great terribleness and signs and wonders. He brought us into this place and has given us this land that flows with milk and honey. And now I have brought the firstfruits of the land which You, O Lord, have given to me."[69]

"That was beautiful," Rahab told Salmon later.

"I've rehearsed it for many years," he told her, "while wandering in the wilderness, dreaming of the day that I would have the fruits of the land to offer to the Lord. And as I worked the land, day by day, I rehearsed. I've looked forward to this for a long time."

Rahab joyed in Maachah's lively young son and beautiful tiny daughter. She spent many hours at Maachah's home, talking and laughing with Maachah. Yet, each time that she was again alone, she felt the emptiness of having no child.

On one day's visit, Maachah's flushed cheeks told Rahab that there was something to be told. Maachah hurried her to the courtyard, where the autumn sun painted everything in hues of gold and silver, and they sat upon a bench.

"Pagiel's master has offered Jasper the price for Elshima," Maachah announced. "He has worked hard for his master so his master has agreed to pay her price. They will be wed next month and she will be leaving me." Maachah ended sadly.

---

[69]Deuteronomy 26:1-10

"I'm so happy for her!" Rahab said. Then, putting her arm around Maachah's shoulders she comforted, "I know that she's very dear to you and is such a help to you with your little ones. You will miss her sorely. But I'll come and help you when you need me."

"Oh, no," Maachah interjected. "I'm strong and well, now, and can easily manage but two children. I'm only sorry to see her go. She has been such a dear friend."

"I married and left your tent, and I hope that I'm still your friend," said Rahab with mock injury.

"You're the dearest friend I know," said Maachah softly, "but you're free to come and go. Elshima will be bound by service to her new master. I'm happy for her, though. She loves Pagiel so."

Elshima and Pagiel were wed on a beautiful autumn day. Maachah's eyes, red and wet with her tears, shone in happiness for Elshima. Elshima quietly accepted each congratulation and seemed quite relieved when all her friends had left.

As Elshima prepared to leave Maachah's home to go with her new husband, Maachah hugged her tightly. "I will miss you so, dear Elshima. Come and visit us when you can. Jared and Jemimah will miss you, too."

Elshima raised her tender eyes shyly and said softly, "You've been so very kind to me. I've been very happy in your home. I would be glad to be welcome here and visit when I can." She lowered her eyes quickly and Maachah knew that in bondage, Elshima would not be free to visit often.

Miriam's son was born on a golden day in late autumn. Rahab again resented the sun's shining for Miriam. She dutifully took the small gown she had sewed to visit the new mother. As she walked to Miriam's house she prayed, for she knew that she would far rather stay home. "Thank You, Lord, for this new life that You have given. Thank you for blessing Enan with a son." She paused and then added, "And Miriam, too. Help me Lord, as I face her with her child in her arms. I fear that she will taunt me for my childlessness. And Lord, give me patience to wait until Your time to bless us with a child."

Miriam's family filled the house, smiling and talking, all at once, about the beautiful child that had been born. Miriam sat against cushions smiling and cuddling her child. A searing pain shot through Rahab's heart and for an instant she let herself wonder why such a woman as Miriam should be blessed with a son, when she, who loved the Lord so, had been denied the joy. Then, just as Miriam raised her eyes to meet Rahab's, she remembered the cruel suggestion of Miriam, that it was her past life which prevented a child.

"Hello, Rahab," Miriam said with mock enthusiasm which Rahab was sure escaped the notice of the others in the room. "So you have come to see Enan's son. He is beautiful and looks just like Enan." Miriam turned her baby toward Rahab for a full look.

"He is beautiful, Miriam. Here, I made something for him," Rahab said softly.

Miriam took the gown from her hand and tossed it carelessly aside. "I suppose you meant well," said Miriam. "I do plan to only dress my son in the finest. Made by the finest. Thank you for your thoughtfulness."

Rahab's cheeks burned and she wondered at the listeners. Did they know what Miriam had said? Did they care? They continued their happy conversation as before. Rahab excused herself and fled the room and the house. Tears stung her eyes as she ran carelessly along the road. She could not see the way before her well and suddenly collided with a small form, which staggered before her. Wiping her eyes to see, she found Elshima before her, bearing a large load upon her head.

"Oh, Elshima! Please forgive me! I wasn't watching my way. Are you alright?"

"Yes, yes," Elshima assured her, lowering her load to the ground. Then she touched Rahab's elbow lightly and said, "Are you alright?"

Rahab dabbed again at her tears and said, "I'm fine, thank you. These tears were in my eyes before I bumped you." Elshima looked at her with concern, but said nothing.

Suddenly Rahab felt compelled to confide in the gentle Elshima. "There is one who torments me, and I cannot be near her without distress. It was she who caused my tears."

Elshima simply stated, "Miriam."

"How did you know?" Rahab asked.

"I've seen how she speaks to you and the look of enmity in her eyes," Elshima answered softly.

"She has a son," Rahab stated. "And I, who have been married longer than she, have no child."

Elshima smiled sweetly and said, "I'm not wise. But I think that the enemy of God and ours would have you fret about being childless. Certainly the Lord wouldn't. He will bless you in His time."

"You're wiser than you think," answered Rahab. "My husband has said the same, and he's very wise. But what do you mean? Who is the enemy of God and ours?"

Elshima looked surprised at her question, but answered in the same soft tones, "God's enemy is the one who hates and seeks to destroy us. It was he who tempted our first mother, Eve, to disobey the Lord."[70]

Rahab remembered the reading of the books of Moses, and hearing the story of the first man and woman, Adam and Eve, and their fall into sin because of disobedience to God. After a moment of thought she said, "Then I must be careful not to give God's enemy cause to rejoice over me. Thank you, Elshima, you've helped me very greatly." As the two women parted, Rahab knew that she had a friend in Elshima. She knew, too, that she had learned something very important. She must trust God and give His enemy no cause for triumph.

---

[70]Genesis 3

When Salmon entered the house in the evening he held her in his arms and asked, "Did you deliver your gift to Miriam today?"

Rahab leaned against him without speaking for several moments. She finally spoke with difficulty. "Yes, I did."

"And is Elimelech as wonderful as his father claims?" Salmon asked.

"All babies are wonderful, Salmon," she answered.

"Yes, they are. And Miriam, how was she?" Salmon asked.

Rahab wished that they could discuss the child alone. But she must answer. "She looked well, and happy."

"What is troubling you?" Salmon asked, continuing to hold her against him.

"Am I troubled?" she asked, trying hard to control her voice.

"Yes, you are. Are you troubled that Miriam has a child while your arms are empty?" Salmon asked gently.

"Yes," she whispered against him.

"What else?" he asked.

"Else? Is there something else?" she asked.

"Yes, something else troubles you. Didn't Miriam accept your gift?"

Rahab began to shake against him as she repeated Miriam's words to her.

"Did you consider that she may have meant that the garment made by you was of the finest, made by the finest?" Salmon asked gently.

"No, Salmon, she didn't. She carelessly tossed my garment aside."

Salmon was silent for a moment. Then, forcing her to look up into his loving brown eyes he said, "Then we must pity Miriam. She doesn't value those things in life of greatest worth. She may never change, Rahab. But you are not responsible for her words or actions, only your own. Miriam must see in your life consistent kindness and constant effort to be friendly. She must see love in your life."

"Love?" Rahab asked. "How, Salmon? How can I love such a woman? She hates me."

"When you learn to love one who hates you, you have learned real love, such as the love of the Lord God for us. This kind of love comes only from God. Continue to ask Him for this love."

Salmon stood holding her for awhile, and then he added, "We both want a child, Rahab. Enjoy the babes of others until the Lord blesses us with children. Enjoy them, Rahab."

Rahab stood against him and wondered at his words. Yes, she would be much happier if she would only enjoy the wonderful babies of others instead of mourning in self-pity when seeing them. Yes, she must rejoice in Miriam's child in spite of Miriam.

Rahab began to practice Salmon's counsel to her. She found the joy in each moment of life, even when in Miriam's presence, and learned that she was much more content. The months passed busily through the winter and into a new year. She watched the children of her friends grow and she forced herself to enjoy the happiness of mothers around her.

The third year of living in the Promised Land was the tithe year. At the end of the harvest, instead of taking the tithe to present it before the priest, Salmon laid it up within his gates, to be given to the Levites, widows and orphans, and the poor of the land about them.[71] Rahab experienced a new attitude toward those in her town, as she worked daily to hand out their goods to the needy. She saw people, lonely, hurting, sad, come to her gates to receive of Salmon's tithe. She was glad for this experience. She was so protected by Salmon's love, she knew, and by the life that he had built for her. Thankfulness

---

[71]Deuteronomy 26:12

overwhelmed her, and she thanked the Lord, again.

As the tithe year drew to an end, Elshima brought forth a daughter, and named her Naomi.

CHAPTER 8

Baby

The years passed with labour and joy. Maachah bore two more daughters, each strong and rosy. She loved all of her children dearly, but her most tender expressions of love were shown to Jemimah, who, although frail and weak, had great strength in her love and care for others.

Miriam still flaunted the pride over her son before Rahab, yet as the years passed and no more children were born to Miriam, she seldom spoke to Rahab of her childlessness. Rahab began to hope that perhaps Miriam would mellow, and that she would no longer be an enemy.

Rahab was surprised to answer an urgent knock at the door late one evening to find the boy Elimelech standing before her, breathing hard. "My father wants Salmon and you to come quickly," he said breathlessly. "My mother's brother and his wife are hurt." He turned and ran into the darkness.

Salmon and Rahab hurried to Enan's home, where they found Miriam's family weeping in the crowded room. Enan came to Salmon's side and whispered, "Miriam's brother and his wife were travelling from Shiloh and were attacked by robbers. They were both badly beaten. His wife has died. The physician has been called, but the life is ebbing from Miriam's brother." He looked at Rahab and said, "Will you go to Miriam, Rahab? Her mother is here, but she, too, is distraught with grief."

Go to Miriam? Comfort her? Rahab was the last person Miriam would want to see at such a time. But she nodded to Enan, and asked before leaving, "What of her brother's baby?"

"The child is well," Enan answered. "His mother hid him behind a tree when the attack came."

Miriam and her mother sat sobbing in a corner near the wounded man. Rahab walked slowly toward them, praying for words that would not anger Miriam, nor bring from her the familiar cruelty. She stood beside them silently for a moment, until Miriam raised her eyes to see her.

"Rahab," she stated simply. There was no bitterness. Rahab knelt at her side and said softly, "I know that there is little that one can say to ease the pain, Miriam, but please know that Salmon and I wish to help you any way that we can."

"How would you know the pain I feel? Your brother lives," Miriam asked, and her question was sincere, spoken through her tears.

"I thank the Lord that the life of my brother was spared. I did have a friend, a very dear friend, who wouldn't come to safety to my house at Jericho's destruction." Tears welled in Rahab's eyes as she thought of dear Zaphnath, gone so many years, now. "This friend was the very dearest that I had. No words can soothe such pain. But the Lord God of heaven and earth can give sweet relief when we lean upon Him."

"You've ever talked about the Lord," said Miriam, "as one would about a friend. I've never known the Lord that way, so I doubt that I will have such comfort from Him. Go now, Rahab, and let us grieve alone."

Rahab walked back to join Salmon. She knew that Miriam's words had been much kinder than usual for her, and at such a time as this, too. Enan was speaking with Salmon as she approached, "I will offer to take the child and raise him as my own, in Miriam's brother's name. Miriam's parents are aging, now, and it may be too large a task for them."

Enan and Miriam did indeed take her brother's son, Nathan, to raise. Miriam was again seen walking through the streets of Bethlehem with a child in her arms, but the proud look of the days of Elimelech's babyhood was vanished.

Rahab had carefully, through the years, timed her daily visits to the well of Bethlehem so as to avoid encounter with Miriam. But one day they met, face to face, at the well's edge.

"Hello, Miriam," Rahab said pleasantly. "I hope that all is well with you."

Miriam's face bore a solemn expression. She spoke in monotone, "Enan is well. Elimelech is well." She paused. "Nathan is well. But I am reminded of my brother each time that I look into his face."

"It's very good of you to care for him," Rahab said.

"I don't care for him," said Miriam. "I feed and clothe and bathe and provide for him because he is my brother's child. He is not the son of Enan, and I cannot care for him."

Rahab was astonished at Miriam's words. She, who had no child, would be happy beyond words to care for a baby. And she would love him. Her heart suddenly ached for the small Nathan. He would grow up without the love of a mother. Why should Miriam be given the gift of a child when she would not love him? Rahab did not care to say anything else to Miriam, and since Miriam was leaning over the well, drawing the cold water into a jar, Rahab turned and walked away.

A soft breeze ruffled her skirts and her long, black hair, as Rahab stood atop the flat roof of her Bethlehem house looking out over the town to the left and the fields upon the hills to her right. Eight years had passed since she and Salmon had taken this house as their own. For six years Salmon had laboured with joy to sow his land, reaping his harvest and offering to the Lord his tithes and offerings before the Tabernacle in Shiloh. The seventh year was the Sabbath Year. Salmon had not sown his fields nor pruned his trees, for that which grew of itself was food for the poor of the land and the beasts of the field. Yet, they had fared well upon the harvest from the sixth year.[72]

Jared ran by on the street below, followed by his two younger brothers, Elika and Zelek, who were running hard to keep up with his long legs. He waved and shouted a greeting to her and was echoed by his brothers. She smiled and waved back. Jasper's sons were strong and healthy. But dear Jemimah, now

---

[72]Exodus 23:10,11

seven years old, was frail and often ill. Maachah's face, so accustomed to a happy smile, would often crease with concern about her little daughter. Jasper's large hands, rough and playful with his sons, were gentle and careful when they held his little girl.

Rahab's face clouded suddenly as she watched Miriam striding by below with Elimelech at her side and the small Nathan in her arms. Elimelech was truly a darling child, friendly and lively, yet Rahab was always reserved in her feelings of love for him. Salmon had told her to enjoy the children of others, and Maachah's children, and the small Naomi were indeed a delight to her. But she could find small pleasure in Elimelech, for his mother's sake.

Salmon had come home one day with happy news. Pagiel had served his master for seven years, so according to the law of the Lord, on this year he was to be given freedom. His master planned to furnish him with a flock of his own and the fruits of the trees and field. Salmon had arranged to sell Pagiel fields for his own use. Great excitement filled the homes of Jasper and Salmon over Pagiel's coming release.

Yet, although she was happy for her friends, Rahab's own private pain remained. She was still childless.

Salmon startled her from her reverie as he approached from behind and put his arms around her, laying his soft brown beard against her face. He held her a long time. When finally he let go, she turned and was surprised to see distress in his brown eyes.

"Salmon," she said softly, "why are you troubled?"

"Pagiel will not be free," he said.

Fear clutched at Rahab's heart. Something was wrong, terribly wrong. "Why, Salmon?"

"Someone went to his master, today," Salmon said sadly. "They explained to him that the law of God says that if a Hebrew servant comes to his master alone, he must depart alone, although he has a wife and children. If he desires to remain with his wife and children, he must have his ear bored through with an aul, and wear an ear-ring to show that he is bound to his master for the rest of his life."[73]

Rahab gasped and sat heavily upon a stool. "Is it true, Salmon? Does the law of God say that?"

"Yes," he answered.

"Why would the Lord do such a thing to Pagiel?" she asked, breaking into sobs.

Salmon knelt beside her, taking her hands away from her face and holding them in his own strong ones. "Rahab," he said, waiting for her to look into his sad brown eyes, "The Lord's doings are sometimes beyond our comprehending. We must obey Him, although we don't understand. The secret things belong to Him. Those that He has revealed are for us and for our children."[74]

"But it seems cruel, Salmon, that in order for Pagiel and Elshima to remain together he must enlist himself into slavery for life!" Rahab said through her sobs.

"It must have seemed cruel to our father, Abraham, to be told to sacrifice his son," Salmon said softly, reminding her of his story at Jerusalem. "Yet the Lord had a purpose and Abraham saw His love and His mercy. The Lord will give to Pagiel His love and His mercy to endure what he must. We must only trust Him."

Rahab sat and sobbed softly until her heart began to slowly mend. Salmon could always explain things to her, and his faith in the Lord never faltered. Yet, she knew that he, too, was pained by this.

"Who told Pagiel's master?" she asked him.

"That is no matter. When one tells us the law of the Lord, that is good," he answered.

---

[73]Exodus 21:1-6

[74]Deuteronomy 29:29

"Who told him, Salmon?" she insisted.

Salmon did not answer her. Suddenly she remembered a form walking by on the street below, walking importantly and urgently.

"Was it Miriam?" she asked.

"It is the law," Salmon answered her.

"Miriam!" Rahab shouted, rising from her seat and clutching the battlement of their rooftop. "She has filled my life with her hatred and now she will hurt Elshima and Pagiel!"

Salmon pulled her to him, his brown eyes charged with severity, but he spoke calmly and evenly, "It is the law, Rahab."

Rahab fell against him, again sobbing. "We must pity Miriam," Salmon told her, softly stroking her hair.

"Why must we pity Miriam, and not Pagiel and Elshima?" she asked.

"Because Pagiel and Elshima trust the great God of heaven and earth. They will find comfort in Him. Miriam does not."

Again, Salmon's gentle words against her wrath calmed her heart. His wisdom to see through the fog of human misunderstanding to the great God in Whose hands were all their lives awed her. She wanted to trust the Lord. But she wanted to understand, too.

Jasper and Maachah, Salmon and Rahab stood with Elshima and sadly watched as Pagiel stood at the door of his master's house and the judge of the city bored a hole through his ear with an aul. A gold earring was inserted into the bleeding hole and sealed. Pagiel was now a servant for life.

For three days, Rahab had risen feeling ill, nauseous, weak. She forced herself to cook Salmon's breakfast, to sweep her floors and wash her dishes. But when she sat before her loom, the discomfort forced her back to her bed. On this third day, as she dragged her feet toward the well, she broke into tears without knowing why. She put her jug on the ground and sat upon it, sobbing into her hands. Suddenly there was a soft touch on her shoulder. She looked up to see Elshima standing before her, heavy with her second child.

"Hello, Elshima," Rahab said, quickly dabbing the tears from her eyes. "Don't get close to me. I haven't been well for three days."

"Is that why you were weeping?" Elshima asked softly.

"I don't know why I wept," Rahab admitted.

"Could I help you fetch your water?" Elshima asked.

"Oh, no, dear Elshima. It's more than you should do to carry your own. Salmon has offered to help me today, but he has much work of his own and I'll be alright."

Elshima stood silently before her for a moment. Then she asked softly, "Are you ill when you rise, and nauseous?"

"Yes," Rahab answered. "Do you know someone else who is ill?"

"Yes," Elshima said. "I know several. I was ill, myself. But it will pass in a month or two."

"A month or...," Rahab stopped mid-sentence and rose to her feet. "You don't mean... do you think I..."

Elshima laughed a light, breezy laugh and nodded her head. "It may not be, Rahab, but it sounds like you're expecting a baby."

"I must tell Salmon!" Rahab cried.

"Wait, Rahab," Elshima caught her arm as she turned to leave. "Perhaps you should wait until you know for sure. How sad Salmon would be if you told him that he will be a father and you are indeed only ill."

"Elshima, Salmon and I have waited so many years to have a child. If I'm but ill, we cannot be more disappointed than we've ever been. I wouldn't sadden him for anything. But I must share even my hope with him."

Rahab ran quickly down the slope of the hill toward Salmon's fields, pausing occasionally to let a wave of nausea pass. Salmon was not to be found at his near fields, so she ran on until she topped a rounded hill, and stopped to rest beneath a gnarled tree. Two caves entered the rock atop this hill. One was wide and shallow, one deep and narrow. Salmon and his shepherds sometimes found shelter from the rain in the shallow cave, which afforded them a view of the fields.

Rahab stood and searched with her eyes but did not see anyone. Exhausted beyond further travel she staggered to the shallow cave and collapsed on the cold stone floor in tears. She cried pitilessly and then began to wretch. Her misery was so heavy she could barely breathe, when suddenly she was in Salmon's arms and he spoke in alarm.

"Rahab! What's wrong? Why are you here when you're so ill?"

She could hardly speak for her sobs, but she finally said, "Oh, Salmon, I only wanted to share with you what Elshima said. I met her at the well and she told me that many women are ill and nauseous when they are going to have a baby!" Rahab stopped, breathless, and waited.

Salmon continued to look into her eyes with a question in his brown ones. Slowly the concern relaxed from his features and a light of hope came to his eyes. He smiled and asked softly, as if afraid to speak the words, "Do you think so, Rahab? Can it really be?"

Rahab remembered Elshima's warning and quickly said, "Well, the symptoms are similar, but of course I don't know at all, yet. I may only be ill. I don't want you to hope, Salmon, and then be disappointed. I only wanted to share with you what Elshima said."

The smile did not fade from Salmon's face, and his brown eyes danced. Without warning he swept her up into his arms and kissed her, disregarding her foul condition. Then he marched away from the caves and down the hillside with long strides. He carried her all the way up the hill to Bethlehem and to their home, as she buried her head against his shoulder and rested in his strong grasp.

The next day Rahab found Maachah at her door and

invited her in. Maachah entered with her children and they began to run about the house. She sat holding her youngest daughter on her lap, with Jemimah leaning against her.

Rahab smiled, eager to tell Maachah her secret, but Maachah sternly waved her to silence and spoke. "Rahab, Elshima came to me today quite distressed. She told me about your conversation at the well, and she is concerned that she has now given you the hope of a child when that may not be the cause of your illness at all. She is sorry that she spoke as she did."

"Thank you, Maachah. You're a good friend. Please assure Elshima, if you see her before I do, that I will try hard not to hope until I really know. And if not, then I won't be more disappointed than I ever am."

As the days passed and each morning brought nausea and illness, Rahab's heart warmed with desire. Finally there could no longer be any doubt. Salmon was to become a father! Rahab's joy and anticipation far outweighed her physical misery and weariness. Yet, she awakened each morning feeling ill, as the days passed into weeks, and the weeks into months. She could rarely eat and she knew that instead of putting on weight, she was losing it. Maachah came each day and helped as much as her lively offspring would give her opportunity. Elshima shyly smiled her congratulations with relief.

Maachah answered the door one morning to greet a disgruntled Arod at the door. He stepped inside hastily and demanded to see Rahab. "She is quite ill, Arod. May I take her a message?" Maachah asked.

"I wish to speak with her myself," Arod answered curtly.

Maachah led him to the couch where Rahab reclined, pale and weak. When Arod saw her, he gasped and some of the irritation drained from his rigid face.

"I see you are ill," he said. "You haven't delivered to me any linen for too long. I've come to learn the reason."

Rahab smiled weakly at Arod and spoke, "Oh, please

forgive me, Arod. I'm carrying a child, and am quite ill. I've been ill for some time and unable to weave. I forgot that an order was due to be delivered. Will you forgive me for not informing you?"

The hard lines of Arod's face had softened and he stammered an apology for his brusqueness.

"If I'm able, as soon as I'm better, I'll bring you more linen. But I don't know when that will be."

"And after the birth of the child?" Arod asked.

Rahab's brow wrinkled as she answered, "I hadn't yet considered that. Perhaps you should find a new source of linen."

"Well," replied Arod, the hard lines returning to his face, "I doubt that I shall find such fine linen as yours. But if it must be, so be it."

Rahab awoke one morning feeling fresher than usual, so decided to walk outside in the morning air. She knew that it was not the right intent, but she wanted very much to meet Miriam, today. She was beginning to bulge with her long awaited child, and she wanted to flaunt it before Miriam, as Miriam had flaunted her child before Rahab. But when she did, indeed, meet Miriam, the anticipated enjoyment vanished. Miriam stood before her austerely, and the hopeless expression she wore was reflected on the face of the small boy who stood beside her, clutching her skirt.

"I congratulate you upon your child," Miriam said slowly.

"Thank you, Miriam," Rahab answered, awkward now as she faced her. "The Lord has blessed us greatly after our years of marriage."

"Well," Miriam said with a hint of her animosity of old, "I see that the Lord has chosen to bless you, with your soiled past, rather than this true woman of Israel."

Rahab ignored the smear and answered, "But you have a child, Miriam. You have Elimelech and now Nathan."

Miriam laughed bitterly, glancing toward the sober child at her side. "Elimelech is truly a blessing. But God has scourged me with this child."

Anger rose in Rahab's heart and she spoke without caution, "Nathan is a dear child, the child of your brother. Enan loves him and is always good to him. Why must you feel so toward him, Miriam? And why must you speak so within his hearing?"

"It was never my desire to give Enan only one child." Miriam said slowly, bitterly. "This child isn't Enan's. He will raise him in my dead brother's name. I loved my brother, but I cannot love his child. Yet, I'm the one who must look after him every day. I must feed and clothe him, and be near him always. It's a torture for me."

Rahab was suddenly swept with nausea, but she breathed in quick gasps and spoke. "We are relatives also, Miriam. We will take Nathan and raise him, if you'll let us. He has lost his parents, Miriam. He needs to be loved."

Miriam looked at Rahab defiantly. "He is loved by Enan," she said. "He is my brother's child and will not be raised by a harlot!" Miriam grabbed Nathan's small hand and pulled him quickly away. Rahab watched them go, her heart aching for the child, her mind puzzling over the woman.

Everyone was greatly concerned as the months progressed and Rahab continued the illness. It did not pass as she had been assured by many mothers. Salmon hired a woman to do the housework and he would stay at Rahab's side, wiping her brow and face and trying to comfort her through her misery. The physician gave her extracts which she swallowed and promptly vomited out. Maachah brewed exotic teas from far lands, yet nothing kept the food in. Rahab grew daily weaker, until she began to fear for the life of her child.

Salmon had carried her to the rooftop one quiet evening to enjoy the coolness and the starlit sky. She lay limply upon the couch and looked into the sky. Memories of a night long ago filled her heart, memories of a young Canaanite harlot standing upon the wall of a doomed city, praying to the God of heaven and earth Whom she had only just come to know. God had answered those prayers, however impossible they had seemed. And He would answer again. Rahab felt certain that the Lord had not given her a child only to be lost before it could come to birth.

"Oh, Lord," she prayed in a whisper, "I have rejoiced and thanked you repeatedly for this child that you have given to Salmon and me. You know, Lord, how sick I have been, unable to eat, and growing thinner and weaker each day. I fear for my child's life, Lord. I don't ask for my own sake, for I can bear what is necessary. But I ask for my child, Lord, that I may soon be well, and able to eat and nourish this precious one who is harbored within me. Please, my Lord. I don't deserve Your smallest concern. But in Your great mercy, please spare my child."

Rahab awoke in the morning to find herself in her bed, not remembering being carried there in Salmon's strong arms. She lay still for several moments, knowing that something had changed, yet not able to identify what it was. When she arose on trembling legs and walked to the window to breathe the fresh morning air she knew. She was not nauseous. For the first morning since she had been with child, she did not feel ill. She was extremely weak, but she was not ill.

Salmon hovered around her all morning, cooking a soft, warm breakfast and encouraging her to eat it slowly. She did, and filled up quickly, but was not swept with the familiar nausea. When Salmon showed signs of planning to stay with her for the day, she said, "I'll be well, now, Salmon. Last night I prayed and asked the Lord to take away my illness for our child's sake, and He did. I'll be well now."

Salmon's deep brown eyes searched hers. Then he smiled and gently hugged her. "You are a woman of great faith," he told her. She shook her head, laughing softly, but he continued, "You have ever said that I have great faith. But I've prayed for you and our child these months to no avail. And now the Lord has answered your prayer."

Rahab held Salmon as closely as her bulging frame would permit and began to gently weep against his shoulder. "Salmon," she said softly, "don't you see that God has also answered your prayers?"

"Why do you weep?" Salmon asked into her hair.

"Because I'm so happy that we shall finally have a child." Rahab released Salmon and sat heavily upon a stool. She had been so occupied by her illness, but now she wanted to talk to Salmon about Nathan. "Salmon, have you lately seen Miriam and little Nathan?"

"I often see them walking together. Why do you ask?" Salmon said.

"When last I spoke with Miriam she expressed to me, within Nathan's hearing, that she considers him but a burden and does not care for him," Rahab answered.

"I have sensed a hopelessness about the little child," said Salmon. "He is her brother's child. Why wouldn't she care for him?"

"I cannot understand it," said Rahab. "But it is true, and Nathan will be hurt deeply by it."

"Enan loves him as he does his own son," Salmon said. "We must pray that Miriam will learn to love him."

Because she had so long been ill, Rahab now savored each moment. She did not again become nauseous, and felt wonderfully well, only clumsy and uncomfortable. But she already loved the child she carried beneath her heart. A swift kick in the ribs would often cause her to catch her breath in conversation, but she would smile at the expressions of concern. She thrilled at the almost constant movement. Her child was alive and active. She praised the Lord.

"What if our child is a daughter?" Rahab asked Salmon one evening.

"I would like to name her Shiphrah," he answered, "after my mother."

"And if our child is a son?" she asked.

A light came to Salmon's brown eyes as he answered, "Our son would be named Boaz."

"I like it," said Rahab, "but why do you choose Boaz?"

Salmon was silent for a moment. When he spoke, it was with difficulty. "My friend. His name was Boaz. He died in the wilderness."

The dear old face of Rahab's friend, Zaphnath, came to her mind suddenly. The tears overpowered her and she wept as if with a broken heart.

"Rahab, what's wrong?" Salmon asked her gently.

"When you spoke of your friend I suddenly remembered Zaphnath, in Jericho," she sobbed. "He died, Salmon, because he wouldn't come to safety at my house!" Rahab's sobs could not be controlled.

Salmon took her into his arms and held her. He had no words to soothe the pain of her memories. He rocked her gently, as a child, for many minutes, until her tears ceased and she was asleep against him.

When the long awaited day arrived, Rahab faced her labour with excitement, for when it was finished, her child would be born. She remembered the kind face of Maachah near, and the soothing voice of the midwife coaxing her to push. She was swept with nausea, reminding her of her months of suffering, but the midwife smiled and assured her that it meant the time was near. Then suddenly, in a relieving whoosh, Rahab discovered that her son was born.

Salmon's joy over his son was boundless. Rahab had always desired to bear him children, but she had little known how dearly he had yearned for a son. He was now utterly fulfilled.

For seven days Rahab was unclean according to the law of the Lord. On the eighth day her tiny son was circumcised and identified as one of God's chosen people.[75] Rahab carefully dressed her tiny son in the soft garments that she had lovingly formed during the last impatient weeks. Her friends brought gifts for Boaz, and she was lost in her joy, when she saw Miriam standing before her soberly. In her hand she held a small, soft garment which seemed very familiar to Rahab. Rahab smiled and took the proffered gift.

"Thank you, Miriam, for coming to share in our joy." She hesitated slightly and then added, "And thank you for the gift."

"I have not come to share in your joy," Miriam said flatly. She glanced toward Enan, who laughed with Salmon. "He has come to share joy. There is no joy in my life."

Rahab's exquisite happiness about her child made Miriam's forlorn words stranger than ever. The small Nathan stood gravely at her side, clutching her skirts. Elimelech, now nine years old, was talking and laughing with his father and Salmon.

"Miriam, you have many reasons to be happy, and few for sorrow," Rahab chided gently. "A child can give so much joy, if you will let him." She looked at the quiet child and smiled. Big, round, dark eyes watched her, but there was no smile in return.

"There is no joy in my life," Miriam repeated. Then, taking the hand of the small Nathan, she led him away.

But there was joy in Rahab's life! Each moment was a delight, caring for Boaz. When he slept in his small basket, Rahab often wished to rouse him, so that she could play with him. But she sat instead beside the basket and watched his tiny chest rise and fall with each breath. She wondered at the fine, long lashes which lay against his cheek, and the fragile fingers curled beside his soft hair. Rahab knew that a woman could know no finer joy than to be a mother.

---

[75]Leviticus 12:2,3

And at such times of contemplation, Miriam's sad face and Nathan's expressionless one would come to her mind. Miriam had allowed herself to lose even the joy of Elimelech in her deep wretchedness. One day, when the face of Miriam was in her mind, Rahab began to pray.

"Oh Lord, You Who have blessed Salmon and me beyond our dreams, I thank You again for giving to us our son. And I now beseech You, Lord, for Miriam. And for Nathan. You alone know the depths of her bitterness and despair. I cannot understand why she has no love for the dear child whom You gave to her. But she doesn't. Oh, Lord, touch her hardened heart in some way, awaken within her the joy of life, and let her love Nathan. And Nathan, Lord," Rahab sighed. "He is so small and cannot understand. I cannot understand. But Nathan's tender heart is being badly beaten by Miriam. I thank You that Enan loves him and shows his love freely. I plead with You, oh Lord of heaven and earth. Don't let Nathan be destroyed by Miriam's contempt."

When Boaz was forty-one days old, Salmon and Rahab took him to Shiloh to offer there the sacrifices required by God's law, a lamb for a burnt offering and a young pigeon for a sin offering. These were given to the priest at the door of the Tabernacle of the Congregation and he offered them before the Lord to make an atonement for Rahab.[76]

Rahab could truly join with her friends, now, in discussions about infants and children. She saw life differently now; her eyes always saw where Boaz was, her ears always heard his cry. She was now a mother.

The peaceful morning air was shattered by a quick knock at her door. Rahab answered swiftly to find Elshima in a heap upon the ground. Much alarmed, Rahab helped Elshima to her

---

[76]Leviticus 12:6

feet, and tried to understand the message, garbled by sobs.

"Pagiel, Pagiel, Pagiel," Elshima sobbed. "Pagiel's eye. He has...hurt...his...eye! Badly."

With horror Rahab finally understood her words. She tried to speak calmly. "Where is he?"

"The...physician," Elshima stammered through her sobs.

Rahab tried to think clearly. "Go to him," she said. "I will get Salmon."

Rahab bound Boaz firmly to her back and ran down to the fields seeking Salmon. She saw him talking with a group of men in a far field and began to scream, "Salmon! Salmon!"

Salmon turned and saw her. He ran with quick strides to her side and caught her in his arms. "What is it!" he asked, deeply concerned.

"Pagiel has hurt his eye badly," she said, panting heavily. "He is at the physician's home now."

"Walk slowly back home," Salmon instructed her. "When you have gotten your breath, tell our friends."

Pagiel was moved to his house and laid in bed. Rahab and Maachah tried to sooth the weeping of Elshima and calm her two small children. When the doctor had done all that he could do, he departed. Everyone gathered around the injured man's bed. Pagiel slept with a thick, blood-soaked bandage over his left eye.

"He told me that his master struck him in the face," Salmon said soberly. He knew that he was badly hurt before he fainted from the pain. But he has lost his eye."

Anxious days followed. Pagiel tossed and screamed through his fever, and his hands had to be bound so that he would not tear the bandage from his eye. Jasper and Salmon took turns at his side. Rahab and Maachah cooked and cared for the children. Elshima sat at Pagiel's side, holding his hand and speaking to him in soothing tones.

Many times Rahab began to pray, "Oh Lord, help." She could find no other words, so she repeated the simple prayer again and again throughout the weary days, as they watched and waited.

Rahab was kneading bread in a trough in the courtyard. All suddenly seemed strangely still and fear clutched at her heart as she wiped her hands and hurried inside. She was flooded with relief as she entered the room and saw Pagiel sitting up in the bed, talking with Salmon. The Lord had heard and answered her simple prayer!

Rahab was glad to be back about her usual routine at home. As she rounded a corner carrying a large bowl of fruit, she almost collided with Salmon. He was grinning widely as he took the bowl from her and laid it aside. Then, grasping her by the waist, he twirled her around, laughing. Breathless, she laughed, too, and then asked, "Is there a cause for so much happiness?"

He laughed again and answered, "I have every cause for happiness and none for sorrow!" Then his brown eyes smiled into hers and he said, "I just sold to Pagiel the land that I had planned to sell him years ago, before his ear was auled."

Still out of breath, Rahab said, "You did! How wonderful! It was good of you, Salmon!"

"I was bound by my word to do it, Rahab. You see, the law of the Lord says that if a man smites his servant's eye so that he loses it, he must let his servant go free for his eye's sake."[77]

"Oh how wonderful!" Rahab exclaimed. "How wonderful the law of the Lord is!"

"It's the same law which bound Pagiel years ago," Salmon reminded her.

"Yes," she said thoughtfully. "It's the Lord's law, and it is good."

---

[77]Exodus 21:26

Chapter 9

Disease

Rahab tried to keep her balance in the press about her and held tightly to Boaz's hand. All of Israel had gathered at Shechem to hear Joshua. The brave leader of Israel, who had led the mighty armies of the Lord to conquer the Promised Land, was now one hundred-ten years old. He stood atop a platform and raised his hands into the air. The multitude hushed to hear his words.

"The Lord God of Israel says to you, 'In old time your father Terah, the father of Abraham and Nahor, lived on the other side of the river and served other gods. I took your father Abraham from the other side of the river and led him throughout the land of Canaan and gave him Isaac. I gave Isaac Jacob and Esau. I gave unto Esau Mount Seir as a possession, but Jacob and his children went down into Egypt.'"

"'I sent Moses and Aaron, and I plagued Egypt. I brought your fathers out of Egypt, and you came to the sea, and the Egyptians pursued after your fathers with chariots and horsemen unto the Red Sea.'"

"'And when you cried unto the Lord He put darkness between you and the Egyptians and brought the sea upon them, and covered them, and your eyes have seen what I have done in Egypt. And you dwelt in the wilderness a long season.'"

"'I brought you into the land of the Amorites, which dwelt on the other side of the Jordan, and they fought with you. I gave them into your hand that you might possess their land, and I destroyed them from before you.'"

"'Then Balak the son of Zippor, the king of Moab, arose and warred against Israel, and called Balaam the son of Beor to curse you. But I would not hearken unto Balaam, so that he blessed you still, and I delivered you out of his hand.'"

Rahab felt a strange sensation as Joshua continued the

message from the Lord, "'You went over Jordan and came to Jericho and the men of Jericho fought against you. I delivered into your hand the Amorites, the Perizites, the Canaanites, the Hittites, and the Jebusites. I sent the hornet before you, which drove them out from before you, not with your sword, nor with your bow.'"

"'And I have given you a land for which you did not labour, and cities which you did not build, and you dwell in them. You eat of vineyards and oliveyards which you did not plant.'"

"'Now therefore fear the Lord, and serve Him in sincerity and in truth, and put away the gods which your fathers served on the other side of the river and in Egypt, and serve the Lord. If it seem evil to you to serve the Lord, choose you this day whom you will serve; whether the gods which your fathers served that were on the other side of the river, or the gods of the Amorites, in whose land you dwell. But as for me and my house, we will serve the Lord.'"[78]

The answer of the people thrilled Rahab, as with one voice they said, "God forbid that we should forsake the Lord to serve other gods; we will serve the Lord, for He is our God, and His voice will we obey."[79]

Joshua wrote the words from the Lord in the book of the law of God and took a great stone and set it on end there under an oak tree beside the Sanctuary of the Lord. Then he said, "This stone shall be a witness unto us because it heard all the words of the Lord which He spoke to us. It shall be a witness unto you, lest you deny your God."[80]

One thing bothered Rahab's heart as they walked homeward from the wonderful hearing of the words of the Lord.

---

[78]Joshua 24:1-15

[79]Joshua 24:16-18

[80]Joshua 24:26,27

The Lord had admonished the people to put away the gods from among them. Rahab was burdened by this, so she asked Salmon, "Do people of Israel truly serve the gods of this land?"

Salmon pursed his lips and then said sadly, shaking his head, "Yes, I fear that some do."

"But why?" asked Rahab, unable to comprehend.

"They don't trust in the Lord God of heaven and earth. Perhaps they desire to see their god. Perhaps they serve other gods in hopes of power or recognition. I don't know why, but they do, and the Lord has commanded them to put away their gods."

"Salmon, I cannot believe that anyone would turn from the true God to serve idols."

"But it's true, Rahab," he answered gently. "They don't trust in the Lord."

"But the Lord took care of them for forty years in the wilderness. The Lord has given them this land and their homes and all that they possess. How could they not trust Him?" she asked.

"Indeed the Lord gives life and breath, sunshine and rain, food and drink to all men. Yet, I fear that there are few who truly trust in the Lord," Salmon said.

Boaz listened silently to the conversation of his parents as they walked along the road toward Bethlehem. When he finally spoke, deep concern etched his young voice. "Mother, I know that the Lord God loves me. You have told me that He loves everyone. But why does He love some more than others?"

Rahab was startled by Boaz's question, and she looked at Salmon, her eyes asking for help. Salmon smiled and put his arm around his son's shoulders. "Why do you think that the Lord God loves some more than others?" he asked.

"Well, Father, you and Mother love me dearly and Nathan has only his Uncle Enan who loves him," was Boaz's simple answer.

"Do you think that means that the Lord loves you more

than He loves Nathan?" asked Salmon.

Boaz was silent in thought for several minutes. "Doesn't it, Father?" he asked.

"Boaz, Nathan's parents died when he was just an infant. The Lord God loved and cared for him so much that He gave Nathan to Enan and Miriam to raise, in the place of his own parents. Whenever God gives a child to someone, He intends for that child to be loved and cared for. But people do not always do as the Lord intends for them to do. Be thankful to the Lord for the love of your parents, Boaz, but do not think that the Lord loves Nathan less than He loves you."

"I am happy, Father," Boaz continued. "Nathan doesn't seem to be happy at all. His eyes look so sad, and he doesn't play with the rest of us."

"Well, Boaz, I think that you should pray for Nathan, then. Pray that the Lord will give him joy, and take away his sadness," answered Salmon.

"Can I Father? Does the Lord answer such prayers?" Boaz asked.

"He does indeed," answered Salmon.

"Oh, Father, I will!" exclaimed the young boy excitedly, glad that there was a way to help.

"Salmon, you are so wise," Rahab whispered to him. "I sure didn't know how to answer him."

The caravan returning to Bethlehem descended to the Jordan Valley and walked along the waters' edge, the easiest way of passage. Boaz had run with the other young boys to skip stones across the waters of the Jordan, but he came running now and tugged hard on Salmon's sleeve.

"Father, we began to climb a pile of stones over there," Boaz said excitedly, pointing toward the river bank, "And the men told us not to. They chased us all away. Why, Father? What are those stones?"

Salmon knelt on the road before his son and pointed toward the pile. "When the Lord God led us from the wilderness to this land, He opened the waters of the river and we walked across on dry land. The Lord God had opened the Red Sea forty years before and allowed our parents to pass over on dry ground. Boaz, these stones were taken from the middle of the river when it was dry, and they are to remind us that the hand of the Lord is mighty, and that we might fear the Lord our God for ever."[81]

All Israel mourned as the messengers rode throughout the land, bearing the news to each city that Joshua, the great leader of Israel, had died. Rahab was thankful for the opportunity she had had to meet Joshua. She thanked the Lord, also, that she had heard the message from the Lord shortly before Joshua's death.

Rahab joyed in each day of her life. Salmon's lands produced richly and they had more than they could use, so their coffers were filling from the sales of his grains and crops, as well as cattle and sheep. Arod had come to ask about her linen when Boaz was still an infant, but she told him with a smile that being a mother was enough for her, now. He had come again, for several years, and had finally stopped coming.

Maachah and Jasper were happy with their busy family. Jared was grown and farming with his father. All but one of their other children were strong and healthy and a constant joy to them. The frail Jemimah, who knit all their hearts together tenderly with her gentle love, was often ill. But she would smile through her pain and suffering, and try not to be a burden to her busy mother.

One day Maachah knocked on Rahab's door and quietly motioned for her to come and see. Rahab followed her. Maachah stopped suddenly and pointed toward an olive tree, beneath which Jemimah, now eighteen years of age, sat. At her side sat Nathan, watching her intently, and listening as she spoke. Suddenly, he threw back his head and laughed, the clear,

---

[81]Joshua 4:21-24

sparkling sound ringing through the autumn air. Rahab looked at Maachah in amazement and whispered, "Nathan is laughing! I didn't know that he knew how."

Maachah nodded her head vigorously, tears shining in her eyes. "Yes, they have become fast friends, you know. He is good for my Jemimah, also, for he doesn't demand anything of her but her company."

The two women continued to watch the girl and the younger boy from the distance. Rahab remembered Salmon's suggestion that Boaz pray for Nathan that the Lord would give him joy and take away his sadness. "Thank You, Lord, " she whispered.

As Rahab walked back from the well with her jug perched atop her head, the rain soaked her from head to foot. It had only been dripping when she had left her house, and she thought how she could have waited a few moments more and caught her water from the rain. As she approached the main street of the town, she heard a wail rise from one of the houses and stopped still. She had not heard such a wail since the fatal days of Jericho, when the children had been offered to the fires. The wail rose again, and Rahab knew that it came from Miriam's house. Leaving her jug standing in the street, she ran as quickly as her wet dress allowed and knocked upon the door of Miriam's house.

A servant opened the door somberly. Rahab asked quickly, "May I enter?" The servant nodded and Rahab ascended the steps to a wide room where she found Miriam clutching Enan hysterically. Two men pulled the man and his wife apart. Rahab recognized them as Levites who lived in Bethlehem. She tried to hear above Miriam's wails what was being spoken.

"He must go to the priest in Shiloh. We have determined that he has leprosy, but he must go to see the priest," said one of the men.

"No!" Miriam shrieked. "No, it cannot be!"

One of the Levites noticed Rahab and motioned for her to approach. As she did so Miriam saw her and became furious.

Rahab could barely hear the man's instructions above Miriam's screeches. "Please find Enan a ride to Shiloh. He must go today, quickly."

Rahab was glad to escape the house, but she ran toward Salmon's barns numbly. Enan! Leprosy! Her mind could not fully grasp what she had heard. When she found Salmon she stammered the message through her tears.

"I will take him with a fast beast to Shiloh," said Salmon. "You go to Miriam."

Rahab looked into his eyes uncertainly. "Go to her," he repeated. Then he turned and hurried out into the rain.

Rahab went to her house, first, and took Boaz to Maachah's home, quickly explaining to her the terrible news. Then she walked to Miriam's house, arriving sodden at the door. She stood outside in the rain, unwilling to enter and face Miriam. "What shall I say to her Lord?" she prayed. "She has never desired my comfort before. Help me."

Enan was gone with Salmon. The two Levites had gone. Elimelech and Nathan sat quietly at a table. Miriam strode angrily through the room, clutching and throwing objects about her in a rage, and screaming senselessly. Rahab stood aside, hoping to avoid the whirling missiles. The two young men sat silently. Rahab stood silently. The minutes passed and suddenly Miriam's rage faded. She stopped in the middle of the room and glared at Rahab. "The Lord of Whom you always speak has smitten my Enan with leprosy."

Rahab and Miriam stood, the one glaring in accusation, the other praying frantically. Salmon would know just the thing to say. But Salmon was on a swift trip to the priest in Shiloh and only she was there before Miriam to speak.

The door opened and Miriam's mother dashed into the room, taking Miriam into her arms and sobbing about Enan's awful fate. Feeling awkward watching the two grieving women, Rahab moved to the table and spoke to Elimelech.

"Would it help if Nathan were to come home with me?"

she asked.

Elimelech looked up at her with red eyes. His handsome young face was clouded with his grief as he nodded. "Yes, thank you," he said.

Rahab nodded toward Miriam and asked, "Shall I tell her or will you?"

"When her tears subside I will tell her," Elimelech answered. "Thank you for your concern. My grandmother and I will take care of her now." He looked at Nathan and said, "Go with Rahab, Nathan. Stay until I come for you."

Nathan rose obediently from his seat and walked out of the sorrowful room. The heavy rain greeted them as they emerged from the house, and they walked along, heads down, toward Rahab's home. Just before they reached the house, Rahab felt a tug at her elbow. She stopped and looked at Nathan, who at thirteen was as tall as she. His usually sad face bore a deeper sorrow and he spoke loudly through the rain. "I love Enan. He is as a father to me. Why must he have leprosy?"

Rahab wished that he had waited until they were inside the house. She wished that she had an answer for him. But she did not. They stood in the rain, the tears and raindrops mingling on their faces, and she did not have an answer for him. Then Nathan spoke quietly, yet Rahab heard his words above the rain, "Without Enan, I have no one."

In sudden compassion Rahab gathered Nathan into her arms and said into his ear, "There are many who love you, Nathan." She looked into his somber eyes and said, "And we must pray for Enan. I know that the Lord can heal. We must pray." Then she led him into the dryness of the house.

Salmon returned late the next evening. He sadly entered the house and sat before the fire. Boaz leaned against Salmon's knee. Nathan sat quietly, waiting. When Salmon spoke his voice trembled.

"The priest pronounced Enan unclean. Enan rent his clothes before the priest and bared his head. He must wear a covering on his upper lip and cry, 'Unclean, unclean.'"[82] Salmon's voice broke as he spoke the last words and he covered his face with his hands. Rahab rose and went to his side.

Nathan, who was staring expressionless at the flames spoke softly and said, "Is Enan home? I wish to go to him."

Salmon lowered his hands from his face and looked at Nathan. His voice was calm when he spoke. "Enan is defiled and unclean. The law of the Lord says that he must dwell alone, outside of the town."

Nathan jumped to his feet, and Rahab was surprised to see his eyes flash and his jaw set in determination. "Then I, too, shall dwell outside the town with him."

Salmon stood and put a hand on Nathan's shoulder. "There are many ways that you can help Enan at this time. We will build lodging for him. He will need his daily sustenance. Enan will want you and Elimelech to farm his lands and care for Miriam."

Nathan still wore the look of determination as he said, "But I must go to him. He will need me."

Salmon's hand was still on Nathan's shoulder. He said kindly, "Nathan, Enan's disease is a terrible thing. If anyone goes near him, they too, can become diseased."

"I don't care!" Nathan said loudly. "I would rather be diseased than to be separated from Enan."

"Yes, I believe you, Nathan. But Enan would not want you to become diseased," said Salmon. "He will wish for you to help Miriam."

Nathan relaxed and looked into Salmon's eyes. "You know Enan well," he said. "If you think that he would wish me to stay, I will. I want to do everything I can. I will help Miriam, and Elimelech."

"And pray for Enan, Nathan," Rahab said.

---

[82]Leviticus 13:45,46

Nathan looked at Rahab, and his eyes were now lit with a fire, uncommon to him. "Yes," Nathan said to her, "I will pray."

When Nathan had returned with Elimelech to Miriam's home, Boaz took his father's hand and said, "Father, if you had leprosy I would want to be with you, too." Salmon embraced his son and held him for several minutes.

"We must try to help Nathan, Boaz," Salmon said. "We must try to help Miriam, too. Life will not be easy for any of them."

When Boaz had gone to his bed, Salmon led Rahab to their rooftop. He stood with his hands on the battlement and looked into the fields below the mountain. Rahab stood at his side with her hand on his.

"I have seen men die in battle," Salmon said. "I watched as friends and loved ones died in the wilderness. But what has happened to Enan is worse than death." Salmon turned to look into Rahab's eyes. "He is my friend," Salmon continued. "I have never suffered as I suffered when I heard the pronouncement of the priest and watched Enan tear his clothes. I've taken him to the caves on our land. I'll build him shelter on his land, tomorrow. I'll be the one to take his food and clothing to him. It will be good for only one to have contact with him."

"And I will try to help Miriam, if she'll accept my help," determined Rahab.

Salmon smiled slightly at Rahab, and putting his hands on her shoulders he said, "I knew some in the wilderness who had leprosy. They never recovered, but died in their loneliness. But I know that the Lord is able to heal Enan. I have taken a Nazarite vow before the priest in Shiloh."

"What does that mean?" Rahab asked.

"I will separate myself unto the Lord to pray and fast for Enan. The law of the Lord says that one who vows the vow of a Nazarite must separate himself from wine and strong drink. I may not eat grapes, moist or dried, or the juice of grapes. God's law says that all the days that one separates himself no razor shall come upon his head, but he shall let the locks of the hair of his head grow."[83]

"How long, Salmon?" Rahab asked.

"Until the Lord answers my prayer," Salmon said softly.

"And if it's the Lord's will for Enan to be leprous until his death?" she asked.

"Until the Lord answers my prayer, Rahab. I believe in His power," Salmon said.

Life, which had been so wondrous and happy, altered completely.

Salmon and Elimelech built a small, sturdy room of stones in the shelter of some tall trees on a gentle rise. From the rise Enan would be able to see and his fields and the town atop the hill. Miriam and Nathan saw to the comforts Enan would need. A bed was fashioned for him with many warm blankets. Soft rugs covered the floor. A chair and a small table stood by the bed. A lamp for light stood on the table and a cheerful fire flickered on the hearth. Nathan laboured tirelessly to supply a large stack of firewood for Enan's use.

Each day Miriam lovingly prepared food for Enan and packed it into a basket. Salmon took the food and many other gifts from Enan's family to the cottage on the hill. He laid them on a flat rock near the cottage and receded a few paces. As Enan collected the offerings from the rock, the two friends would shout messages to one another.

Nathan threw himself into the task of helping. He worked long hours in the fields. He chopped wood and carried burdens for Miriam. Yet, with all his business, he could sometimes be found at Jasper and Maachah's home, sitting with Jemimah, talking and laughing with her.

Boaz, who had run through his boyish days joyfully, now

---

[83]Numbers 6:2-5

became pensive, sitting for hours at a time in thought, and then asking hard questions.

"When will Uncle Enan be well again?" Boaz asked one day as he looked up from the labour of writing his Hebrew characters.

Rahab knelt beside a tub scrubbing clothes. She stopped and pushed a wisp of hair from her face with a sudsy hand. "In the Lord's time," she said.

"Does the Lord's time take long?" Boaz asked.

"The Lord will know when it is time." Rahab reached her wet arms to embrace her son. "The Lord God loves Enan. He will heal him when it is the right time."

"If the Lord loves Enan, why did He make Enan sick?" asked Boaz.

"The Lord loves everyone, Boaz, even those who are wicked and do not love Him. But Uncle Enan does love the Lord. God knows how to take care of those who love Him," Rahab answered.

"Nathan said that Aunt Miriam is very angry with the Lord for making Enan sick," Boaz said.

"We must pray for Aunt Miriam. This is very difficult for her, and she has never learned to trust in the Lord's love," Rahab told him.

"May we pray now, Mother, for Aunt Miriam and Uncle Enan?" the child asked.

Rahab wiped her hands against her skirts and together mother and son knelt before the Lord God of heaven and earth and prayed for Miriam and Enan.

Salmon worked in his fields and helped in Enan's. He worked silently and returned home with little to say. Rahab's heart ached as she watched him sit and stare into the fire, praying, she was sure, for Enan. His hair began to lengthen and she tied it in the back to prevent it from getting in his way. He often mounted the stairs to their rooftop to stand beneath the stars and pray.

One starry evening Rahab followed him to his rooftop perch and stood beside him. He stood silently for awhile, leaning upon the battlement of the roof. Then he reached his arm to pull her near and held her against him. She felt him tremble and knew that he was weeping. They stood thus for a long while in the starlight, the strong Salmon weeping silently against her as she gently stroked his long brown hair.

Salmon took a deep breath and stood straight, looking into Rahab's eyes in the darkness. The familiar twinkle was absent from his deep, dark eyes. She could see his lips purse beneath his moustache. His beard was wet with tears as he spoke, almost inaudibly in the quiet darkness.

"Today Enan's hands were bound so that he could scarcely carry his food from the rock." Salmon paused, struggling with his emotions. "He only asks about his family. He does not complain. And his faith in the Lord is not shaken." Salmon's voice broke with his last words. With great difficulty he continued. "Would my faith be so great if my adversity were so heavy? I see my friend corrupting away, and he encourages me in the Lord." Salmon paused again, regaining his composure, and looked once more into Rahab's eyes. She saw deep determination in his eyes as he said, "Enan is very concerned about Miriam. He feels her closeness and love in the things that she sends to him each day. But he cannot speak with her. He doesn't know how she is handling her pain and grief." The determination in Salmon's eyes intensified as he said, "I told Enan that you, Rahab, will try to help Miriam through her suffering."

"But Miriam does not want..." Salmon placed his finger quickly to her lips and his eyes were almost fierce as he said, "I told Enan you will try to help her. You must try, Rahab."

Rahab riveted her eyes upon his brown ones. Salmon had always asked the impossible of her concerning Miriam. Yet, she knew that the Lord had helped her, through the years. Never mind that Miriam still scorned her. Salmon had often told her that she was responsible for her attitudes and actions, not

Miriam's. Rahab breathed deeply and silently nodded consent.

Boaz had gone to the fields with Salmon and Rahab knew that she had no excuse to remain home. She knelt in her courtyard among the fragrant autumn blossoms and implored the Lord to help her as she faced Miriam. Miriam had never desired her help, or even her presence. Yet, she must go, for Salmon's sake. For Enan's sake.

She found Miriam kneading bread and stood uncomfortably, watching the rapid movements of her hands, not wanting to speak, for fear of the response. After several moments, Miriam stopped and plopped the dough onto a board, covering it with a cloth. Only then did she seem to notice Rahab's presence.

"So, you have come," Miriam said. "Do you come to gloat that your husband is strong and well, while mine slowly dies?"

The familiar twinge hit Rahab's heart, and she desired only to scream at Miriam for her foolish words. She wished mightily that she may simply turn and leave. But she was there to comfort Miriam, who did not desire her comfort. Praying silently, "Help, Lord," she spoke quietly and slowly.

"I have come to aid you in any way that I can. I will gladly do anything that you want me to." Then she added, "I will work in a separate room if you wish."

Miriam looked at her with her icy blue eyes squinting and her mouth set grimly. When she spoke, it was in a hoarse whisper, but seemed to be shouted nevertheless. "This bread is for my dear, helpless Enan. My hands only will touch his food." Rahab felt Miriam's eyes on her hands and wished to hide them, but she stood still. "What have I else to do than my housework?" Miriam continued in the whispered shout. "You will gladly do anything that I wish? Then leave me! That is what I wish!"

Rahab knew that this was her cue to turn and leave, as her heart longed to do. But she had been instructed to help Miriam. It was Enan's desire. It was Salmon's command.

"Miriam, I desire to be here no more than you wish me to be. But Salmon has promised to Enan that I would come to help you. To comfort you," Rahab said.

"Ha!" Miriam laughed aloud, roughly. "You! You are come to comfort me? And how, pray tell, would one such as you comfort me?"

Rahab knew as she stood before Miriam that she detested her, and the feeling was mutual. And Miriam was right. How, indeed, could Rahab comfort her? But Rahab stood her ground and answered quietly, "There is no way for me to comfort you, Miriam, that's true. But the Lord God, Who loves you dearly, can comfort you. He alone understands the pain you know. He alone can ease it."

Miriam's contorted face relaxed briefly and then set again with hard lines. She brushed the flour from her hands upon her apron, wiping her hands back and forth over and over as she said, "Perhaps the Lord God loves you, Rahab, but He does not love me." She then looked at Rahab with her cold blue eyes and said, "Why the Lord God should love a heathen harlot before a true Hebrew woman I do not understand."

For years Miriam had shown her contempt with her voice alone, and had not used that dreadful title. As she spoke it, every drop of venom in her heart was poured into the word. Rahab's heart was pierced through with the pronouncement of it, and she felt the hot color rise to her face. But the message of Miriam's words was more important by far than Rahab's pride. So she pushed the insult aside and said, "Why should you believe that the Lord God does not love you, Miriam?"

Miriam stared at her through squinted eyes. Rahab wondered if an answer would ever come when Miriam finally spoke. "I was able to give Enan but one child, and now the Lord has stricken Enan with a slow death," she said bitterly.

Rahab cried silently to the Lord for words. She, too, had but one child, but that would be of sorry comfort to Miriam. "Yes, Miriam, you have a strong, healthy, loving son. A child, a son, is a blessing from the Lord."

Miriam raised her finger to point it at Rahab. "Do not tell me that Nathan was a blessing from the Lord," she stated. "I have suffered in heart from the day that he came into our home. The Lord dealt me a severe blow indeed the day that He took my brother's life and the life of his wife and gave to me the burden of raising my brother's child."

Rahab's eyes burned with her tears, and she knew that she would now speak the words that she would later wish to retract but would be unable to. "I have never understood you, Miriam, but in the matter of Nathan you astound me. I, and many other women whom I know, would have been so happy to raise Nathan. He is healthy and strong. He is obedient. He has never done anything to cause you grief. Yet his whole life you have been nothing to him but a grief. He has lived in the pain of knowing that you did not care for him. He has suffered more at your hands than if you had beaten him daily for his life!"

Miriam did not move. Rahab held her breath. She had said it and there was no taking it back.

When Miriam spoke her voice was mocking with kindness. "Thank you, Rahab, for the great comfort that you have brought to me."

Shame suddenly replaced the rage in Rahab's heart. It was true. She was a miserable comfort to a woman whose husband was decaying in leprosy. She dropped her eyes and spoke softly, barely audibly. "Forgive me, Miriam." She said no more, but raised her eyes to look into Miriam's blue ones.

"Rahab, what is the use of us speaking with one another. We detest one another. It's an utter waste of our time, mine and yours. I'm sure that you have much more useful things to do, for your husband, perhaps. I bid you farewell." Miriam turned away and Rahab knew the visit had ended. What would she report to Salmon of the visit? Surely she had not helped Miriam.

As they sat at the table eating their evening meal, Salmon's eyes alone asked the question that Rahab did not want to answer. She tried to avoid his gaze, but knew that she must speak of it. When Boaz had finished his meal and been excused, she folded her hands under her chin with her elbows on the table's edge and made herself look into Salmon's eyes.

"I went to Miriam, today," she told him. Salmon did not speak, but watched her intently. She licked her lips and continued, "She was not happy to see me, Salmon. I fear that I was sorry comfort for her."

Salmon continued to watch her, and then asked gently, "What message shall I give to Enan?"

Rahab wished to escape this conversation, but she must answer him. What message, indeed, could she give? She licked her lips again and said, "Miriam fills her days with busying herself about her housework."

Salmon raised an eyebrow and continued to watch her. His gaze discomfited her, and she tried to say more. "She prepares the bread for Enan with love and wishes that her hands alone touch it."

Salmon leaned back and his eyes softened. "Are you telling me that Miriam does not wish your help with her housework or her baking?"

"Yes," was all she answered.

Salmon leaned toward Rahab and asked, "And did you have any words of comfort for her?"

"I told her that the Lord God loves her dearly. I told her that He understands her pain and can ease it," she said.

Salmon nodded slowly. "And her response?" he asked.

Rahab sighed. "She doesn't believe that the Lord loves her. She perceives what she counts as trials to be evidence of His lack of love for her."

"What does she perceive as trials?" Salmon asked.

"Enan's leprosy, of course," Rahab said, feeling easier now that they were simply conversing. "And having only one child." She paused. "And Nathan."

"What did you say to her?" Salmon asked.

Rahab felt strangely that Salmon already knew the answer and was waiting only for her confession. Why must he know each word of her conversation with Miriam? But he was still leaning toward her, waiting for her response.

Rahab could not continue to look into Salmon's gaze. She lowered her eyes and her voice and said, "I scolded her for her attitude toward Nathan and she told me there was no use of my being there and asked me to leave."

Salmon was silent. Rahab could not look at him. She sat still, staring at her hands. When Salmon finally spoke she found herself looking at him. "You trust in the Lord, Rahab, but how do you imagine you would feel if I were stricken with leprosy and must leave our home and never see you but from afar?"

Rahab's heart was heavy within her breast and she felt the terrible injustice of Salmon's question. Her world would come apart if such a thing were to happen to them. But Salmon could not understand that no matter how she empathized with Miriam, Miriam did not desire her comfort, or her presence.

"Salmon, I know that Miriam's life is difficult far beyond my understanding, but I am not the person to help her," she said.

"Who is the person to help her?" Salmon asked.

"Her family, someone she trusts and respects," Rahab said.

"And whom of her family and friends will encourage her in the Lord?" Salmon asked.

"Surely there's someone, Salmon," Rahab said.

Salmon shook his head. "Enan is very concerned because he fears that Miriam has none to encourage her to trust the Lord in this trial. He knows that you know and trust the Lord, Rahab. That's why he requested that you help her."

Rahab looked at him angrily. "He must be aware of the disdain in which she holds me. He must know that she will not listen to me." She paused, breathing deeply, angrily. "He must know that she hates me!" she almost shouted at Salmon.

Salmon continued to watch her and she broke into tears.

"Salmon, she called me "harlot" again. She hates me, Salmon. Please don't make me go to her again!"

Salmon rose from the table and left the room. He ascended the stairs to his rooftop perch. When he had gone Rahab wept bitter tears of self pity. When her tears had subsided she stared into the fire on the hearth. Surely she was a selfish woman. Salmon had taken the vow of a Nazarite, and perhaps it would be years. She herself had a life full of the blessings of the Lord. Why couldn't she find a way to help Miriam? She rose from the table and ascended the stairs to stand beside Salmon. He had loosed his hair and the night breeze blew it across his face as he leaned on the battlement, staring across the hills.

Rahab pushed his straying hair aside and kissed his cheek. Then, leaning her head against his shoulder she spoke softly. "I'm a selfish woman, Salmon, I know. Please forgive me. I do want to help Enan. If I can help him by being a comfort in some way to Miriam, I do want to try. She really doesn't want my help, Salmon. But I will try. I will try," she repeated.

Salmon smiled at her in the starlight and said, "I love you, Rahab."

Boaz was immersed in thought once more as he and his parents travelled home again from the observance of Passover. "Father," he asked at last, "What is the meaning of these testimonies, and statutes and judgments, which the Lord our God has commanded us?"

Salmon smiled at the question of Boaz, nodding his head. "God knew that you would ask such a question, Boaz."

"Did God tell you so?" Boaz asked, awed.

"He did, Boaz. God said, 'When your son asks you about these things, tell him.'" Salmon continued to smile as he led his family out of the caravan of travellers to sit beneath a tree.

"Tell him what, Father?" Boaz asked, sidling up close to Salmon's side.

"We were Pharaoh's bondmen in Egypt and the Lord brought us out of Egypt with a mighty hand. The Lord shewed signs and wonders, great and sore upon Egypt, upon Pharaoh, and upon all his household, before our eyes. And he brought us out from there that He might bring us in to give us the land which He sware unto our fathers. And the Lord commanded us to do all these statutes, to fear the Lord our God, for our good always, that He might preserve us alive, as it is at this day. Boaz, it will be our righteousness if we observe to do all these commandments before the Lord our God, as he hath commanded us."[84]

Boaz smiled broadly. "I know all about how the Lord God took our fathers out of Egypt, Father."

"Yes, I know, my son," Salmon said softly, ruffling the boy's brown hair. "But the Lord God wants me to remind you often, so that you will never forget."

"Oh, Father! I will never forget!" Boaz threw himself into his father's arms, and the family of three embraced.

---

[84]Deuteronomy 6:2-25

CHAPTER 10

Waiting

Elshima shook her head slowly. "She would not give him permission," she said sadly.

"I'm sorry for Naomi's sake," Rahab said softly. "And for Elimelech's." Her voice hardened as she said, "But I'm not surprised that Miriam opposes their desire to marry."

Elshima looked sadly at Rahab and her eyes asked, "Why?"

"You know the burden that life is for Miriam with Enan so sick," Rahab said. "She is disagreeable about everything."

Elshima nodded her head in sympathy, but Rahab's heart wanted to cry out that Miriam had always been disagreeable to everything.

When Elshima had gone, Rahab pulled a shawl over her shoulders against the early spring air. She knew better than to do what she intended, but Miriam was already angry, so what would it matter? For almost three years Rahab had tried every way that she could to help and comfort Miriam. Even Salmon seemed almost resigned to the truth. Miriam would not be comforted by Rahab. Miriam would not listen to Rahab's encouragement to trust the Lord. So now, Rahab would go to her and speak her mind, no matter the consequences.

Rahab stepped out of the gate and walked quickly along the street. Her mind whirred. She knew her motivation was wrong. But she did not want to think about it. As she neared Miriam's house she felt suddenly guilty that she would do this knowing it was wrong. She tried to ignore the nagging thought that she had not prayed, that she knew this was not the Lord's way.

She was so wrapped in her determination that she did not see Salmon and ran against him in the street. He caught her from falling and asked, "To where are you hurrying?"

Rahab stood startled, looking at Salmon and wondering what she could tell him. So she stated lamely, "Miriam will not allow Elimelech and Naomi to marry."

Salmon looked at her with a question in his eyes but said nothing. Rahab knew he would disapprove, but she said, "I am going to see Miriam."

"May I go with you?" Salmon asked, turning toward Miriam's house and walking along.

Rahab hurried to keep up and mumbled, "Of course you may come."

Salmon knocked hard on the door when they reached Miriam's home. Elimelech opened the gate to them, his eyes sad and his countenance sober. Salmon greeted him cheerfully and strode up the broad stairs to the wide room where Miriam sat warming herself before the fire. Salmon seated Rahab beside him and reached to hold one of Miriam's hands, which were folded on her lap. Miriam looked at Salmon with a question in her blue eyes.

"Enan?" she asked simply.

"Enan is no worse," Salmon told her. "As always he sends his love to you and Elimelech and Nathan."

"That's good," Miriam said, looking away from Salmon's brown eyes into the flames on the hearth before them.

The three sat in silence, listening to the crackling of the flames. As Rahab sat in the stillness her heart cried out and thanked the Lord that Salmon had met her in the street. Sitting here now, seeing Miriam, Rahab knew she would have caused disaster according to her plans. Finally Salmon spoke, his deep, calm voice interrupting the quiet.

"Elimelech desires to marry Naomi," he said.

Miriam looked at him sharply and drew her hand away from him. Her face hardened with determination and she said in a hoarse whisper, "Enan's life is a living death."

"Elimelech will continue to care for you and his father after he is wed," Salmon told her softly.

"How can he think of his own happiness when his father is corrupting away every day?" Miriam's words fell like icicles from her lips.

Rahab knew that her response would be to shout at Miriam's absurdity, but Salmon recovered Miriam's hand and spoke gently, the concern and care evident in his voice, "I know that I cannot understand your suffering, Miriam, nor Enan's. Rahab and I can watch, and care, but we cannot really know your pain." Miriam glanced quickly toward Rahab, and Rahab again thanked the Lord that He had not allowed her to come here by herself.

"Elimelech has also borne a great weight of suffering and pain," Salmon continued tenderly. "He has devotedly tilled the fields for his father and cared for you, also, Miriam. He's a good son. I know that you love Elimelech dearly. I know that you want the best for your son. For Enan's son. I know that you want him to be happy, Miriam."

The hard facade of Miriam's composure cracked and crumpled. Rahab had seen it slip before only when Enan became leprous. Miriam covered her face and wept against Salmon's strong shoulder, sobbing. When she spoke her voice trembled and cracked through her tears.

"Her parents are slaves! And Elimelech is descended of princes!"

"Pagiel is a free man, Miriam. His freedom was dearly bought many years ago," Salmon answered her.

"But he was a slave. Elshima was a slave!" Miriam hissed.

Salmon patted Miriam's shoulder silently for a moment. When he spoke his words were very quiet, but they seemed to ring in the stillness of the room. "My father was a slave to the Pharaoh of Egypt. My mother was a slave as a confectioner in the palace."

Silence again. An ember dropped, hissing, and sending a small shower of sparks upward. Miriam's quiet sniffing ceased.

She still leaned against Salmon's shoulder, his hand patting her. When she spoke her voice sounded distant.

"My father was a slave to the Pharaoh of Egypt. My mother slaved in Egypt, also." Sitting upright and reclaiming her hands to fold into her lap, Miriam quietly asked, "Will you take Elimelech with you to Enan, today, Salmon? He should have his father's permission and blessing."

As Salmon and Rahab walked away from Miriam's house toward their own, Rahab wondered again at Salmon's ability to deal with Miriam.

"How do you always know just what to say to her?" Rahab asked.

"I love her," he answered. "I look beyond her unpleasantness and see a soul in need of love and compassion."

"I have tried, Salmon, to love her, but I fear that I've failed," Rahab said sadly.

"Stop trying," said Salmon. Rahab grabbed his arm and turned him to face her.

"Stop trying?" she asked.

"Yes, Rahab. Stop trying. God loves her. Let Him love her through you. He wont fail."

"I don't understand, Salmon," Rahab pleaded.

"Look beyond her unpleasantness and see a soul in need. Let God love her through you," Salmon said.

The marriage of Elimelech and Naomi on a warm late spring day was festive in a reserved way. Elshima and Pagiel were very happy. Maachah and Rahab flitted about serving the guests. Miriam sat nobly and accepted the congratulations of those present. The bride and groom went to the cottage on the hill and, keeping a safe distance, exchanged shouted messages with Enan.

Salmon seldom spoke about Enan's physical condition. He often spoke, though, of Enan's love for the Lord and unfailing faith in God's love for him. Rahab always felt an almost reverent awe when Salmon spoke of Enan's strength of soul. She wondered often if her faith would remain strong and firm if she faced such adversity. And then she would think of Miriam, bearing Enan's affliction as well, yet without knowing the love of the Lord in her lonely life.

Salmon bore his vow of a Nazarite gravely. His hair had grown long and heavy, and Rahab would wind and plait it to keep it out of his way. She sometimes would look at him and wonder if he must bear his vow for the rest of his life. She never voiced her question, however, for she knew that he would bear it until Enan was healed or dead. She believed in the Lord's ability to heal, but she found it difficult to believe that it would actually happen to Enan. And although she knew that he suffered terribly from his loathsome disease, she could not wish his life shortened for Salmon's sake. And so life continued, and Rahab often missed the carefree days before Enan's illness, when the heaviest burden Rahab knew was Miriam's smirking hatred.

Elimelech and Naomi would visit occasionally, and Rahab was pleased to see how happy Elimelech was. He would talk in lively conversation unless he spoke of his parents. Then his voice became low and sad. Yet, Rahab noticed that Naomi could easily bring him back to happy conversation. "She's very good for him," Rahab thought to herself.

When Elimelech and Naomi had a son within the first year of their marriage, Miriam once again could be seen walking through the streets of Bethlehem with a child in her arms. Rahab spoke with her as infrequently as possible, but she saw a hint of happiness light the shadows on Miriam's face. Miriam devoted her days to the baby Mahlon, eventually moving to Elimelech's house to dwell there and care for the child. Rahab admired the strength of the young mother, Naomi, in giving her child into Miriam's care so that she may have some happiness.

Nathan, who was not yet quite twenty years old, was left in charge of the house as well as the lands of Enan. The sad, quiet boy had grown into a man of quiet strength. His young shoulders almost stooped beneath the burden of grief he bore for his uncle Enan, yet he could be found laughing and joyous when sitting at the side of the fragile Jemimah.

As Rahab straightened herself at the well of Bethlehem one morning, she saw Maachah hurrying toward her. Mixed emotions played on Maachah's face. "Oh, Rahab, I'm so glad to find you!" Maachah sat Rahab beside her on the mouth of the well and spoke quickly in her excitement.

"Nathan has asked for Jemimah's hand in marriage! We are so happy about it. Surely, Nathan is very young, but he has shown that he is a man who can take care of things. And he makes our Jemimah so happy! Nathan understands so much, and he knows her frailties, and he loves her in spite of them and wants to take care of her." Maachah paused and her voice shifted to grayer tones. "Nathan has not yet spoken to his aunt. He desires to accompany Salmon today to speak with Enan. He is sure of Enan's blessing, but he fears Miriam's reaction."

"And with good reason," Rahab said. "Do you remember how she opposed the marriage of Elimelech and Naomi? She has never cared for Nathan's happiness, so she has no cause to agree to his marriage." Seeing the trouble in Maachah's eyes, Rahab hurried to try to say something encouraging. "But Miriam seems to be happy these days with her grandson. Perhaps she will be agreeable."

Enan gave his loving assent to Nathan's desire to marry Jemimah. He could not arrange the wedding in the customary way, so shouted agreements were reached with Jasper, as they had been with Elimelech. Rahab expected to hear from Miriam as the plans for the marriage were made. But Miriam had found a niche for herself caring for little Mahlon, and she seemed totally oblivious to Nathan's coming marriage.

For a week before the marriage Rahab and Maachah cooked and prepared the feast. On the day of the wedding Rahab helped Maachah ready her brood and they went to the feast at Enan's house. Great mirth filled the rooms and Rahab was so happy for the solemn young man and his fragile bride. Nathan left his bride's side and approached Rahab. Drawing her aside he asked in whispers, "Where is my Aunt Miriam?" Only then did Rahab recognize why all was so pleasant at the marriage feast. Miriam was absent.

Rahab shrugged and answered, "I will find her."

After a quick search of the large rooms, Rahab exited onto the street and walked toward the home of Elimelech and Naomi, who were both at the marriage feast. "Perhaps Miriam stayed at home to care for Mahlon so that Naomi could enjoy the feast," Rahab told herself. Yet she feared a deeper cause, knowing that Mahlon was full old enough to attend a marriage feast.

Rahab pushed the gate open and found Miriam sitting in the shade of the courtyard watching her small grandson play. Miriam looked up quickly and her face suddenly steeled. Rahab tried to smile and seated herself on a seat facing Miriam.

"Nathan missed you at his wedding feast," she said quietly to Miriam.

"Nathan?" Miriam asked, raising her eyebrows. "Nathan would not miss me."

Miriam's answer puzzled Rahab. Could Miriam think that her lack of love for Nathan was reciprocal? Rahab quickly prayed for wisdom and felt a strength as she spoke.

"Yes, Miriam, Nathan missed you. He wishes for you to share in his happiness."

"I have never derived happiness from Nathan. Why should I now?" Miriam asked.

"Not your happiness, Miriam. Nathan's happiness. He's very happy today and he wishes for your presence at his wedding," Rahab answered her.

"But I cannot," Miriam answered sweetly, looking toward small Mahlon. "I must see to my grandchild."

"I will stay with Mahlon if you do not wish to take him to the wedding feast. But please go, Miriam. Do this for Nathan."

Miriam sat motionless, staring at the playing child. Then

she slowly turned to Rahab, the familiar smirk in place upon her features. "I most certainly will not leave my grandchild," she pronounced, "with a harlot."

The familiar weight of heart at the cruel words tempted Rahab to a harsh reply. But breathing a silent prayer she instead said, "I do regret that you feel that way after so many years, Miriam. I am sorry, too, that you will not go to Nathan." Rahab stood and turned to leave, but was stopped by Miriam's voice.

"And do you really think that Nathan will suffer at all if I am not there?"

"I do," Rahab answered, and as she left she caught a glimpse of Miriam's face set in a cruel smile.

Jemimah took up residence in the wide house of Enan, radiating her happiness about her. Maachah worried for her health as she busied herself about the household tasks. Rahab's concern, however, was that Miriam would return to her house and turn her wrath upon the young woman who had come into her home. For the moment Miriam seemed content to remain at Elimelech's home, caring for Mahlon, and sending her tokens of love to Enan from there.

Boaz was no longer a child. At fifteen he was tall and firm and bore a strong resemblance to his father. He loved to work at Salmon's side throughout each day, returning home in the evening tired and happy. Rahab would often sit and watch him talking and would joy in the man he was becoming. Salmon told her that he and Boaz talked often of Enan and his terrible disease. They prayed together in the fields, and Boaz's faith that the Lord would someday heal Enan amazed even Salmon.

Evenings had ever been a time of teaching in their home, Salmon retelling the wondrous stories of God and His people, Boaz listening and learning. Boaz could recite most of the law of God, and as her son learned, Rahab also learned. Boaz had learned to write in a neat, close hand the script of the Hebrews. In the fields Salmon had taught his son to count and calculate, and at his age Boaz could already bargain well in the market place. Often in the evening the house would ring with two strong voices and Rahab's sweet treble as the songs of God's people were sung.

Rahab's long black hair was becoming streaked with gray. Her face had lost its firm youthfulness and wrinkles appeared around her eyes. She knew that she was aging and that she would bear Salmon no more children. But she sincerely thanked the Lord for her son.

Another son, Chilion, was born to Elimelech and Naomi. Miriam seemed to have found a fresh burst of youth and truly seemed happy. She could be seen carrying her new grandchild in her arms, the small Mahlon scurrying along beside her, grasping her skirts. When Rahab chanced to meet her, Miriam would babble excitedly about her grandchildren. However, Rahab detected a dark shadow lingering about the edges and assumed that it was caused by the horror of Enan's burdens.

Maachah came to Rahab's house one morning early, joy and sorrow mingled upon her face. Rahab escorted her to the courtyard, where they sat among the fragrant blossoms. Rahab asked after Maachah's many children and Maachah burst into tears.

"Maachah, whatever is wrong?" Rahab asked, putting her arms around Maachah's shoulders.

Maachah spoke brokenly through her tears. "Jemimah is with child! She is so ill, like you were when you carried Boaz. But my Jemimah is not strong. Oh, Rahab I fear for her!"

Rahab pursed her lips, remembering the days and months of illness and weakness, and her own fears for her child. "The Lord brought me through it, Maachah. He can bring Jemimah through, too. I will go to her and see what I can do to help."

Because she knew the agony of illness while carrying a child, Rahab devoted herself to the care of Jemimah. Often nothing could be done but to sit and speak comfortingly to her. Jemimah tried to continue caring for herself as normal, but she finally resigned to lie in bed and let others care for her. She grew daily weaker and thinner, until she seemed to be scarcely alive.

With all of her hard work to aid Jemimah, Rahab often fell into bed at night exhausted, but she never forgot to pray. One evening Rahab followed Salmon onto the rooftop, where they stood together watching the night sky and the soft movement of night around them. She sighed and leaned her arms on the battlement, laying her head upon them.

"Jemimah is so ill, Salmon. I pray for her almost constantly. Yet, months have passed and she only grows worse. Her child is growing, but Jemimah wastes away. How long, Salmon, before the Lord will help her?"

Salmon remained silent and motionless beside her, but she saw that his eyes were closed. She waited in the darkness until she wondered if he had forgotten her question or fallen asleep. Finally he spoke, his voice quivering slightly.

"I have prayed now for years for the healing of Enan. I will admit to you, Rahab, that my faith often falters. I wonder if the Lord will ever heal him. I know that the Lord is able. At the first I knew that He would heal Enan. Now I don't know."

In all the years that Rahab had known and loved the man standing beside her she had never heard him speak as now. His was always the faith and the strength, unshaken, unquestioned. Rahab put an arm around Salmon's shoulders and leaned her head against him. Together they stood, each with a friend in desperate need of God's intervention, each with a deep, unspoken prayer in the heart.

One weary day as Rahab stood in the sunshine hanging clothes to dry for Jemimah, Miriam appeared and stood watching her. Rahab felt her presence before seeing her and turned to face her. She merely said, "Hello, Miriam," and returned to the laundry. Upon finishing she walked toward the house, but Miriam hurried ahead and barred her way.

"Why are you here?" Miriam demanded.

"To help care for Jemimah," Rahab said. "Why are you here?"

"This is my house," Miriam returned haughtily. "And now that I am here you may leave."

Rahab continued toward the house until Miriam's shrill voice stopped her. "I said you may leave!" Miriam screamed.

"I will say farewell to Jemimah," Rahab said and entered the house amidst Miriam's protests.

Miriam, who had not seemed to notice that Nathan had a wife was suddenly overcome with concern for Jemimah. She received Maachah's company in caring for the ailing young woman, but Rahab was no longer welcome.

A cold wind was blowing across the hills of Bethlehem and Rahab knew that winter would soon be upon them. She thanked the Lord once again for the warmth and safety of her house against the winter storms. With a brisk fire crackling on the hearth Rahab began to knead the bread for their supper. The heavy burdens with which she lived seemed to lift and her heart felt light and happy. Salmon and Boaz would return soon from the fields to sit before the fire and eat. She loved them both and they brought her so much happiness. She hummed a tune as she turned the dough in her hands, and she found that she was smiling.

The door opened and closed quickly with a rush of cold. Rahab looked up with the smile still on her face to see Salmon standing alone by the door. He did not move toward the fire or remove his cloak, so she hurried to him, rubbing her hands on her apron.

"Is something wrong, Salmon? Where is Boaz?" she asked, looking toward the door.

"He is safe," Salmon said. He did not remove his cloak, but he led Rahab to the fire to sit beside him. His hands were cold as he held hers and spoke. "Boaz learned of your days in Jericho, today," Salmon said softly. "He left the field alone and did not return."

All the light of the day was suddenly dark around Rahab. A hard ache began to grow and engulf her as her mind whirred with Salmon's news. She closed her eyes and struggled to find words for the questions in her heart.

"How?...Who?" was all that she could ask.

"Boaz was told today that Jemimah is so ill and near the point of death because you were allowed to care for her," Salmon said sadly. After a pause he said, "No, he was told today that Jemimah is so ill because a harlot was allowed to care for her."

At the bitter word Rahab looked into Salmon's eyes and breathed, "Miriam!"

Salmon rubbed her warm hands and nodded his head. His voice was soft and even when he spoke. "She told him your history from her point of view."

"How did Boaz happen to speak with Miriam, today?" Rahab asked, the anguish for her son just beginning to dawn.

"The fields we sowed bordered those of Elimelech and she brought his noon meal today," Salmon said.

"Oh, Salmon! That woman is hateful beyond imagining!" Rahab let herself weep as Salmon sat quietly with her. She stopped crying suddenly and looked through red eyes into Salmon's troubled brown ones. "We should have told Boaz long ago, ourselves, Salmon," she said.

"I have told him long ago, " Salmon answered.

"You have told him? Then why...?"

Salmon interrupted saying, "I told him that you worshipped a heathen god in the city of Jericho. I told him how the Lord God used you to help Enan and me to escape. I told him that the Lord spared your life and those of your family because of your faith in God."

"You did not tell him that I was a harlot?" Rahab asked.

"You are not a harlot, Rahab, and Boaz did not need to be told."

Rahab took a deep breath. "But Miriam thought he needed to be told," she said. "Where could he have gone, Salmon," Rahab asked, suddenly concerned only for Boaz.

"He likes to sit in the caves and think sometimes. He could be there," Salmon told her.

Pulling her cloak closely around her, Rahab hurried through the cold darkness of Salmon's fields to the hillside of the caves. Salmon, carrying a torch, could not keep up with her quick pace and called for her to slow for him.

When they reached the crest of the hill they found Boaz standing against the stone wall, watching their ascent. Salmon lit a fire in the mouth of the cave and placed two large, smooth stones near the fire. Then he retired into the darkness to wait and pray.

Rahab approached her tall son and put her hands gently on his arms, which were crossed on his chest. She saw in the firelight the streaks on his face and the pain in his brown eyes, so like Salmon's, but he would not look at her.

"Boaz," she said softly. "Please look at me."

Boaz looked down before looking into her eyes. As he gazed at her Rahab suddenly felt a stranger to the tall youth before her. But she smiled slightly and searched for words. Salmon would know exactly what to say, but this was her task alone.

Rahab nodded toward the fire and said, "Will you sit by me near the fire?"

Boaz stood firm, so Rahab stood before him in the cold wind and said through the tears that were stinging her eyes, "Miriam told you some things today that hurt you, Boaz. What she told you was true. But I would like you to let me tell you myself."

Boaz had continued to look at her without a word. Now he gently pulled his arm away from Rahab and brushed away a tear that had found its way down to his nose. He sniffed and spoke in a cracked voice. "Is it true, Mother? Were you a harlot in the city of Jericho?"

The word pressed hard against Rahab's heart as she answered her son. "Yes, Boaz. I was a temple harlot, a priestess of the gods Baal and Ashteroth." Boaz looked away, but Rahab spoke on gently. "I believed as I was taught by my parents and the priests of the gods that the gods demanded certain sacrifices of us to prevent their wrath against our people. I dedicated my life fully to Baal and Ashteroth, but I was not happy. Although I was well known I was lonely and friendless but for an old Egyptian man, named Zaphnath." The memories were very painful, but Rahab continued. "He told me of a time in Egypt, when the God of the Hebrews sent horrible destruction upon the land and then led His people across the Red Sea on dry land. When we in Jericho heard that the Hebrews had entered our land and had defeated two kings, we feared greatly."

"When Enan and your father came to my house seeking refuge from the soldiers of the King of Jericho, I knew that the Lord God of the Hebrews had sent them. I believed what they told me, that the Lord would destroy the city. I believed that the Lord would spare me and all that would be in my house with me. The Lord brought my family to me. The Lord spared us from the destruction of Jericho."

The hard lines of Boaz's face had softened and he was again looking into her eyes.

"I didn't deserve the salvation of the Lord," she continued. "But in His great mercy He saved me alive." She paused, praying for the right words. "I am not a harlot, Boaz. The Lord has forgiven my sin and made me a new woman. Can you forgive me, Boaz, for what I was?"

Boaz suddenly put his arms around his mother and sobbed against her. "Mother, please forgive me. You didn't wrong me. I guess I was just so shocked when Aunt Miriam told me. And she blamed Jemimah's illness on you. I'm sorry, Mother, please forgive me."

When Boaz finally released his grasp, Salmon, Rahab, and Boaz walked together toward their home, leaving the fire burning at the mouth of the cave.

CHAPTER 11

Redeemed

The mourners stood in a cluster about the grave, somber, some weeping, a few sobbing in loud wails. Rahab stood with Salmon near Jasper and Maachah, sharing their grief, yet unable to ease it. Nathan knelt at the graveside, bowing his body over the silent reminder of his precious Jemimah. Miriam stood behind him, gently rocking the motherless infant Elzabad. Enan had left his solitary retreat and stood apart from the mourners, bearing even his grief alone.

As the mourners began to walk slowly away from the grave Miriam approached Rahab. Miriam's eyes glared at her with a wild stare. She stood before Rahab and, clutching the sleeping child to her with one arm, stretched the other toward Rahab, her finger almost touching Rahab's nose.

"It was because of you!" Miriam hissed. "You marred our family with your presence in our home! You are the cause of her death!" Miriam's voice had risen to a scream and the babe in her arms awoke and began to cry.

Rahab felt weak and empty. Jemimah had died. The Lord had not delivered her. Rahab's heart was broken and aching. And before her stood the hatred of Miriam in animated fury. She looked at Miriam without response and turned to leave.

"You, Harlot! You are the cause of her death!" Miriam shrieked.

"No, Aunt Miriam, you are wrong." Rahab stopped her retreat and turned at the voice, to see Boaz standing before Miriam.

"My mother had no more to do with Jemimah's death than you, Aunt Miriam. The Lord God of Heaven chose to bless us with Jemimah for only a few years, and now he has taken her from her suffering." Boaz spoke evenly, softly, with apparent love for the "aunt" before him. Rahab marvelled at how like Salmon he was.

"Yes, the Lord God of Heaven has chosen to leave me with another child to raise that I do not desire," Miriam said, quieting.

"You need not raise Nathan's son," Salmon spoke. "We will take him."

Miriam turned toward Salmon and looked at him silently. Then, turning toward Rahab Miriam said, "I will raise the child for Nathan." She was in control of her voice, now. Holding her head high she strode away from them.

"Thank you, Boaz," Rahab said as he joined her and Salmon to walk home. He smiled faintly at her, but did not answer.

Although the sun still shone in the sky, the sunshine had departed from life. Maachah's grief was heavy and Jasper seemed to age rapidly. Maachah's children moved about quietly, each mourning in his private way. Rahab wanted to help them, but the loss was a heavy blow to them.

Nathan, who had known much lonely grief in his life, quietly went about his tasks. The smiles that Jemimah had brought into his life were there no longer. He held his tiny son in silence and then returned to his somber existence. He began to visit Enan frequently, sitting or standing nearer than thought safe, yet desiring Enan's company and comfort above all else.

Maachah and Rahab walked together to Miriam's house to see the small Elzabad. While accompanying Maachah, Rahab could enter the home peacefully. She sat quietly while Maachah held her grandson lovingly, and watched Miriam. A dark shadow hung about the room that felt oppressive to Rahab. The shadow seemed to follow Miriam as she moved, spreading a gloom about her.

One cold, windy day when Rahab saw Miriam walk quickly past the well she left her waterpot behind to follow. Keeping behind her, hopeful of not being detected, Rahab waited in the shadows and watched as Miriam went into the shop of the apothecary. When Miriam emerged she pulled her robe around her tightly and proceeded away from the town toward the mountains beyond. Rahab paused only for a moment, remembering her waterpot and her tasks awaiting her, but pushing the thoughts aside she continued to pursue Miriam.

The path which Miriam took became steep and the footing difficult. Jagged stones made the path slippery, although it was dry. Roots protruded from the ground, causing Rahab to watch each step to avoid tripping. Several times she almost lost sight of Miriam, but managed to follow her through a narrow valley and to the crest of the mountain. There Rahab stayed behind a tree and watched in horror.

Three men in flowing robes stood atop a raised, circular platform. Upon this platform was a smooth, black image of stone. Rahab recognized it as an image of Baal. Next to it was a tall yet narrow altar. Miriam approached the altar slowly. She mounted the steps to the platform and knelt low before the image, her hands grasping the smooth stone. She then raised herself slightly and laid a kiss upon the hem of the stone garment.[85] When Miriam arose she offered a packet to the men.

Rahab gasped as the truth dawned. These men were priests, but not of the true God. Miriam was offering incense upon the altar to Baal! Rahab was clutched by fearful memories as she watched the ceremony. Although it was still daylight, the mountaintop seemed dark with oppression beneath the tall green trees. Rahab turned and fled as quickly as she could back down the perilous path.

At the foot of the mountain Rahab waited. Finally she saw the form of Miriam descending the path. Rahab waited until Miriam was almost beside her and then stepped out to bar her way. Miriam gave a startled cry and stopped abruptly.

---

[85] I Kings 19:18

"Tell me where you have been. Tell me what you have done," Rahab demanded.

Miriam looked at her curiously and replied, "Why is it your business where I have been?" Rahab noticed that the dread title was not added. She felt the tension in Miriam's voice.

"I followed you to the grove at the top of the mountain," Rahab told her.

Miriam stood silently with the cold wind whipping her skirts. Her eyes were fierce and her graying hair was straying in wild wisps about her face. "Then you know where I have been," she said coldly. "You know what I have done."

"Why?" Rahab cried with anger and confusion.

Miriam looked steadily into Rahab's eyes. "You cannot imagine the agony of my life! You do not know how it is to have a husband dying for years of leprosy!" Miriam paused but did not take her fierce gaze from Rahab. "I go to the mountain to offer incense and implore the gods for Enan."

Miriam looked away and tried to pass Rahab in the path, but Rahab grasped her arms firmly and would not let her go. Miriam did not struggle. She stopped and stood still, but would not look back into Rahab's eyes.

"The Lord God of Heaven and earth alone can help Enan. He only has the power to heal him and bring him back to health," Rahab said. "And to you," she added. "Pray to Him, Miriam. Beseech the true and living God for Enan."

Miriam's eyes, still fierce, looked back into Rahab's pleading ones. "Salmon has prayed all these years for Enan, even taking upon him that horrible vow," Miriam said.

"I know," Rahab said softly.

"Has it helped? Has it given my Enan his life back?" Miriam asked accusingly. She did not wait for a reply. "No! Praying to your God has not helped him. He has lived too many years in his torment. I must find a way. I am willing to do anything to help him."

Rahab did not release Miriam. The two women stood in

the cold wind, one steeled in bitterness, the other weeping.

"Why do you care, Rahab? What is it to you if I implore the gods for Enan?" Miriam finally asked.

"Because your idolatry could bring God's wrath upon us, as He promised when you first entered this land,"[86] Rahab answered.

Miriam's eyebrows raised and she bore a look of, "I thought as much."

But Rahab continued, "And I care for your sake, Miriam." Rahab heard the words she spoke and knew that it was true. She really did care. She stood in the cold wind facing her bitter enemy, and she knew that she loved Miriam.

"For my sake? Why? I have always held you in contempt," Miriam said.

"Yes. And I have felt that contempt, and it has hurt."

Miriam's hard face smiled slightly.

"Miriam, the Lord has thrown our lives together because of the men we love. I am part of your life and you are part of mine. Miriam, Enan loves and trusts the Lord God of heaven and earth, surely you know that," Rahab said kindly.

Miriam dropped her eyes to her hands which were reddening in the frigid air. When she raised her eyes to Rahab's, tears brimmed and spilled over, running down along her nose.

"Yes," she said quietly. "Enan's faith in his God has not been shaken, even though he has been stricken with leprosy and has lived a life of agony and loneliness." She looked full at Rahab and only grief and despair were in her eyes. "But I don't know his God, your God. I cannot know Him."

"You can, Miriam, " Rahab said softly. Then, wondering if she had been heard above the whistling of the wind, she repeated louder, "You can!"

"How can I know your God?" Miriam asked.

---

[86]Deuteronomy 27:15; 28:15

The chill wind still blew about them forcibly, but Rahab was no longer cold. She felt warmed from the inside as she sat beside Miriam upon a mossy rock and told her the story of how she herself had come to know and trust the Lord. She reminded Miriam of many of the wondrous works the Lord had done for His people. Then she said kindly, "Faith is to take the Lord God at His word. Believe what He has said. Trust in His love for you. Love Him."

Miriam wept.

That evening, sitting by the warm fire, Rahab told Salmon the events of the day. He wiped his eyes with the back of his hand and leaned his elbows on his knees, gazing into the flames.

"So the Lord has finally taught you to love Miriam," he said. "And He has finally taught Miriam to love Him. Enan will be very happy when he hears this." He paused and then continued, his voice saddening, "But now that we know about the altar in the grove on the mountain, it must be reported to the judges and officers at the city gate. If we allow it to continue we are guilty ourselves."

He looked into Rahab's eyes for a moment. Then he asked gently, "Did anyone else besides you see Miriam go to the mountain to offer?"

"I don't know," she answered.

"If there are but two witnesses to one's idolatry," Salmon told her, "we are responsible to report that one to the elders at the gate. Such a one must be stoned to death."[87]

Rahab's face blanched as she looked into Salmon's eyes and said in dismay, "I saw Miriam. Must I..."

"No," Salmon interrupted. "A person will be condemned to death for idolatry only if there are two or more witnesses."

Rahab closed her eyes and sighed, relieved. "Thank You, Lord, that I followed Miriam alone to the mountain. I would not

---

[87]Deuteronomy 17:2-6

want her to be stoned to death. She now knows the error of her way and she trusts in You."

Salmon met with the men of Bethlehem at the gate of the city. He soberly told them the tale as they shook their heads and commented to one another. Then, with Rahab leading them up along the steep and treacherous path, they followed bearing mallets, ropes, axes and coals of fire. As they moved along they were joined by others of the city, men, women, and children.

When they topped the mountain, most of the people stopped in dismay, seeing before them the grove and idol, watching the priests of Baal as they offered incense upon the altar. Attracted by the noise, the priests looked toward the advancing crowd and suddenly scattered, running between the trees of the grove. The men with Salmon ran after the priests, shouting excitedly. When they returned to the altar they led the priests of Baal bound with ropes. While several men stood watch over the priests, the others pulled down the idol of Baal and beat it to dust with mallets. The altar and circular platform were also pulled apart and beaten to dust. The trees of the grove were felled and pulled into a heap upon the dust of the altar and image. There the men of Bethlehem burned the grove. All the people who had climbed the mountain stood in the cold evening air and watched the flames ascend, the only sound the crackling of the flames against the green wood.

Then the priests of Baal were led to the crest of the mountain and the people gathered in a circle around them. Memories of her first days in the camp of Israel at Gilgal returned to Rahab as she and the people of the city of Bethlehem obeyed the Word of the Lord in stoning the priests of Baal and covering their dead bodies beneath a heap of stones.[88]

When next Maachah and Rahab visited the baby Elzabad at the home of Miriam, Rahab no longer felt the dark shadows

---

[88]Deuteronomy 17:7

lurking about Miriam. Nathan sat beside Maachah, sweetly reminiscing about their dear Jemimah, helping each other's hearts to heal.

Miriam called Rahab to her, a first in her life. "I have prayed for Enan's healing," she said. "I have asked the Lord God to bring him back to me." She paused. "How long must I pray before Enan will be healed?"

Rahab had no answer. Salmon had prayed for years for Enan's release from leprosy. But she didn't wish to shake Miriam's newfound faith in God. "Help me to answer her," she prayed.

"Faith is to believe that the Lord will work in His own perfect time," Rahab said. "To trust is to believe in His love, for you, for Enan."

Miriam looked at Rahab for a moment and then said quietly, "Then faith in God does not guarantee Enan's recovery."

"Faith in God is not a magical thing, which to have insures answers to your prayers," Rahab said carefully. "Prayer is the petition to our all powerful and all loving Father. He knows what is best for us, and He answers us in His love."

"But it couldn't possibly be the best for Enan to suffer all his life with leprosy," Miriam said. "It cannot be God's will for him to die of leprosy."

Rahab could find no words to answer Miriam's plea. She looked at Miriam and for the first time noticed the gaunt, thinness of her features and the hollow sadness in her eyes. Following an impulse that was strange to her, Rahab reached her hand out to Miriam's. Miriam did not pull her hand away as Rahab thought probable. "Would you like to pray now for Enan, together?"

Rahab felt Miriam tremble. Her enemy of many years stood hand in hand with her, and Rahab knew that the hatred for her had vanished from Miriam's heart. Miriam had come to trust the Lord God of heaven and earth just as Rahab, many years ago had turned from idolatry to trust Him. The two women who had ever been enemies now found a bond of love as they knelt together in their common faith in God.

Rahab stopped from hanging clothing on the line and looked about her courtyard. The sun streamed down warm and bright upon the flowers which tumbled over the wall and crept into every corner. Birds chirped and sang in the treetops and Rahab shaded her eyes to watch a pair of birds flit to the edge of their nest and push insects into the open mouths of their babies.

Rahab was suddenly interrupted from her thoughts by the quick grasp of Boaz's strong hands on her shoulders and a whiskery kiss against her cheek. She turned around to see him smiling down at her from the height of his twenty years. She started to speak, but he interrupted her with a jovial question.

"How would you like to take a trip to Shiloh?" he asked.

Startled by the unexpected question, Rahab said, "Now? Why?" They had all taken the journey to the Tabernacle only a few weeks before to offer the sacrifices of the Feast of Weeks.

Boaz tried to wear a somber countenance through his smiles. "My father will go to the Tabernacle to conclude the days of his separation as a Nazarite before the Lord."

Rahab knit her brow in confusion. "But, Enan," was all that she could say before Boaz burst into laughter and hugged her, spinning her around, and shouting,

"Enan is healed!"

When Boaz released her from his spinning grip she fumbled for the stone bench and sat down. Boaz stood before her with his arms folded across his chest and grinned, while nodding his head. "Yes, mother, it's true."

Everyone in Bethlehem came to see the caravan off to Shiloh. Men, women, and children chatted gaily as they accompanied Enan and his family along the road. They stopped and turned back only after they had walked several miles from the city. Tents, food, and other necessities were packed into donkey drawn carts. Jasper and Maachah walked along with their children who were going on the trip. Enan walked along surrounded closely by his family. Miriam clung to him, happy and smiling in the sunshine. Elimelech and his family walked beside him. On the other side Nathan held Elzabad's hand as they walked, or hoisted him onto his shoulders when he became weary. Rahab smiled at the joy radiating from Nathan as he walked along, conversing with Enan. Salmon, Boaz, and Rahab walked along together, following Enan's family. Friends and acquaintances wished them well as they waved and returned to Bethlehem.

The weariness of the journey to Shiloh faded quickly in the morning light as Enan stood before Eleazar outside the city of Shiloh, at the side of a running stream. Eleazar, now ancient in years, moved slowly through the motions as he examined Enan to establish that he was indeed healed of his leprosy.

Eleazar then asked for the two clean birds for Enan's cleansing. Elimelech stepped forward to help with this part of the ceremony. Eleazar commanded Elimelech to kill one of the birds in a vessel of clay over the running water. Eleazar then took cedar wood, scarlet, and hyssop which Enan had brought, and dipped them, as well as the living bird, into the blood of the bird that had been killed. Eleazar sprinkled the blood upon Enan seven times and pronounced him clean. Everyone was smiling as Eleazar released the live bird in the open field.

Enan and Miriam returned to their tent, where Enan shaved all the hair from his body. He then washed himself and his clothes.[89]

Rahab, Boaz, and Salmon then went to the door of the Tabernacle of the Congregation. There Salmon gave to the priest, Phineas, the son of Eleazar, his offering to the Lord. It was a male lamb of the first year for a burnt offering, an ewe lamb of the first year for a sin offering, and an unblemished ram for a peace offering. He also offered a basket of cakes made of

---

[89]Leviticus 14:2-8

fine flour and oil and wafers of unleavened bread anointed with oil, and drink offerings.

The priest sacrificed these offerings before the Lord. Then Salmon shaved his head there before the Tabernacle and put the hair into the fire beneath the peace offering. Rahab watched as the long, heavy tresses fell away from Salmon's head, and she saw a smile of relief cross his face, as he stood straighter and taller in his newfound freedom.

Phineas took the sodden shoulder of the ram and one of the unleavened cakes and one unleavened wafer out of the basket and put them into Salmon's hands. The priest then waved them before the Lord for a wave offering, signifying that the vow of Salmon's separation unto the Lord as a Nazarite was fulfilled.[90]

When they had returned to their tent Salmon repeatedly exulted in the loss of his heavy knot of hair, and Boaz teased him for his baldness.

Enan could not enter into the city of Shiloh, but had to wait seven days to complete his cleansing. On the seventh day Enan had to once again shave off all his hair, beard and eyebrows and wash himself and his clothes in water. On the day following he took two unblemished male lambs and one ewe lamb of the first year to the door of the Tabernacle. He also brought fine flour and oil.

Eleazar the priest presented Enan and his offerings before the Lord at the door of the Tabernacle of the Congregation and there waved them for a wave offering before the Lord. He killed one of the male lambs for the trespass offering beside the altar and caught some of the blood in a bowl. This blood Eleazar put on the tip of Enan's right ear, on his right thumb, and his right big toe.

Eleazar then dipped his right finger into the oil, which he had poured into his left hand. He sprinkled the oil seven times

---

[90]Numbers 6:13-21

before the Lord and put oil on the tip of Enan's right ear, the thumb of his right hand, and on his right big toe. The remainder he poured upon Enan's head.

After the trespass offering, the sin offering was made, and atonement was made for Enan. The burnt offering was then killed and burned on the altar with the meal offering.

At the conclusion of the ceremonies Eleazar pronounced Enan clean.[91] Miriam was the first to embrace him in rapture and was followed by each one, exulting in the blessing of the Lord upon his life.

As they walked along the road returning to Bethlehem, Rahab looked at those about her and smiled. Jasper and Maachah walked along chatting with Nathan, the small Elzabad astride his father's strong shoulders. She watched Nathan nod and smile. Nathan, who had suffered so much with such strength, had now found a happy peace in the healing of Enan.

Elimelech and Naomi, Mahlon and Chilion walked beside Enan and Miriam in a close pack. Rahab watched Enan's bald and beardless head turning toward each of his family in turn to hear their excited messages of love and just to view them. Rahab thanked the Lord that Enan, whose faith had ever been strong in his God, could now embrace and once again live among his loved ones.

Rahab and Boaz each walked at the side of Salmon. Rahab shaded her eyes to look up, and marvelled at the similarity in the men she loved. Salmon had covered his bald head as a shield from the sun, which lit the sky and trees, flowers and grass, with a brilliance that Rahab could feel. She wondered if she could hold one bit more joy without bursting and suddenly a hymn of joy sprang from her lips. She sang alone for a moment, and then one by one her fellow travellers joined her in praising the Lord.

---

[91] Leviticus 14:9-20

CHAPTER 12

Bereaved

Rahab straightened her back in her garden and shaded her eyes to search the row of trees to her right and the hills to her left. A shuffling behind her tightened a knot in her stomach and she whirled around to find Miriam standing between rows of cucumbers. Miriam's face was twisted in sadness, and Rahab's alarm melted into sudden concern.

"I didn't mean to startle you," said Miriam.

"Salmon's fields were raided twice just last week," Rahab answered. "I do want to save my garden from marauders." Letting go the handle of her hoe, Rahab stepped closer to Miriam and asked softly, "Have they decided to leave after all?"

Miriam could only nod her head as she began to weep. Leaving her hoe behind, Rahab took Miriam's hand and led her from the garden. The two women walked along the road and climbed toward the city in silence, but for the sniffing of Miriam. When they reached the gate of the city, they sat in the shade beside the well.

"I feel that it is my fault," Miriam said sadly.

"Elimelech has decided to take his family away to Moab to escape the famine we suffer because of our marauding enemies. How could that be your fault?" Rahab asked.

"The Lord told us at the beginning in this land that we would be given into the hands of our enemies if we turned from Him to idols. The famine we now suffer is because of me. Because I turned to idols," Miriam said as she broke into tears afresh.

Rahab sat quietly for a moment, watching those who passed in and out through the gate of the city, which was now guarded by walls, tall and strong. She did not look at Miriam when she spoke.

"Yes, it is because you turned to idols," she said. Then,

looking straight into Miriam's eyes she added, "But not only you, Miriam. So many of Israel have turned from the true and living God to worship idols. That's why we sow and our enemies reap. That's why we suffer famine." Then, reaching to take Miriam's hand again she said, "But then you didn't know the true and living God as you do now. His mercy is great, Miriam. He has forgiven you."

"Then why must my son leave if God has forgiven me?" Miriam asked through her tears.

"I cannot answer that," Rahab told her. "Perhaps Elimelech's faith is shaken because of our troubles. But, Miriam, you must keep trusting in the goodness of the Lord."

Elimelech's family and friends walked sadly from the city with him as he and Naomi left with their two tall sons to sojourn in the land of Moab. Elimelech embraced his father and his mother and promised them that they would return as soon as things were better there in Bethlehem.

Those who had accompanied them out of the city stood atop a rise and watched them leave, the only sound the squeaking of the wheels of the oxcart carrying their belongings.

As Rahab and Maachah walked beside Miriam back toward the city of Bethlehem, neither knew what to say, how to comfort her. Enan came to Miriam's side and putting his arm around her shoulders, led her home.

Rahab and Maachah walked along together quietly, arm in arm, and Rahab detected a halting in Maachah's gait. "Are you alright?" she asked.

Maachah waved her comment away. "Just getting old, Rahab. We are not either of us young women anymore, you know!" They chuckled together over this fact, yet concern continued to gnaw at Rahab. By the time they reached Maachah's home, she was labouring with her breathing and Rahab gently made her lie down. Running back quickly to the men who were talking by the well, Rahab grasped Jasper's arm in alarm and told him to come quickly.

The day had been a weary one, watching Miriam's grief as her children went away. But Rahab was not prepared for what she found as she hurried back to Maachah's house, with Jasper close behind. There on the bed lay Maachah, an expression of sweet peace on her face, but instantly Rahab knew that the sweet spirit of Maachah was no longer there. Jasper entered the house to find Rahab weeping on the floor beside Maachah's still form.

Never, since the destruction of Jericho, had Rahab known such grief, such loneliness. Maachah had been her friend, her sister. Maachah had loved her from that first day after the awful night of her flight from Jericho. Maachah had accepted her from the first, and had taken her into her family when others scorned her. Maachah was a part of her life as real as Salmon and Boaz. And Maachah was gone.

After the body of Maachah had been lovingly laid in the grave, Rahab went to the caves on the hill, where so many years before Boaz had fled in his pain. She smiled when she saw the two large rocks still in the mouth of the cave where Salmon had placed them. Sitting upon one of them she stared out over the fields towards the forests on the mountains beyond. She loved this land. Her heart warmed in gratitude once more that God had spared her in His mercy from the demise of Jericho and had made her one of His own children. She breathed a prayer of thanks for Salmon, for Boaz, knowing that they were gifts from the Lord that she could never deserve.

A soft tread brought her from her reverie to find Miriam standing beside her. Rahab offered her the other stone as a seat.

"Rahab," Miriam said softly. "I, too, miss Maachah, but I know that you and she had a special love. I cannot know your pain. But I have known pain, Rahab. I know the empty and lonely heart of grief. There is nothing that I can say or do to ease the pain, but please know that I will pray that He Who can will ease it."

Rahab smiled at Miriam and the tears that came to her eyes were not those of sadness for the loss of Maachah, but tears of joy for the miracle before her, that her foe had become her friend.

The marauding bands from Mesopotamia increased their attacks. Fear haunted the city of Bethlehem as the foodstuffs were taken, and starvation seemed imminent. Final doom seemed ready to fall upon the city when one day a band of mounted soldiers approached the gate of Bethlehem. Rahab remembered the days so long ago when she and the city of Jericho had watched in fear as the army of Israel approached. But Bethlehem was a city of the Lord. Surely He would protect them. Yet her heart reminded her that the danger upon them was inevitable. God would keep His Word.

A captain of the band spoke with the elders at the gate. He was, he told them, an emissary from Chushanrishathaim, king of Mesopotamia. He promised that all scavenging upon the land would cease if a levy was paid regularly to Chushanrishathaim. To the frightened and hungry elders it seemed a small price to pay. So peace returned to Judah, but Israel served another king.

It was a normal day, like any other. Rahab had awakened to praise the Lord for His mercy upon her. After breakfast Salmon and Boaz had gone with Nathan and Enan to cut timber for a new barn which Enan was raising. Rahab had done her morning duties and then sat in the sunshine of her courtyard to spin linen thread at her wheel.

When Rahab answered the urgent knock at the door Boaz fell into her arms, weeping like a little child. He knelt before her in the doorway and grasped her waist, pressing his head against her. Dread filled her as she stroked his head and waited for him to quiet and tell her what broke his heart.

Finally Boaz looked up into Rahab's eyes and sobbed, "My father has been killed!" Rahab went limp and Boaz was suddenly on his feet, holding her, lifting her into the room and onto a couch.

"Mother," Boaz said softly, stroking her cheek. Rahab opened her eyes and looked into the red, puffy eyes of Boaz.

"Mother," he repeated gently, "Father was struck in the head with an axehead which slipped from the helve. Father is gone."

Rahab lay still, her mind in a fog. She understood the words of Boaz with her mind, but her heart had not yet comprehended. Boaz sat beside her, gently stroking her cheek while tears streamed down his own. Slowly the haze cleared and the truth stabbed its way into Rahab's heart. Salmon was gone! She must go see him. She must know.

Holding her arm tightly, Boaz guided his mother to the wooded lot where the men had felled trees all morning. There a group of people parted to let them through. Rahab had seen those she loved in death before, but never had it been Salmon. There he lay on the leaf strewn ground. The blood that had flowed from the gash in his head had turned his grayed hair rust, but an expression of peace rested on his handsome features. Rahab knelt beside him and touched his face. "Salmon," she said softly. But she knew he would not answer. She knew he would not open his deep brown eyes and smile at her. Salmon was gone to his God.

Rahab fell upon Salmon's prostrate form, weeping. "No, Salmon, no," her heart cried. "Don't be gone. I need you. How will I live, Salmon?" Boaz pulled her gently away and she watched as Enan and Nathan carefully lifted the lifeless body to carry it home.

Through constantly streaming tears Rahab washed and prepared the body of her beloved Salmon for his burial. Miriam came and silently helped her. When Rahab's grief overtook her, Miriam led her away to a seat, and Enan, Jasper, and Nathan completed the preparations.

As Salmon's body lay upon a bed awaiting burial, friends and family came to weep and mourn with Rahab. A warm arm went around Rahab's shoulders and she looked up to see Miriam's sad smile. Miriam sat beside her silently for a moment. Then she spoke in a wistful, faraway voice. "I will miss Salmon. He was so good to me. I never doubted that he cared for me.

And he was so good to Enan, suffering such discomfort and shame for so many years. He was a very unselfish man, Rahab. God was as real to him as if he and God walked and talked together each day." New tears began to course down Rahab's cheeks, but she did not mind Miriam speaking of Salmon. It was true. Salmon and God had walked and talked together each day.

Miriam tightened her grip on Rahab, and leaning toward her whispered, "Will you forgive me, Rahab?" Rahab looked at Miriam through her tears, but before she could speak Miriam said, "Please forgive me. You were also always kind to me. I know that I made it difficult for you." Miriam lowered her eyes as she whispered, "Forgive me for using that wretched title. I'm so sorry!" Miriam broke into weeping.

"I forgave you long ago, Miriam," Rahab answered.

Miriam continued to weep, so Rahab put her arm around Miriam's waist and said, "Please, Miriam."

"Enan and I must leave!" Miriam blurted out.

"Leave? Where? Why?" asked Rahab.

Miriam straightened herself and looked toward Salmon's body. "Don't you know, Rahab? It was Enan's axe which killed Salmon. We must flee tomorrow to the city of refuge at Hebron."

The awful reality of Miriam's words came to Rahab. She had not thought of to whom the axe belonged. It had been an accident, and no one was at fault.

"Please forgive Enan!" Miriam pleaded. "Please forgive us!"

"There is nothing to forgive, Miriam. Enan loved Salmon as a brother. And you need not leave and go to a city of refuge," Rahab said kindly.

"It is the law,"[92] Miriam told her. "We will leave in the morning."

---

[92]Numbers 35:22-25

It was very difficult for Rahab to watch her beloved Salmon be laid to rest beneath the earth, although she knew he was not there. As friends and family wept beside the grave, Boaz began to sing the song of joy which Rahab had sung on the return trip from Shiloh when Enan and Salmon had been released from grievous burdens. His strong, clear voice rang out over the fields and hills of Bethlehem. One by one others joined to sing, until a choir lifted the song to God.

After everyone else had left the tomb, Boaz stood apart as Rahab continued at the graveside. As evening came, he put a shawl over his mother's shoulders and retreated to stand apart again. Then Rahab felt someone beside her and turned to find Nathan sitting in silence. She knew not how long he had been there.

"Nathan," she said.

"We can never know each other's grief," Nathan said. "But I have known grief, Rahab. I only wish to share in yours. You need not talk. Please just know that I care." Nathan sat quietly beside her, but suddenly Rahab did not want to be silent. She wanted to talk to this young man who had also loved and lost his heart's desire.

"Thank you, Nathan. It's such a lonely feeling, isn't it?" She did not expect an answer to her question.

"When you are one, and part of you is torn away..." Nathan's voice drifted into the silence about them.

"More of my life was lived with Salmon than before God brought him into my life," Rahab said. "He's so much of my life I just don't know how I can live, now, without him."

Nathan sat in quiet for awhile before he spoke. "I cannot comprehend how those who do not trust the Lord can live when they are parted from one they love." Nathan paused, watching the glow of the western sky. "The hand of God alone lifts me up each morning and guides me through each day." He paused again and looked at Rahab, although she kept her eyes upon the grave before them. "And the Lord, in His infinite love, has taught me the many reasons that I have to rejoice in Him. The emptiness for Jemimah will remain with me all of my days. But I know a joy deep in my soul which comes from the Lord alone. That is how you, too, Rahab, will live without Salmon."

Rahab was thankful, now, for her spindle and loom. Yet, although her hands flew busily through the linen, and Arod was supplied with more than he could handle, her mind was left too free to think, to remember, to miss Salmon. Boaz worked hard each day but was never too tired to sit and talk with Rahab at the evening fire. As the days spun into one another and a commonness fell upon her life, Rahab began to sense a loneliness that she never would have thought possible. She missed the presence, the comradeship of Miriam.

Almost every evening was concluded with a rooftop vigil. Rahab leaned upon the battlement and prayed to the Lord of heaven and earth. She prayed for Boaz, Jasper and his children, Nathan and Elzabad. She would often grip the cold stones and plead on behalf of Enan and Miriam. They had known such hardship, and now separated by many miles from all family and friends, they suffered once more. And she prayed for the return of God's people to faith in Him, and their release from serving the king of Mesopotamia. Each evening, sometimes after hours of intercession, Rahab would go to her bed at peace with herself and God.

Evening was closing one more day, and Rahab brought the evening meal to Boaz to eat before the fire. She sat beside him, watching him eat until he slowed and looked away from the flames into her eyes. He smiled and leaned back.

"Mother," he said, "I would like very much to make a journey to Hebron. I have business there. I thought that perhaps you would like to accompany me."

Rahab was instantly on her feet, hugging him and laughing. "How did you know, Boaz, that I would desire to go?" she asked.

Boaz laughed, also, and said, "I desired your company,

Mother. And I know a woman in Hebron who will enjoy it, also."

Rahab was able no longer to walk the miles between the cities of Israel, so Boaz carried her to Hebron in a wagon drawn by oxen. Several months had passed since Enan and Miriam had left to sojourn in Hebron, but Rahab missed Miriam as though it had been much longer. They left in the early mists and rode silently until the sun rose. Boaz pulled the oxen to a halt and together they watched the hues brighten and then blend into the new day.

"When I was young," Boaz said, "my mother would not desire to cross the street to speak with Miriam. Today she rides many miles with me to visit her."

Rahab smiled and sighed. What Boaz said was true. God had wrought a miracle, indeed.

"When as a lad I would help my father work in the fields, he often stopped to pray for you and Aunt Miriam," Boaz said. He looked into Rahab's eyes. "I believe that God has answered his prayers. He prayed always that the Lord would teach you to love her."

"Yes," Rahab said softly, "The Lord has taught me to love her."

Boaz smiled broadly, his beard parting to show white teeth gleaming in the sun. "My father was so pleased and happy when you and Miriam became friends."

A warm peace washed over Rahab. She thanked the Lord of heaven and earth that she and Boaz could converse with ease about Salmon. She watched her son as he started the wagon forward again, noting how like Salmon he was. Not quite as tall as Salmon, Boaz was broader, stout and strong. But his eyes were Salmon's. And the love for his Lord so like his father's.

About an hour passed with pleasant words and memories, when Rahab looked Boaz squarely in the eye and asked, "Son, do you ever hope to marry; to give me grandchildren?"

Boaz watched the horizon before them, clucking to the oxen as they plodded steadily. "From a small lad I saw you and my father love each other dearly and joy in being married until you were parted," he said slowly. "I have never met a woman with whom I believed that I could share such a life. When I was young the young women seemed to me so frivolous. Now I am far past marrying one of the frivolous young ones, there are few unmarried women. I cannot desire to wed a woman put away from her husband. And perhaps there is reason those still single remain so." Boaz glanced sidelong at his mother and grinned.

"Your father had no brothers," Rahab reminded him. If you die childless, Boaz, your father's inheritance..."

"Mother!" Boaz interrupted her with a loud laugh. "I'm not yet decrepit. Would you have me marry a woman I cannot love wholly so that my father's inheritance will not be forfeited?"

Rahab laughed as well, but answered him. "It's important in the plan of God that a man give his inheritance to his son." She paused, remembering. "It was important to your father," she said.

Boaz looked into his mother's serious gaze. "Since it is important to God, Mother, He will see to it that I find the fit woman. I believe that. Don't you?"

Rahab replied only with a smile.

Hebron was a city of the Levites, whose inheritance was in the Lord alone, and the offerings of the people to the Lord. They had been given cities throughout the tribes of Israel as their homes, but the surrounding lands belonged to the tribes. The population of Hebron was a strange mixture of the holy and the marred. Those of the tribe of Judah who had caused the death of another by accident fled to Hebron for refuge. The elders of the city judged them as to their innocence, and they were allowed to live within the city walls in safety, forfeiting only their liberty to leave the city.

The days in Hebron fled all too quickly. Rahab and Miriam talked through the hours, each knowing that the memories of most of their years would not be mentioned, each thankful that all was now changed. Close embraces and many tears closed the visit as Rahab and Boaz began the homeward journey early on the morning following the Sabbath. They all knew that only such visits would allow them fellowship, for Enan could not traverse beyond the city walls.

Rahab was lost in thought when a rider ran by swiftly on the road to Hebron, leaving a cloud of choking dust.

"A courier with a message of great importance," Boaz told her.

Rahab and Boaz saw sadness veil the faces at the gate of Bethlehem. Boaz hailed an elder there.

"The high priest, Eleazar, has died," the man told him.

Boaz looked at his mother's face and watched her sadness at the news fade and a smile light her eyes as he said, "This sad news will be most welcome in Hebron, and in all of the cities of refuge throughout Israel. The death of the high priest signals liberty for the refugees."[93] He paused. "Enan and Miriam will be free to return to Bethlehem."

With Miriam's return, Rahab found herself often at Miriam's door. The comfort of Miriam's friendship far outweighed the pain of the years past. Rahab joyed as she watched the pleasure which Miriam found in Nathan's son, Elzabad, who was now almost grown. Yet Miriam spoke often of her two grandsons, Mahlon and Chilion, whom she missed dearly. She had received news that they had both married.

Joy had returned to the nation of Israel, for the Lord had delivered them from the oppression of the king of Mesopotamia by the hand of Othniel, the nephew of Caleb.[94] Miriam hoped that Elimelech and his family would soon return to Bethlehem.

One morning Rahab knocked upon Miriam's door and

---

[93]Numbers 35:25-28

[94]Judges 3:8-11

found her sitting red eyed and somber in her courtyard.

She looked at Rahab and whispered hoarsely, "Elimelech is dead!" Her grief pressed heavily upon her and Rahab felt its weight as she said, "Mahlon and Chilion are dead." She stared at a flower nodding in the breeze. "Why has the Lord smitten me thus?"

As Rahab comprehended Miriam's woeful words, she had no answer. She, too, watched the flowers bob gently in the sunshine. Her heart cried out to the Lord for words. "When Salmon went I, too, wondered, why. It is beyond our power to understand why, Miriam. But we must not doubt God's love for us." She paused, remembering the painful days when first she lived without Salmon. "I may have known God's love then, in a way I never knew when I had Salmon. The comfort of the Lord is His love."

"Enan has told me much the same," Miriam said. "He has ever found solace in the Lord." She looked at Rahab, her face wet with tears. "But these are my grandsons, my son!" she cried. "My children are dead!"

Miriam went to her bed and Enan lovingly cared for her. She would speak to visitors, but she never arose from her bed. Rahab went everyday to Miriam's home to cook and clean, and sit at Miriam's side.

Nathan passed quietly through the room one day as Rahab sat by Miriam's bed. Suddenly Miriam was sitting up straight, calling loudly to him. "Nathan! Nathan! Come to me."

Nathan approached the bedside silently. Rahab saw for the first time his grayed head and stooped shoulders. She had not noticed him aging. He was always Nathan, strong and silent, sad and lonely. He knelt beside his aunt and took her hand.

Miriam spoke in a thin voice. "You have been good to me, Nathan. You helped so much when Enan was sick. You have worked hard, and you kept your uncle's fields for him when we were in Hebron. You have been so good," she repeated. "But I have treated you so vilely! Forgive me, Nathan!" Nathan held her against him as she wept. "I could have joyed in you as a son. Instead I let bitterness toward God become bitterness toward you. If I could only start again, and change it all. Please forgive me, Nathan!"

Nathan closed his eyes and stroked her hair. When he spoke his voice was husky and choked. "Thank you, Aunt Miriam, for taking me into your home when my parents died. Thank you for food and shelter and clothing. Thank you for raising my son after Jemimah..." His voice broke in a sob.

"Will you forgive me, Nathan?" Miriam implored.

"Yes," Nathan said simply, and together they wept.

CHAPTER 13

Bride

Naomi had returned. The whole city of Bethlehem was stirred by her arrival. Naomi, who had left so many years ago with her husband and two sons to sojourn in Moab, had come again to Bethlehem a widow and childless. With her was a daughter in law, the wife of Mahlon, whose name was Ruth. Rahab's heart ached for Naomi, for bitterness consumed her. She had asked to be called no longer Naomi, but Mara, meaning "bitterness". [95]

Rahab slowly ascended the stairs to her rooftop perch, stopping three times to catch her breath before she reached the top. Her three score and twelve years prevented speed, but nothing could keep her from her favorite place of prayer and contemplation. A servant ascended the stairs at her side, ever ready to stop a fall, but Rahab dismissed her at the top. Grasping the battlement Rahab stood and surveyed Bethlehem. The city had changed so since her early days there. Many new houses had been erected and the wall surrounding them locked out danger, but also blocked Rahab's view of the fields beyond, where Salmon had laboured in love, and where Boaz now worked.

Bethlehem would never again be as it had been for Rahab, for Salmon was gone. Dear Maachah and the dear friendly Jasper had passed. Naomi's parents had died while she was in the land of Moab. And Rahab's beloved enemy, Miriam, had succumbed to her grief, followed shortly by Enan, ever faithful, ever trusting in his God. The people walking the streets below Rahab were young. Even Boaz was not considered a young man among them.

Rahab heard a commotion below and watched the

---

[95]Ruth 1:20

servants loading food into a cart for the noon meal of the labourers in the field of Boaz. Boaz, astride a tall black steed, accompanied the servants to the field, chatting with the driver. The cart wheels groaned beneath the load, for much provision was needed to feed the reapers in the large, vast fields of Boaz.

Without summoning a servant to assist her, Rahab descended her stairs slowly. She sat in her courtyard at her loom, but her stiff fingers would not allow much work, and she drifted into sleep in the warm sunshine.

"Mother." The warm voice and gentle nudge awakened Rahab. Boaz sat on the stone bench across from her, grinning as he had when young in some boyish prank. A servant brought fruit and nectar on a tray and left. Boaz lifted a pomegranate and cracking the shell with his hand, began lifting out the tangy, flesh covered seeds. He continued to grin.

Rahab leaned toward him saying, "What is it, Boaz? You have something to tell me."

"Many gleaners[96] followed the reapers today in my fields," he told her.

"Yes," she said, nodding and waiting.

"I spoke with one of them today, Mother."

"As you often speak to those who glean in your fields," Rahab said, still waiting.

Boaz turned to look full into Rahab's eyes. "Her name was Ruth, the daughter in law of Naomi."

Rahab nodded again.

"I told her to eat with my reapers, and to follow close after the maidens who reap for me," Boaz said. He looked away quickly at a bee buzzing a flower and added, "She has been good to her mother in law since the death of her husband. She left her mother and father and her land to come to a people she does not

---

[96]Deuteronomy 24:19

know."

Rahab smiled and said, "Yes, Boaz, Ruth has been kind to Naomi. It was good of you to help her."

Boaz looked again at Rahab. "She has come to trust the Lord God of Israel," he said.

Rahab remembered through the years to the time when she, a young pagan woman, had come to trust the Lord God of Israel. "I would like to meet this young woman," she told Boaz.

"Perhaps you will, Mother," Boaz answered, the boyish look still capturing his bearded face. "Perhaps you will."

Throughout the barley harvest and the wheat harvest, Ruth the daughter in law of Naomi continued to glean in the fields of Boaz. Daily Boaz returned home with content on his handsome face. He often had tales to relate to Rahab about events concerning Ruth, or words exchanged with Ruth. Rahab watched her son and wondered at his fascination with the young widow.

As the sun set one evening Boaz returned home with heaviness. He sat eating without speaking. When he had finished and the servants had cleared away the meal, Rahab reached her frail hand to grasp his large, strong one. "Do you want to tell me what burdens you, Boaz?"

"Do you know the law of the kinsman redeemer, Mother?" he asked.

"Tell me, Boaz," Rahab answered softly.

"The lands of Elimelech may be purchased from Naomi by a near kinsman," Boaz told her. "But at the time the lands are redeemed, it must be bought of Ruth, also, and the near kinsman must take her to wife and raise up a son in the name of her dead husband, to inherit the lands of Mahlon and Elimelech."[97]

"And do you wish to do the part of a near kinsman to

---

[97]Numbers 27:11; Leviticus 25:25; Deuteronomy 25:5,6

Ruth?" Rahab asked gently.

Boaz looked at Rahab sadly. "Ruth is so young, Mother. She would not desire a man of my age to redeem her," he said. "Besides that, there is a closer relative than I. He is young, Mother. It is Nathan's son Elzabad. He has the right to redeem the land and raise up seed to Mahlon."

Rahab watched her son's pain and suddenly realized that Boaz was in love with the young Moabitess. He had found that woman, although young, with whom he desired to share his life. Yet he feared that his hope would not be realized. Rahab squeezed his hand and stood. He stood with her, and she led him to the rooftop.

"Your father and I often came here to pray," she said. "Here we prayed for a child." She smiled at him. "Here we prayed for Enan. Here I prayed for Miriam. The Lord answered all of those prayers, Boaz. He still listens. Do you want me to pray here with you, about this matter?"

"Yes, Mother." Boaz and Rahab knelt together on the rooftop, and sought the heart of their God.

The following day began the winnowing of the barley harvest. In the evening Boaz stayed with the other men at the threshing floor to guard the grain. Rahab did not expect to see him again until the completion of the threshing, yet Boaz arrived home early the next morning. He seemed much agitated as he washed himself and changed his garments. When he had combed his hair and beard, he kissed Rahab and smiled wryly. He blew out a deep sigh and finally spoke.

"I'm going to the gate this morning, Mother. There I will tell Elzabad of the land of Naomi which must be redeemed and about Ruth," Boaz said, his voice faltering.

"I will pray for you, Boaz. But why do you go today, now?" she asked.

Boaz closed his eyes to prevent the mists forming there. "She came to me in the night, at the threshing floor," he said.

"Ruth?" Rahab asked.

"Yes, she came to me and asked me to do the part of a near kinsman to her! I'm not young, but she asked me, Mother," Boaz said, an edge of excitement in his voice. Then he lowered his eyes and added somberly, "Yet, Elzabad may choose to redeem. I must go, now, and find him."

Rahab paced the room after Boaz had left. Then, snatching a shawl against the early morning air, she hurried as fast as her feet would toward the city gate. There she lingered near the well but could see the events unfold. Boaz sat among the elders and judges at the gate. Elzabad sat beside Boaz, and they were deep in conversation as the elders listened. After several minutes of discussion, Elzabad bent over and removed a shoe. Then standing, he handed the shoe to Boaz. From her lookout by the well Rahab could hear Boaz as he stood holding the shoe aloft and exclaimed, "You are witnesses this day that I have bought all that was Elimelech's, Mahlon's and Chilion's from Naomi. You are also witnesses that I have purchased Ruth the Moabitess, the wife of Mahlon, to be my wife, and to raise up the name of the dead upon his inheritance, so that the name of the dead will not be cut off from among his brethren."[98]

Rahab began the shuffle home, smiling to everyone she passed. Before she reached her gate Boaz fell in beside her, taking her arm and helping her along.

"Did you hear, Mother? Elzabad declined to redeem the land and marry Ruth because it would mar his own inheritance." He stopped and grabbed her around the waist. "Mother," he almost shouted, "I have redeemed the land. And I will marry Ruth!" He swung her around and she stood laughing and gasping, hugging her son in his great joy.

The marriage feast of Boaz and Ruth was unprecedented in grandeur in the city of Bethlehem. All of the city was called to attend. The servants worked for days in advance to prepare the

---

[98]Ruth 4:9,10

food and ready the banquet rooms. As the guests passed by to greet the bride and groom, Rahab suddenly felt very lonely. All of the friends of the family were there. Boaz beamed with happiness and Ruth radiated joy. Even Naomi smiled happily, satisfied in the marriage of her daughter in law.

But Rahab wished to turn and find Salmon beside her, smiling and laughing at his son's marriage feast. She desired to look across the room and see Maachah corralling her young and chatting gaily with another guest. Rahab closed her eyes and imagined what she and Miriam would discuss, for Miriam's grand daughter in law was now Rahab's daughter in law. Although in a crowded room, Rahab felt alone, apart, lonely for the loved ones long departed.

"Thank you, Lord," she prayed. "Thank you for giving Boaz a wife, and such a wife, who loves you, Lord. Thank you that although I miss my friends so dearly, I do have the wonderful memories. Thank you, again, for saving me from Jericho. Thank you for all the years as Salmon's wife. Thank you for the love of friends I have always known. And thank you for Miriam. She was ever the thorn in my life, yet when she turned in faith to you, she became my friend. Thank you, Lord. You came into my life with a miracle and you have worked so many since. Thank you."

When the wedding feast had ended, Boaz went to kiss his mother and found that she had gone to the bosom of Abraham.

EPILOGUE

The Scriptural account of Rahab is given to us in the book of Joshua, chapters 2 and 6. Hebrews 11:31 says, "By faith the harlot Rahab perished not with them that believed not, when she had received the spies with peace."

The story of Ruth, Rahab's daughter-in-law, is told in the Scripture in the book of Ruth.

The genealogical record[99] shows that Rahab's son, Boaz, had a son named Obed. The son of Obed was Jesse, whose youngest son David became the great and godly King of Israel. Thus, the Lord God of heaven and earth used a pagan harlot, who truly believed in the Lord, in the family tree of a king, and eventually of the Saviour, the Lord Jesus Christ.

---

[99]Matthew 1:5,6